Praise for *Scene of the Grime*

"[A] delightful, sassy tale filled with eccentric, interesting characters that add to the whodunit."
—The Best Reviews

"The first Grime Solvers Mystery, introducing cleaning expert Sky Taylor, has lots of promise—an interesting main character, a charming Massachusetts town with plenty of secrets, and several possible love interests for Sky. Readers will enjoy getting to know Sky and the people of Pigeon Cove. Several great cleaning tips are also included."
—Romantic Times

"*Scene of the Grime* is a well-written, fun, delightful novel. The characters are vividly drawn and the dialogue sparkles. . . . I very much enjoyed reading this book and look forward to the next Grime Solvers Mystery."
—MyShelf.com

"[A] light, enjoyable read—and the cleaning tips [are] spot on."
—Gumshoe

DIRTY DEEDS

A GRIME SOLVERS MYSTERY

Suzanne Price

AN OBSIDIAN MYSTERY

OBSIDIAN
Published by New American Library, a division of
Penguin Group (USA) Inc., 375 Hudson Street,
New York, New York 10014, USA
Penguin Group (Canada), 90 Eglinton Avenue East, Suite 700, Toronto,
Ontario M4P 2Y3, Canada (a division of Pearson Penguin Canada Inc.)
Penguin Books Ltd., 80 Strand, London WC2R 0RL, England
Penguin Ireland, 25 St. Stephen's Green, Dublin 2,
Ireland (a division of Penguin Books Ltd.)
Penguin Group (Australia), 250 Camberwell Road, Camberwell, Victoria 3124,
Australia (a division of Pearson Australia Group Pty. Ltd.)
Penguin Books India Pvt. Ltd., 11 Community Centre, Panchsheel Park,
New Delhi - 110 017, India
Penguin Group (NZ), 67 Apollo Drive, Rosedale, North Shore 0632,
New Zealand (a division of Pearson New Zealand Ltd.)
Penguin Books (South Africa) (Pty.) Ltd., 24 Sturdee Avenue,
Rosebank, Johannesburg 2196, South Africa

Penguin Books Ltd., Registered Offices:
80 Strand, London WC2R 0RL, England

First published by Obsidian, an imprint of New American Library,
a division of Penguin Group (USA) Inc.

First Printing, July 2008
10 9 8 7 6 5 4 3 2 1

Copyright © Penguin Group (USA) Inc., 2008
All rights reserved

OBSIDIAN and logo are trademarks of Penguin Group (USA) Inc.

Printed in the United States of America

PUBLISHER'S NOTE
This is a work of fiction. Names, characters, places, and incidents either are
the product of the author's imagination or are used fictitiously, and any resemblance to actual persons, living or dead, business establishments, events, or
locales is entirely coincidental.
    The publisher does not have any control over and does not assume any
responsibility for author or third-party Web sites or their content.

For Mickey,
whose heart was as fierce
as our love for her is great

Chapter 1

"Our guests are the *loveliest*. I wish they'd leave," Chloe Edwards said, her snowflake earrings sparkling in the glow of the exhibit hall's overhead fluorescents.

I looked at her, a tray of drained and half-empty wine-glasses balanced in my hands. On my last visit to my ex–flower children parents' house, I hid out for a while browsing the New Age section of their personal library. Besides reeking of patchouli incense, it takes up most of their shelf space and is the place to go if you're eager to be schooled in alternative medicine, dream interpretation, holistic diets, chakras, channeling, and yes, Tantric sex therapy—there are loads and loads of books on that subject. But considering that we happen to be talking about my sixtyish mom and dad here, and that I'd rather not fall back on my old habit of grinding my teeth, I think I better truck on to my major point, if you don't mind.

Said point being that I'd read a little about Zen koans while thumbing through one of their books. As I understand it, these are riddles that defy rational solution. A Buddhist teacher will relate a koan to his student, and the student will meditate on it and try to extract profound meaning from what seems superficially meaningless. The general idea is to open the mind to new insights and ways of thinking.

Which is pretty much what it's like interpreting Chloe-speak. What she'd said seemed to contradict itself, sure. But if you knew Chloe like I do, you'd realize that it didn't in the least. Chloe is actually the sharpest and most insightful person I know, and most of what leaves her lips makes good sense. You just need to put yourself in a Chloe state of mind to catch it.

Standing beside her in the large exhibit room on the ground floor of the Art Association building, I took a quick head count of the stragglers around us and then glanced at the people filing out the door.

"We're doing okay," I whispered. "Pretty much everybody's left."

Chloe checked her wristwatch and frowned a little. "That won't cut it, Sky. It's almost eleven o'clock at night, and my invitation clearly says the exhibit runs till ten. You can't finish tidying up until the last of them goes home."

I couldn't argue. It *was* getting late, and I was going to have my hands full getting everything done. But when Chloe had offered me the job of doing cleanup for that evening's event, I'd felt compelled to accept—never mind that I already had wall-to-wall bookings with the huge number of local inns holding Christmas and New Year's functions. I mean, let's be honest. My newspaper column's fun, but it isn't as though I can exactly pay my bills on the cup of coffee I'm paid for writing it. Also, I knew Chloe had gone out of her way to finagle the gig for me, and I didn't want to seem unappreciative, considering her gala was the most prestigious—and best-paying—hobnob in town.

In Pigeon Cove, it's a seasonal tradition for the Art Association to hold a themed holiday bash about a week before Christmas, with a different member of the board of trustees selected to host the affair each year. This year it was Chloe's turn, and she'd done a bang-up job—especially considering that a group of the town's most influential businesspeople had lobbied for the exhibit to be given the anything-but-artful title "Pigeon Cove's Growth and Expansion in the Coming Year." They'd also done their best to turn the whole wingding into a shameless promotion for various moneymaking projects they had in the works.

Those hotshots hadn't reckoned with Chloe, though. Our local entrepreneurs may have intended to slap poster ads disguised as fine-art prints all over the gallery walls, but she'd outsmarted them. If Chloe was going to be stuck with their commercial pitches—and she knew she would be—she would at least arrange to have the final word on the event's creative mode. And so she'd insisted they use life-sized, three-dimensional multimedia dioramas to qualify. Her stipulation had made some genuine imagination flow from their mental taps, forced them to hire legit artists and craftspeople for the displays, and turned what could have been a long, tedious night into something that was really enjoyable.

Still, I could see Chloe starting to fade after mixing with the guests for hours. Tireless as she seemed, I sometimes had to remind myself she was only human.

"Chloe, you don't have to say good night to every last comer," I said. "Since I've got to wait around anyway, you can leave it to me . . ."

Chloe shook her head.

"You're too easygoing, dear." She glanced over toward the appetizer table. "Look at the Fontaines still eating away! They're overstaying their welcome at your expense."

"Maybe so. But I can't exactly start pushing them out the door."

Chloe's finger snapped up to her chin like an exclamation point.

"No, you can't," she said. "That's the hostess's job, isn't it?"

And with that she started toward a group of admirers lingering by the elaborate Getaway Groves Condominiums exhibit, which featured a stone path, a live topiary evergreen hedge, a flower garden, and even a "snoozing" condo owner on a hammock, in the person of Kyle Fipps. A third-generation real estate developer and wannabe actor, Kyle was one of Bill Drecksel's two major partners in a deal to build a number of fancy condo units at the South End. To the amusement of the viewers around him, he'd apparently gotten carried away with his role and fallen asleep in the display's mock spring gardens, a straw hat over his face.

I quickstepped in front of Chloe now, afraid she'd startle him into tipping out of the hammock.

"Seriously," I said. "How about we give it a few minutes before we shush people off?"

Chloe hesitated a second, then released a sigh.

"All right," she said. "Provided I stay here and help you clean."

I frowned. Besides the gigantic snowflake earrings dangling almost to her shoulders, Chloe had on a bright, Christmassy red silk tunic with matching slim pants and heels—not quite your usual cleaning uniform. Of course, neither was my foxy pleated black minidress, red and white Santa hat, or the color-splashed vintage Peter Max scarf I was wearing courtesy of Mom. But I'd had to put on something decent while picking up after the guests, and had brought a smock in my bag of tricks—that's what I call my cleaning kit—for when I got around to the heavy-duty scrubbing.

"Chloe, don't be ridiculous," I said. "I can take care of things on my lonesome."

Chloe made a stubborn face, her lips pursed. "I'm sure that's true. But as long as I'm here, you won't. Or must I remind you we're supposed to be best fr—" She suddenly broke off and looked over my shoulder. "Why, hello, Finch."

"Salud," Finch Fontaine said from behind me. "I hope I'm not interrupting an important conversation."

Chloe gave her a stiff smile. "Actually, Sky and I were just discussing how much hard work she has ahead of her tonight."

I turned to look at Finch, who'd carried over a plate from the appetizer table. She seemed oblivious to Chloe's unsubtle hint.

"You know, my husband and I have advance-purchased an oceanview unit at Getaway Groves," she said, glancing past us toward Kyle's exhibit. *"L'amour et de la mer,* love and the sea. They nourish my dancing soul and liberate it from the commonplace." She popped a morsel of pricey finger food into her mouth. "The Fippses are superior people. We grew quite close as couples during the transaction. What a shame they're not getting along these days, or didn't you hear?"

"I heard," Chloe said. "Incidentally, Sky can't get started on that work I mentioned until everyone leaves."

Finch smiled at me. "You're so magnificent at cleaning my studios. I'm sure you won't have a bit of difficulty."

I suppose I should have felt flattered. But all I could think was that some people were too clueless for words.

"I honestly cannot decide whether I prefer the foie gras or the *pâté de volaille*. They're both so delicious," Finch said, chewing away. "Although I enjoyed sampling those delectable *beignets de fromage* while the warm appetizers were being served."

Chloe and I stood there watching her in abashed silence. A minuscule woman of about forty-five with a thin, waifish face, sandy brown hair, and soft brown eyes, Finch preferred being called Miss Finch by her dance students at the Fontaine Culture Club, which she'd cofounded with her husband, Humbert, and was touting as a premier center for the advancement of modern dance and song on Cape Ann. To hear Finch tell it, she'd pulled the club together entirely with her own blood, sweat, and tears—the same way she boasted of having made herself a top-notch dancer by working twice as hard as everyone else in the world. Never mind that her biggest claim to fame was having been featured in a Billy Idol video in the mid-eighties; forget that the Culture Club had been financed using her generous family trust fund; and put aside the fact that its board of directors set the whole thing up as a tax write-off while she and Humbert were away on an extended photograpy safari in West Africa.

"So, Chloe, tell me how you felt about my exhibit," Finch said now.

Chloe pursed her lips.

"I enjoyed it," she said tightly.

"It's clever, don't you agree? And executed to brilliant perfection."

Chloe looked at her, took a deep breath. "I can see that a great deal of planning went into it, yes."

"Planning and vision," Finch chirped. "The motif came to me in a burst of inspiration so powerful I was left breathless. It's *sui generis*. Alone, apart, to itself."

Chloe's lips tightened again. I knew she wasn't eager to offend Finch. For all her preening and pretense, Finch was a staunch patron of the Art Association. And I have to admit that her exhibit for the Culture Club *was* inventive enough. Stepping up to a large window frame, you were given a simulated glimpse into the building's main practice studio, where dozens of Barbie dolls were twirling in tights and tutus. Symbolically outside the window, meanwhile, was a tree full of battery-operated finches that would flap their little wings and open and close their beaks in time to various pieces of music playing from camouflaged speakers.

"Finch, I'd love to compliment you some more, but I want to show Sky a few things that need to get done around here," Chloe said pleasantly. She smiled without evident sarcasm. "Also, I believe there's heavy snow in tomorrow's forecast. You might want to get a jump on it heading home."

I bit my lip. A jump? The Fontaines lived right around the corner from the Art Association, and Chloe was well aware of it. But I was hoping Finch would finally catch on that we had things to do.

It turned out she did. Either that or she'd grown bored with us. It was impossible to tell, and I honestly didn't care as she bade us *bonne nuit* and *au revoir*, and then went to separate her husband from the picked-over remnants of the appetizers.

Chloe watched them head toward the coatroom.

"Self-praise is no recommendation," she whispered to me.

"Got that right," I said, my eyes going to the front entrance.

It looked as if people had at long last decided to call it an evening. Possibly, I thought, they'd taken a cue from the Fontaines. But whatever the reason, the exhibit hall entirely emptied within minutes after Finch and Humbert left.

Well, okay. It *almost* emptied.

Glancing around the room, I realized that Morris Silverberg, the ophthalmologist, was still hanging out at his Presbyopic Bocce Ball Court, stuffing a cannoli into his mouth with one hand and adjusting some of the eyeglass frames hanging from the exhibit's giant Christmas tree with the other. But at least Morris had his winter parka on and seemed ready to make tracks.

Unfortunately the same couldn't be said for Kyle Fipps. Over at the Getaway Groves display, he was still out like a light, the straw hat covering his face.

I poked Chloe with my elbow, nodded in his direction.

"Can you believe the guy?" I said. "That's what I call taking performance art to a new level."

Chloe shook her head thoughtfully.

"It could be," she said. "Of course, I did notice him sampling the wine before. The poor man's been going through that terrible divorce with his wife, Lina . . . Maybe he had a bit too much to drink."

I looked at her.

"You think our happy hammock snoozer's *plotzed*?"

Chloe shrugged.

"I don't know," she said. "We'd better check on him."

As we crossed the room to the exhibit, I realized I was still holding the tray of dirty glasses and unsuccessfully looked around for a place to set it down. At the same time, Chloe went walking up the stone path to the hammock and gave it a gentle push.

Kyle didn't stir.

"Kyle," Chloe said quietly, "rise and shine."

He still didn't move.

Chloe glanced around at me, her brow creasing.

"What do you think?" I said.

"I think I'd better treat him to a cheerful little wake-up ditty."

I shrugged. Crazy as it sounds, Chloe's idea didn't surprise me. For that matter, it was fairly routine coming from her.

She turned back toward Kyle, leaned close to his ear, and started singing about Dorothy the Dinosaur munching on some roses and Wag the Dog digging up bones.

It didn't work. Kyle remained absolutely still.

Chloe had gotten around to the part of the song where Henry the Octopus was doing something or other in circles when I decided to walk up the path and give her an assist. Maybe, I thought, Kyle needed a bit more than a kid's song and a tender nudge to get him moving.

"C'mon, Kyle! Nap time's over. Let's go!" I said in a loud voice, lifting the hat off his face while balancing my tray in one hand.

I looked down at him, my jaw suddenly dropping.

Kyle's eyes were open. I mean, *wide* open. And glassy. And his face was a very deep and disconcerting shade of purple.

Standing over him, Chloe screamed, and that was what set off the chain reaction: her scream startling me into dropping the tray, wineglasses spilling from the tray into the fake garden grass. The next thing I knew Chloe had kind of bumped into the hammock, and Kyle had fallen over its side to the floor, dropping heavily amid the strewn glasses and plastic potted plants, sprawling there in a motionless heap.

"Coming through! I'm a doctor!" It was Morrie Silverberg, the eye specialist, thudding over from his indoor bocce court. He stood over the body, looked at me. "Does that man need a doctor?" he asked.

I looked back at him. All things considered—and my dropped tray aside—I felt fairly composed. But then, this wasn't the first time I'd stumbled on a dead body.

"Something tells me Kyle won't be needing any more eye tests, Morrie," I said.

Chapter 2

"You really should let me help out," said Morrie Silverberg. "While I'm available." "I can see what's going on here just fine, thanks."

Morrie nodded down at Kyle. "I'm not talking about you. I'm talking about him."

"Being how he's dead, I don't think he needs a prescription for eyeglasses. And if he *wasn't* dead, I'd send him to the optometrist at the Wal-Mart in Beverly, which my brother-in-law happens to manage. Considering what you charge for a visit."

"What I charge?"

"Uh-huh."

Morrie looked indignant.

"My rates are highly competitive, as I'd urge you to see for yourself," he said. "Also, FYI, I'm an *ophthalmologist*."

"There's a difference?"

"God forbid you ever develop an ocular condition that requires surgery. You'll find out the difference."

In case you're wondering, Morrie was now talking to somebody other than me. I'd dialed 911 on my cell phone after Chloe spilled Kyle Fipps off his hammock, bringing four members of the local police force to the scene. According to Chief Alejandro Vega, who'd arrived in one of their squad cars, an EMS vehicle was also speeding up to the Cove from Addison Gilbert Hospital in Gloucester. In the meantime, Morrie was intent on making himself useful—or else.

As far as that went, the uniformed sergeant who was crouching over Kyle's body on the Getaway Groves exhibit's artificial turf—his name tag read PRATT—clearly fell into the thanks-but-no-thanks camp. I suspected that camp might include everyone in the room, although Pratt did seem unnecessarily hostile.

Now he glanced up at Morrie and frowned. "Listen, my eye doc at the Beverly Wal-Mart can probably handle any condition in the books," he said. "And if there's one he can't handle for some reason, I know they'd take care of me at the Wal-Mart Supercenter in Plymouth without robbing me blind."

"That's very funny."

"What's funny?"

"Your choice of words."

"What words?"

"The words you used there at the end."

"At what end? What are you talking about? Who said any words that were funny?"

Morrie stared at him. "Never mind, Sergeant. I think maybe we've veered off track."

"If *we* have, maybe it's because *you* keep pushing an agenda," Sergeant Pratt said. "And I'm not enthused about it, let me tell you."

Morrie shook his head and gestured down at Kyle again.

"I wanted to examine Mr. Fipps," he said. "Correct me if I'm wrong, but isn't he the reason we're all here sweating with our coats on?"

"You bet he's why I'm here," Pratt said testily. "He's also why the chief's here, plus two other officers and the ladies who found the deceased stretched out in this here hammock." He reached out and patted the spot Kyle's body had vacated when Chloe bumped it. "On the other hand, you seem to think it's the place to start running live infomercials. And making disparaging comments about Wal-Mart, which is the source of my brother-in-law's livelihood, never mind it put clothes on the backs of all those poor hillbillies in the Ozarks. Or don't you know your retail history?"

"Okay, fellas. Enough."

No, it *still* wasn't me chiming in. Rather, it was Police Chief Alejandro Vega, who'd stepped over from a buffet table across the room, where he'd gently pulled Chloe aside to ask her some questions. With his lean build and dark good looks, Vega had convinced just about everyone in the Cove that he was secretly Zorro. The local women fantasized about being flung over his saddle and swept away to his secret cave. As a result, the local men wanted to run him out of town along with the horse he'd ridden in on. For that reason it was no surprise when a poll conducted by my newspaper, the *Anchor*, had found that his approval ratings broke sharply along gender lines.

"Has one of my officers taken your statement, Dr. Silverberg?" he asked.

"No." Morrie shook his head again. "Nor does the sergeant seem the least bit interested in me or my expert medical observations. An apathy I hope hasn't trickled down from the top."

I wasn't kidding when I said the men in town weren't wild about Chief Vega, who really didn't deserve the attitude—and that's coming from personal experience. He'd been decent to me back in the spring, when I'd cleaned my way into trouble with a Chicago hit man. Long story.

Vega appeared to be trying to decide how to address Morrie's implied criticism. As I stood there watching him, an irked Sergeant Pratt sprang up from his knees.

"You can stuff the trickle-down talk where it belongs," he said, jabbing a finger at Morrie. "I'm just not interested in you foisting your business on me."

Morrie blinked at him. "What do you mean *foisting*? Who needs your business? I'm semiretired!"

"Say what you want. I don't appreciate you sticking your nose where it doesn't belong, and while you're at it trying to sell me on a two-hundred-dollar eye checkup," Pratt said. "Plus I can do without listening to your hang-ups about big chain stores, not that they're any different from what I hear out of the rest of you snobs in the Cove."

Vega gave me a quick look and then rolled his eyes skyward. Between Morrie and Pratt, there seemed to be a surplus of huffiness in the air. While I'd figured Morrie's snapping at the chief was an example of the resentment Vega had come to expect from men, Sergeant Pratt's giving Morrie a hard time had made me want to scratch my head.

But Vega's glance told me everything. I suddenly knew without asking that Pratt was from Gloucester, a neighboring town about five miles to the south. I also knew that his antagonism for Morrie—who in spite of being annoying and envious of Vega's looks sincerely *had* wanted to help—was an upshot of the Great Map Flap that had erupted between Gloucesterians and the residents of the Cove right after Thanksgiving, when our chamber of commerce printed up its tourist brochure for the forthcoming calendar year.

That said, I didn't know how anybody could find it timely or appropriate to stand there bickering, given the dreadful situation . . . let alone a couple of ostensibly sane adults, one of whom was a physician and the other an on-duty police officer.

Kyle Fipps was dead, sprawled alongside the stone path cutting through his lush fake lawn. A short while ago, he'd been deep into what his playbill handout called the "Gardening Gentleman" segment of his performance, trimming yew shrubs he had bought at a local nursery and set in wooden planters as stage props. He had used hedge clippers to manicure the shrubs into neat geometric shapes—squares, rectangles, globes, even a spiral—and impressed everyone with his topiary skills. Then he'd gone into the "Gent at Leisure" segment, which turned out to be his show's final act.

Kyle couldn't have been older than thirty-nine or forty. While we were barely acquaintances, I thought he'd seemed in great shape earlier that week at the new Get Thinner Fitness Center, where I was doing my so-so best to melt some extra winter padding off my hips and thighs. That morning, he'd hopped aboard the cross trainer right beside the machine I was working out on, showcasing his iron cheeks in a pair of spandex exercise trunks.

I sighed heavily. Maybe it was Chloe's influence, but lately my thoughts had been taking odd turns in stressful situations, and envisioning a dead man's butt as it had appeared in its active prime made me kind of uncomfortable. Not that Kyle would have been offended. He was very proud of his butt, judging by how he'd liked to admire it in the gym's full-length mirrors. And I couldn't have blamed him. We live in a society that's fixated on butts. With the right rump, it's possible to become a showbiz personality absent any other virtue or talent. There are, come to think of it, celebrities whose booties are much more famously recognizable than their faces.

Now, don't get the wrong idea. I have nothing against presenting a nice rear view to the world. I tried hard to keep mine respectable, and had taken more than a few opportunities to admire the fact that the guy I was seeing, Mike Ennis, was likewise conscientious. But in my opinion being a well-rounded person deserved a tad more emphasis than having a well-rounded bottom. And besides, Kyle was—*had been*—a married man. While he and his wife, Lina, had separated after Thanksgiving because, as rumor had it, his bottom had drawn a bit too much close-up, hands-on extramarital attention, I made it a policy never to get too interested in any butt attached to another woman's husband. Which was something that seemed increasingly rare in Pigeon Cove these days, though I'll admit my perception might have been skewed by the Boston Stripper scandal that had kept Mike out of town the past couple of weeks, chasing a lead that involved an exotic dancer known for her bare-cheeked shenanigans with a local politician.

Then a thought struck me that was thankfully unrelated—or tangential, anyway—to the gratuitous display of backsides and its effects: Had anybody contacted Lina? Regardless of her problems with Kyle, she needed to know what had happened.

I was about to ask Chief Vega about it, but he was busy separating Morrie and Pratt. His hand on Morrie's arm, he steered him toward another town cop who'd kind of wandered over to Morrie's Presbyopic Bocce Ball Court.

"Ronnie," Vega said, "why don't you interview the doc so he can be on his way home?"

The cop looked at Vega. A tall, square-jawed guy of about thirty who'd introduced himself on arrival as Officer Connors, he'd been peering through the so-called Big Eyes viewer Morrie had set up next to his Christmas tree near the court. As best I can describe it, the Big Eyes resembled one of those coin-operated contraptions you'd find at national parks and landmark skyscrapers like the Empire State Building—only a Martian version, with lenses designed to look like, well, a pair of extremely big bug eyes.

"Check out these giant eyeballs, Chief," Connors said, cocking a thumb at the viewer. "You look through 'em and things go in and out of focus."

Morrie, who'd seemed kind of dejected, visibly perked up at his comment. "Did the fuzziness seem worse with objects that were closer to you? Say, those balls at the throwing end of the bocce court?"

"Yeah, matter of fact. They got kind of smudgy."

"That's presbyopia in a nutshell," Morrie said. "An inability to find a point of focal clarity. I designed the Big Eyes to simulate the condition as a *free* public service." He gave Pratt a meaningful glance. "After tonight's debut, the viewer will be at my office for anyone to walk in and use. Though a young man like you probably won't have to worry about it for another ten years, many people over forty suffer from some degree of presbyopia, and I want them to recognize its indicators."

"Sounds like my mom. She's always moving her books away from her face when she reads."

"You bring her into my office and I'll take care of her."

"Thanks, Doc. That'd be great."

Morrie drew his shoulders upright, looking pleased. "I think I'll give my statement to that superb young officer," he told Vega, and started off toward the bocce court.

"Shark bait," Pratt muttered, staring at the younger cop.

Vega stepped sideways out of the sergeant's earshot, motioned for me to join him.

"Sorry about Pratt," he said in a low voice. "This idiotic Cove-Gloucester feud's gotten out of hand."

"No need to apologize," I said. He wasn't to blame, after all.

Vega looked at me. Actually, he seemed to look at the top of my head a second before bringing his eyes down to my face.

"How've you been, Sky?" he asked.

"Present circumstances aside," I said, "I'm okay."

"And your little cat?"

"Toil and trouble, meaning she's okay too," I said.

Vega smiled slightly. "I've been following her exploits in your column."

"I won't tell her," I said. "Skiball already has a bloated ego."

Vega was silent. Was I just imagining that he was staring at the top of my head again? I resisted the urge to pat it and make sure it was still there.

"About tonight," Vega said after a moment. "You were working at the affair, is that right?"

I nodded.

"On assignment for the newspaper?"

"No," I said. "Don't let my clothes fool you. It was strictly a cleaning job. I don't wear a conventional uniform, especially during special events."

"Oh."

"The last thing I want is to stick out like a sore thumb."

"Oh." He hesitated. "I see."

Vega looked a bit self-conscious as he flipped open his notepad, and this time I thought I might know the reason. A lot of people had preconceptions about why I'd gotten into the cleaning business. They seemed sure

I would regard it as a step down from the highfalutin ad career I'd left behind—an assumption that was totally wrong. It was far and away more gratifying. Back when I was a copywriter on Madison Avenue, so many of our corporate accounts budgeted more to advertising and packaging disposable junk than to product development— and the lines I wrote to hype that junk seemed no less worthless and disposable. There were times when I would almost feel guilty at the conclusion of a job, realizing I'd been part of an effort to pull a fast one on the public.

My cleaning service, on the other hand, was something honest and real. I could set my own standards, deliver as promised, and at the same time buy myself the freedom to write what I wanted. Once, the words I typed into my computer had been nothing but clever persuasions. These days they gave expression to my deepest thoughts and feelings. I truthfully couldn't have been prouder of how I earned my living.

Now Vega scribbled something in his pad and brought his gaze back to mine. His awkward moments were few and fleeting, as befit a swashbuckling hero.

"I realize Chloe's pretty upset, and won't keep the two of you much longer," he said. "But I need to ask a few routine questions."

I looked into his deep brown eyes. A thought had suddenly struck me. "You don't suspect that what happened to Kyle was anybody's *fault*, do you?"

Vega shook his head.

"Kyle seems to have died of natural causes . . . I'm guessing heart attack . . . though it's obviously the medical people who'll need to make that determination," he said. "Out of curiosity . . . did you see him behaving unusually at all? Notice anything that might have signaled he wasn't feeling well?"

"No," I said. "Truthfully, I was too busy to pay much attention to anyone. But I did catch some of his routine toward the end of the night."

" 'A Fun Time Out at Getaway Groves'?"

"That was its title, yeah."

"And he was supposed to be, what, puttering around the lawn?"

I nodded. "Mowing, watering the flowers, snipping the hedges . . ."

"And then taking five in the hammock."

"Yes," I said. "Which is when I guess he must've passed away."

"Some kind of time-out," Vega said, shaking his head. "I'm wondering if anyone else might have noticed Kyle was sick . . . Do you have any idea if he mixed with the guests? As opposed to staying on his set, that is."

"Again, not that I saw. But I doubt it."

"Why's that?"

"You'd have to double-check with Chloe or another member of the Art Association's planning committee, but I think it's against the performance guidelines."

"Sky is absolutely right, Chief Vega," said Chloe, coming over from where she'd stood near an hors d'oeuvre table. "When a performance artist is part of the event, we insist on maintaining the fourth wall."

We turned toward the sound of her voice.

"Fourth wall?" Vega said.

"The separation between performer and audience," Chloe said. "It keeps the atmosphere delightfully whimsical."

I wondered if "delightfully whimsical" was a phrase that had ever before been spoken a few feet away from a recently discovered corpse, the sight of which gave me the chills. Not that Chloe looked anything but shaken. Her eyeliner was smeared from crying, and I could hear a tremor of distress in her voice. It was just her nature to be obliging.

"So Kyle wouldn't have spoken with anyone the entire time?" Vega said.

"He could reach through the fourth wall, and over it, but wasn't supposed to shatter it," Chloe said. "You'll never lose your shirt if you keep your sleeves rolled up."

I scratched behind my ear. Normally I was a skilled

interpreter of Chloe-isms, but it took me a few seconds to decipher that one, and another few to sort of halfway figure out how it applied to Vega's question.

He seemed similarly confused as he looked up from his pad.

"So if I understand," he said, and rubbed his chin, "you're saying that he *did* interact with people from the set, but wouldn't have circulated around the hall."

"Yes," Chloe said. "But that isn't the same as mingling. Of course, performers are allowed restroom breaks at any time, provided they hang an intermission sign."

"How about grabbing a bite to eat? At the buffet table, say?"

Chloe shook her head. "That would be like smashing the fourth wall to bits and pieces with a sledgehammer," she said. "I'm sure Kyle must have had something to eat and drink. But if he followed the guidelines, he would have stayed in character on the set."

Chief Vega stroked his chin again. Outside on Main Street, a siren was howling loudly. I guessed it must be the EMS vehicle arriving from Gloucester.

Vega had turned to face me. "Sky, I was just thinking . . . do you remember—?"

Before he could finish his sentence, a pair of men in medical whites pushed through the exhibit hall's entrance.

"Where's the party that needs attention?" one of them asked.

Then they must have seen Kyle for themselves. Without waiting for a response from anyone, they hurried over to the Getaway Groves set, sort of pushed Sergeant Pratt out of the way, and immediately examined the body. After a couple of minutes, the man who'd spoken from the door looked up at the rest of us.

"Anybody here want to tell me what happened?" he asked.

Chloe fidgeted nervously with the neck of her tunic.

"I thought Kyle was asleep, went over to wake him up with a delightful children's song, and accidentally rolled him off his hammock," she said. "But it turned out he wasn't sleeping after all."

The emergency services man stared at her.

"And what did this to him, ma'am? The singing or the fall?"

Vega gave him a pointed look.

"Sorry, Chief," the man said. "Been a miserable night . . . The holiday season's a *creep show* for us. You wouldn't believe what just went down on the highway."

I won't speak for Vega, but I preferred not to know the details. I also wanted to spare Chloe from hearing them.

"Kyle must've been in the hammock for over an hour," I interjected. "We don't know when he died."

The man in medical whites grunted. "Not to split hairs, miss," he said, "but right now we shouldn't be calling this man dead."

"Which isn't to give the misleading impression that he's alive," the other man said. "Since he has no vital signs and is pretty darned blue."

"And besides that, is cooling to room temperature," the first man said. "Nonliving bodies drop about a degree and a half an hour when you leave them sitting— or laid out, as the case may be. It's like when you take a ham out of the oven. You could say Kyle here's been, uh, out of life's oven about that long. But we can't officially pronounce anyone dead at the scene. The law doesn't let paramedics like me make the call—"

"Or EMTs, of which I'm one, for that matter," the second man said. "And before you ask, there's a difference."

"Every paramedic's an EMT, but not every EMT's a paramedic," the first man said. "Beyond that you'll have to look it up, because we don't have time to educate you."

"Though I should mention we both hate being called *ambulance drivers*," said the second man.

"*Hate* it," echoed the first man. "But getting back to your question, miss, we have to consider Kyle here a *likely* DOA until he gets to the hospital and can be examined by a licensed doctor. At which point the doc can confirm what we know but can't say."

Chloe made a sympathetic face. "That seems very dismissive of your training."

He flourished his hand in her direction like a stage magician.

"Thank you very much, ma'am!" he said. "If more people only felt that way, maybe we'd get some respect. And again, I didn't mean to insult you about your singing voice, which I'm sure is beautiful."

I was braced for the two of them to hike Chloe up on their shoulders when a voice from over by the bocce court got everybody's notice.

"Licensed doctor? Did someone ask for a licensed doctor?" His parka still zipped shut, Morrie Silverberg was waddling over from across the hall. "I'm an M.D. and I'm available!"

The emergency services men looked around at us.

"Why didn't anybody tell us there was a doctor in the house?" the paramedic asked.

Chief Vega seemed about to answer, whereupon Sergeant Pratt beat him to it.

"We didn't think you guys were here for his rip-off eye tests," he said, scowling as Morrie brushed past him.

Chapter 3

It was right around midnight when the EMS wagon drove off with Kyle. Morrie Silverberg followed the gurney out the door, and Chief Vega and his men went next. Snowflakes gusted into the exhibit hall as they made their exit, arriving ahead of the weatherman's predictions.

I didn't mind the snow. Snow and New England winters were meant to go together, especially around the holidays. And while Kyle's passing away in the middle of the Art Association's festivities hadn't exactly helped to float my bubble of seasonal cheer, I could console myself with Chief Vega's assumption that he'd died of natural causes. Unlike when I'd stumbled upon a murder at last year's Memorial Day summer kickoff . . . Have I used the term "long story" once too often yet?

Anyway, it was just the third time that winter I'd seen any flakes, unless I counted the gems hanging from Chloe's ears. There was, however, a six-inch accumulation on the ground from earlier in the month. After it came down, an Arctic freeze set in and never left, and as a result there hadn't been any melt. The nice thing was that old snow stays mostly white in Cape Ann, so it was slippery but pretty, and you could admire the town's wintry charm while taking a painful spill. This was in sharp contrast to Manhattan, where it got smudged various shades of gray, yellow, and brown—punctuated with splotches of shuddersome red gunk—within a day. I won't even hint at the unmentionable objects I'd seen sticking out of snowbanks along the curbs, except to say you'd want to be up to date on your tetanus boosters if you fell into them.

But let's not get sidetracked—where were we? Oh, yes. Midnight at the Art Association. Everyone gone from the exhibit hall but Chloe and me. And a whole lot of work to be done. I knew a thorough cleanup would keep me there till sunrise, and the problem was that I was really frazzled and spent. The other problem was that Chloe wouldn't head home without me, and she looked even more out of sorts than I felt.

I figured the best thing I could do for both of us was get some basics taken care of now and return to complete the job early the following morning. I would have to reshuffle a bunch of appointments, sure. But it seemed the most sensible option.

Even so, we wound up staying until almost two o'clock. I was okay with putting off the grunt work, but leaving the place a total mess was out of the question. The thought of dishes lying around overnight with scraps of leftover food and crusting gravy on them would make my eyes pop open in the dark, assuming I could take my mind off Kyle long enough to get sleepy. At the very least, I needed to put things in a semblance of order. Then I could get off to a smooth start when I came back tomorrow.

The first rule of cleaning is to plan an organized attack on the mess. Or on a major campaign like cleaning up after a party, a series of small, efficient raids. Which is to say, don't start by looking at the big picture, but fight one battle at a time. It makes winning the war far less daunting—trust General Sky to know, troops.

I started off with the same approach I'd have taken at home, and that was by clearing the glasses, silverware, and dishes from wherever the guests had put them, meaning every available surface on which something could be balanced, securely or otherwise. There were lots of empty buffet trays around, and I used them to carry the dirty tableware into the kitchen, filling them up one at a time. Then I rinsed the food off everything under the tap and loaded the dishwasher, leaving whatever didn't fit on the rack to soak in the sink.

I was wearing disposable kitchen gloves as I moved around the room, and had stuffed some plastic grocery bags into the kangaroo pouch of my smock to use as trash can liners. Each bag was good for lining a small cylindrical bucket, which was easier than lugging around a heavy-duty trash bag and a full-sized wastebasket while I picked up crumpled, dirty napkins and assorted leftover yukkies along with the tableware. That way, I could carry a tray into the kitchen with one hand and bring the bucket along in the other. Again, it was about organization. Cutting down on my trips to the kitchen helped me make better headway. Once I was finished with an area, I *knew* I was finished with it.

And that was about it. The question I like to ask myself after doing a rush job is: *Would a hungry mouse want to come in here?* If the answer's no, I'm ready to call it quits.

Outside, the snowflakes were cold and wet on my cheeks. Huddled against the wind, I linked arms with Chloe and went down the street to where I'd parked the sunburst orange Dodge Caliber that had replaced my Toyota SUV. I'd liked the Toyota, but a hit man from Chicago had ditched it over a thirty-foot-high ledge into an ocean inlet. When the insurance investigator came to assess the damage, she'd had to look down from the ledge at low tide just to see isolated parts of it sticking out of the water. I think the sight of gulls diving to pluck stranded fish off the SUV's roof clinched it as a total loss.

The Caliber faced where I'd left it against the curb, and I noticed a thin film of white on the windshield as we approached. I had a snow brush in the cargo section, but didn't bother getting it out. I not only reuse supermarket bags as trash bags, but in the winter hang on to those clear plastic bags from the produce section. Usually I keep one or two folded in my purse or coat pocket. When there's just a little snow on my windshield or headlights, I'll put one of them over my glove and dust

off whatever needs dusting. They're a perfect fit, keep
the glove dry, spare me from having to fish around for
the brush, and give me a reason to pat myself on the
back for recycling.

The Caliber started up as if it was glad to finally be
going home. With Chloe in the passenger seat, I was
driving back to the Fog Bell when I realized I'd never
asked Chief Vega the question that had been bugging
me.

"Ooowee," I said, annoyed.

I know. In New York, an exclamation like that would
have gotten me laughed out of town and possibly even
ticketed and fined. But after moving to Pigeon Cove, I'd
realized the opposite was true. I had to watch the four-
letter words in mixed company or risk sending people
into traumatic shock. The problem was that after years
of letting out streams of colorfully foul language when I
got aggravated, none of the usual sanitized interjections
had fit my mouth. "Phooey" sounded too childish.
"Drat" and "darn" had done for a while, but I'd never
really gotten comfortable with them. "For crumb's sake"
was weak and sterile, "fiddlesticks" way too prudish, and
"cripes" a word no one but a Saturday-morning cartoon
character should even consider. "Oh, crud" was passable, and I went with that quite a bit, though I craved
a little variety from time to time.

For the last month or so, I'd been experimenting with
"ooowee," maybe because its association with the old
Frankie Ford song made it kind of seditious. Everybody
knew what Frankie had in mind when he was "ooowee
babying" and "ooowee mama-ing" some girl to let him
take her on a sea cruise—and trying to persuade her she
had nothing to lose. Which *he* knew, and *she* knew,
wasn't exactly true, assuming she hadn't already lost it
and wasn't telling.

Ooowee. Yep, I kind of liked it. A grown woman
could say it without sounding like some kind of, well,
fuddy-duddy. Which was another scarily inoffensive
term.

"What's wrong, Sky?" Chloe said.

I had been quiet a full minute. And I knew my mental detour had less to do with forgetting to ask Vega my question than wanting to avoid the painful memory that raised the question in the first place.

"I was thinking about Lina Fipps," I said. "I'd meant to ask Chief Vega if he called her to let her know about Kyle."

Chloe pursed her lips and hmmmed. "I hear things were very nasty between Lina and Kyle."

I shrugged. "Things are nasty between Lina and almost everyone," I said. Which was true. She didn't exactly have a reputation for being the friendliest woman in town. "My point is, she's still Kyle's wife and ought to be notified."

Now it was Chloe's turn to sit in silence. I drove looking straight ahead into the night as the wipers swatted at the snow, and felt her looking at me, and was reminded why I was always confiding in her. I didn't have to verbalize the thoughts behind my thoughts to have her understand them.

My husband, Paul, had been a couple of years younger than Kyle when I lost him. It wasn't unexpected—we'd been fighting his illness for a very long time. But Paul had seemed to be having one of his better days, and I'd left his bedside at the hospice to get some things done at home.

Then, in the middle of the night, he'd taken a sharp downturn, and there had been an awful mix-up—when she tried to contact me, a nurse on watch had unbelievably called a wrong number and left a message on someone else's answering machine. I didn't find out about Paul until her supervisor wondered why I hadn't arrived and decided to phone again early the next morning. By then, my husband had been gone for several hours.

I would never forget how that felt. Not as long as I lived. And Chloe knew it.

"Lina needs to hear about Kyle," I said, still looking straight out my windshield. An icy layer of precipitation had slicked the blacktop. "Maybe she already has, but what if not? I'd hate to think of her getting blindsided by a condolence call from somebody who assumes she's been told when she hasn't."

Chloe didn't answer for a second.

"I wish Jessie were in town," she said. Her voice was low and thoughtful.

"Jessie Barton?"

Chloe nodded.

"She and Lina are friends."

That surprised me. "How'd that happen?"

"I'm not sure," Chloe said. "She told me Lina was a regular shopper at her store, so it may have started with that."

I drove along, thinking. Jessie had left town at the beginning of December after closing up the August Moon, a clothing boutique she'd owned on the jut of land we call the Gull Wing because of how it sort of curves out into the harbor. There hadn't been much warning. Or even a holiday clearance sale, for that matter. Just her telling everyone that she was ready for a change, and rumors that she'd run off on a toot with some rich guy she met on one of the vacation cruises she took about every other month . . . something that admittedly did fit her modus operandi. Jessie's flings were the stuff of legend. As I'd heard it, she'd left the Cove with a French tourist when she was in her twenties, split up with him right around the time their flight to Paris touched down, and then lived in about ten different European countries in as many years—with almost as many dashing international lovers—before finally coming home to open her boutique.

Still, Jessie's sudden departure had seemed kind of mysterious to me. Her shop had been one of the regular cleaning gigs on my schedule, and we'd come to know each other pretty well. But while I'd gotten some e-mails and a cheerful e-card or two from her since she'd left, they'd all been of the generic how-are-you-I'm-doing-fine variety. The same was true for everybody I'd spoken to—not a single person in town seemed to have a clue where she was. Given her history, though, I hadn't de-

tected any worry. They'd always figured that the August
Moon was a lark and she'd be gone again before long.

"I've got it," Chloe said, pulling me from my little
mental detour.

"Huh? Got what?"

"Marge Millwood is out of bed by five every morning.
I'll set my alarm and call her first thing. Before she can
grab a snow shovel."

I glanced over at her, puzzled.

"Why Marge?"

Chloe shrugged. "She insists on shoveling her own
walk and front steps," she said.

"No, Chloe. Why *call* her?"

"Because she's friends with Grace Blossom."

"The horticulturist?"

"Yes." Chloe nodded. "Who's also friends with Lina.
Lifelong friends, in fact." She paused. "Grace and Lina
were next-door neighbors growing up. Their mothers
were close, and it rubbed off on the girls. You would
always see them together."

"So now you're telling me Lina's got *two* solid
friendships?"

"Yes. Well, actually, the Fippses and the Fontaines
would socialize, too."

I looked at Chloe. "You keep this going, and Lina's
going to almost seem popular."

"I wouldn't go that far . . . I think the connection
there was mostly between Kyle and Finch," Chloe said.
"Anyway, Grace can phone Lina and make certain she
knows what's happened. Learn from yesterday, hope
for tomorrow."

I hesitated. For the second time that night, a Chloeism
had confused me, which was the opposite of their usual
effect. I'd gone way past the stage where they did anything but shed light on things.

"Chloe," I said, "if you don't mind my asking, where
are you getting these new expressions?"

"Is something wrong with them?" She sounded curious rather than defensive.

"No." I hesitated. "Well, sort of. It's just that they don't sound like you."

She shrugged.

"I picked up a book of sentence sermons," she said.

"Sentence sermons?" I repeated, clueless.

Chloe nodded.

"They're very pithy, and I try to use three or four a day," she said. " 'Anger manages everything badly' was one I thought would be more appropriate. But I hate to be too negative under the circumstances. And sermon or not, it does make me sound suspicious."

I was still lost.

"Suspicious of what?" I said.

The wipers *tock-tock-tock*ed. The heater blew. Chloe looked into the snowy night and cleared her throat.

"Never mind," she said. "You told me I was reading too many crime novels. That's why I picked up the book—it was in the swap shop at the dump, or waste drop-off center, or whatever fancy name they call it these days." She pointed out her window. "We're almost home. You have to turn at the next corner."

I looked at her.

"And here I thought the house might have moved from where it's stood since Thomas Jefferson was president," I said. "Come on, Chloe. What's up?"

She sat a moment with her lips pressed together.

"I know you were thinking about your Paul before," she said.

I nodded slowly.

"I guess what happened to Kyle made me remember the night he passed away," I said. "I didn't want Lina to go through anything similar to what I did. Even if she is the Wicked Witch of the West's local stand-in."

Chloe smiled gently and patted my arm.

"I was thinking of Paul as well, dear," she said. "But for a different reason."

I couldn't help looking surprised as I made the turn onto Carlisle Street.

"Paul was sick for so long," Chloe said. "Oscar and I

knew. We could see it the last time the two of you visited from New York. Even before you told us."

I nodded, exhaling.

"He'd lost a lot of weight," I said.

"Yes," Chloe said. "I suppose that's why it occurred to me that Kyle looked very healthy tonight. Odd, isn't it?"

"That he looked healthy?" I said. "Or that he died?"

Chloe didn't say anything. The Fog Bell was just ahead on the left and I pulled into the garage beside her VW Beetle. From early spring through late autumn, when she took guests at the inn, I'd have parked out on the street.

"Chloe," I said, turning off the engine, "about Kyle . . . I'm still not sure what you were getting at . . ."

She unlocked her door and reached for its handle.

"She who thinks twice before she speaks says only half as much," she said abruptly.

"What's *that* mean?"

"I don't quite know, dear. But it's in my new book and I think it sounds wise." Chloe looked around at me. "We'd better take our shoes off in the outer hall. Oscar will be fast asleep and I don't want to make a racket."

Chapter 4

Say you're an artist with a blank canvas, paintbrush in hand, imagining a village that epitomizes coastal New England for your next masterpiece. Better yet, forget the *artist* part and stick to being yourself. Just close your eyes for a second, let your romantic nature soar, and try to visualize such a wonderful place.

There you have it. That's Pigeon Cove. Clusters of two- and three-hundred-year-old houses, mostly Victorians and Colonials set along an idiosyncratic layout of narrow streets and lanes that slope unevenly toward the headlands rearing high above the sea. Behind their well-tended gardens, the exteriors of these residences and inns are subdued—clapboard white, pale yellow, beige, dove gray, and other muted colors meant to convey a traditional reserve that harks back to the Pilgrims. Inside, they're all wood-paneled drawing rooms and parlors, dark-beamed ceilings, stone hearths with crackling logs, and broad staircases leading up to cozy bedrooms with antique furniture and delicate floral wallpaper.

Of the many homes in our historic district, the Fog Bell is the only one that's gloriously pink, bucking a whole parcel of color code ordinances that mandate neutral exteriors. I'm not sure how Chloe finagled her way around the codes. She'd circumnavigated more legislated obstacles to her Chloeness than I could remember, maybe because her personal magic cast spells over even the grumpiest paper pushers at Town Hall. Whatever the source of her ability, I was hoping some of it would rub off on me. I'd put in a bid to become the exclusive cleaning service for the Cove's government offices, and was open to any edge I could get.

During the day, the Fog Bell's distinctive pinkness can't be missed. In the nighttime, when the lights wink off along Main Street, it usually blends in with the town's understated landmark colors. But as I approached it through the side yard, my cleaning kit in hand, the Christmas candles in its windows refracted off the wind-blown snow in the air to give it a soft, rosy shimmer. As worn-out as I felt, I couldn't help but pause to appreciate it. The place scintillated like an open jewel box from its foundations to its eaves.

"Lovely, isn't it?" Chloe had stopped beside me. "It settles me inside. Even when things aren't easy."

I nodded, recalling the wonderful enchanted feeling Paul and I had gotten when we'd first chanced upon the Fog Bell as weekend tourists. When he died, Chloe and Oscar had invited me up from New York to stay with them until I could pull myself together. They'd insisted that if I accepted, I absolutely wouldn't pay room and board for my guest suite. I'd insisted that if I absolutely didn't have to pay room and board, I *definitely* would have to do the housekeeping for Chloe. She agreed, and then I did, and with that negotiation clinched, my new life in Pigeon Cove and the famous Sky Taylor cleaning empire got their simultaneous starts.

It was also the start of how *I* got settled inside. I suppose I might have done it without Chloe. I think I'd have found the strength. I just don't know how long it would have taken, or how hard it would have been.

Standing amid the blowing flakes, I gave Chloe a smile of appreciation for more than she'd ever chosen to ac-knowledge, and then hefted my bag of tricks as we con-tinued over the path to the door. The lavender I'd planted around her house, greenish in spring and sum-mer, was silver-blue in the winter cold. I slipped off a glove while Chloe turned her key in the lock, rubbed my hand over a clump already dusted with fresh snow, and smelled the fragrance on the tips of my fingers. Pity the poor gardener who doesn't realize lavender is an evergreen.

After we'd kicked off our shoes and said good night, Chloe went straight through the inner door that opened to her kitchen, and I turned upstairs.

As I reached my suite I heard Skiball yelling on the opposite side of the door. Though I won't claim this is an exact quote, it sounded something like: *"Yaah-aaiieee-yaaay!"*

Her carrying on didn't worry me—and before anyone calls the animal police, let me explain. Skiball enjoyed shouting her little head off. It meant that she was having fun with a real or imaginary plaything—or to put it another way, battling a member of her villainous rogues' gallery. In my opinion, Ski's noisiness was rooted in insecurity. I was at least her third owner, having inherited her from my dear late friend Abel Monahan, who'd found her hungrily wandering on a deserted blacktop in Florida. She was small for a full-grown cat—tiny, in fact—and her impeccably white paws had already been declawed when Abe stumbled upon her. After he brought her home, he'd noticed some cuts or scratches on her ear and face and guessed she must have gotten them tussling with another cat. But without claws, Ski must have been defenseless in a fight. Maybe she'd turned to yelling as a way to scare off attackers, convincing them she was a crazy kung fu cat.

Be that as it may, Ski usually hollered while engaged in make-believe feline combat, which was probably the only type in which she could come out a winner. One recurrent adversary, for instance, was the evil Mrs. Mouseman, a stuffed white fabric mouse that started out being a Christmas tree decoration. Another of her regular foes was the Metallic Blue Hair Clip Creature, which coincidentally resembled some benign hair clips that came in a pack I'd recently bought. Then there was the Invisible Cat Catcher, whose mysterious stalking presence, though undetectable to the human eye, often sent her scrambling up onto my bed and across my chest in the middle of the night. But her true nemesis, the bane of her existence, was the elusive and unconquerable Taunting Tail Monster.

Most cats, I was told, outgrew chasing their tails by the time they said good-bye to kittenhood. My darling tuxedo, who was about three years old, bickered with hers several times a week. The spats didn't last long and always ended in an impasse. Usually Ski'd grow tired of trying to catch her tail or make it go away, and she'd take a nap.

My guess as I stood on the landing? Skiball was waging war on the Tail Monster right now. The note of exasperation in her hollering clued me in.

I opened the door, went inside, and set down my bag of tricks. Sure enough, Skiball was perched on the armrest of a wooden chair, her head bent forward underneath it so she could espy the Tail Monster flicking back and forth on the other side. She whacked at her nemesis with a forepaw, but the mischievous appendage nimbly flicked out of reach.

"Hi, Ski," I said. "That rotten tail's on your tail again, huh?"

Skiball looked up at me, her hostilities abruptly suspended.

"Sorry I'm late." I unbuttoned my coat. "You don't want to know the fine points, believe me."

"Ee-ee."

"Glad I'm home too. Go back to your grudge match if you want."

But Ski'd had her fill of it. She tumbled off the armrest, came across the room to me, and I picked her up.

When she wasn't engaging an opponent in mortal combat, Skiball liked to hug. As I hefted her into my arms, she sort of climbed onto my shoulder, pushed her face against my cheek, wrapped her front paws around my neck, and clung to it.

Remember those spitty little kids you knew in grade school? Well, Skiball was like that. A spitty little cat. In her most affectionate moments, Ski's mouth filled up with water and made squishing noises. The drooling always followed. I admit to thinking it was sort of cute, but

I unwrapped my vintage Peter Max scarf as the overflow began. I didn't want it getting a spit spot.

Carrying Skiball with me, I peeked into the bedroom and saw that my answering machine was blinking. Ski had turned to eight pounds of mush in my arms, and as I entered the room I gently put her down on a chair before she could fall asleep. She voiced a squeak of protest at our separation, but I wanted to listen to the message and take a hot bath before crawling under my blankets. My feet, ankles, and back ached from working in pumps all night.

I went to the answering machine and hit the playback button.

Sky, hello, it's about midnight, Mike's recorded voice said after a second. There was a lot of background noise. *I'm working a tip, but figured you'd be home by now, and hoped we could talk for a minute. . . . There's something I need to tell you.*

He paused. I hoped he wasn't about to sneak an I-love-you at me. He'd started to say it the morning before he left for Boston, and I'd put a hand over his mouth to shush him. It was an awkward moment considering what we'd been doing in bed for the half hour or so leading up to it, and considering that I'd pretty much instigated the action. Also, he'd been catching his breath and I hadn't wanted to cut off his air. Mike's slim but hard-bodied, and I wasn't sure I'd have been able to squirm out from under him if he lost consciousness.

"Don't, Mike," I said to the answering machine. "Stop. Red light. Dangerous intersection ahead."

. . . Look, I have to run. I just left a message on your cell, so hopefully you've gotten it. Later.

Well, whatever that was about, I'd been spared.

I had no sooner thought that than I wished I hadn't. It was unfair to Mike, and maybe to myself. I cared a lot about him. I missed him when he was away, and wished his arms were around me when they weren't. We had dated for three months before I finally took my wedding band off my left hand, put it on my right as befitting a widow on the make—no, you won't find that language in Emily Post—and then invited him over for a romantic dinner and told him he could leave his car keys in whatever pocket he'd put them.

That first time was passionate and exciting and I'd been ready for it. I'd known I was ready for a while before it happened, and felt comfortable with it every time afterward. But I was also comfortable with keeping things kind of open. I wasn't ready to say I loved him or ready for him to say it to me. I had loved my husband, loved him with every bit of my heart. How could I give any portion of that love to another man without taking it away from Paul?

Sighing, I turned from the machine and saw that Skiball was already curled on the chair with her eyes closed. I tiptoed past her, went back to where I'd left my purse near the door, and fished out my cell phone, a rose pink Sony that coordinated harmoniously with the outside of the inn. I'd left it with my purse and coat in one of the Art Association's back rooms while working and hadn't yet bothered to check my voice mail.

I went into the bathroom, carrying the phone with me. It was good that there had been no "I love you" on the answering machine. Very good, in fact. But now I was wondering what was going on with Mike, what was so important that he'd had to click off in a hurry.

Standing in front of the sink, I looked in the mirror and realized I was still wearing my red and white Santa hat. Somehow it seemed inappropriate headgear for finding a dead body and then dealing with policemen and EMTs. No wonder Vega had stared at me.

I frowned and ditched the hat. Then I put my cell phone on a glass shelf beside the sink and took off my earrings, a pair of small gold hoops I liked to wear when I cleaned because they didn't get in the way of things. Also on the shelf where I'd set the phone was a wire earring tree and a ceramic ashtray with a Japanese picture motif of a log stilt house in a field of snow. I used the ashtray as a receptacle for earrings I'd either worn or tried on and hadn't gotten around to hanging back on the tree.

Though I was exhausted and eager for my bath, I'd noticed that I had two messages on the cell. One was probably Mike's. But I wanted to see who'd left the other.

I reached for the phone, hit the one-touch message-retrieval button, put it in speaker mode, placed it back on the shelf next to the ashtray, and started taking off my face. My mascara was smudged after what had been a long night, so I saturated a cotton square with eye makeup solvent and dabbed it off as I listened to the first message.

Sky, it's Mike. I don't have much time, and it's hard to hear myself speak over all the noise in here.

Hard for me to hear you too, I thought. And that was with him practically shouting into the phone. I realized the racket I'd noticed before was some kind of pulsing electronic dance music.

I'm still in Boston.

Where in Boston?

On Lagrange Street, Mike said. *At the Silk N' Lace gentlemen's club.*

"Strip club, you mean," I said, thinking aloud. The old Combat Zones had been cleaned up except for a handful of them, including the one where our married and currently up-for-reelection city council president Tommy Thompson was supposed to have been seen throwing bills all over the stage at a gyrating employee. This was a couple of weeks before a freelance news photographer took some shots of him at a Celtics game flanked by two young, unnaturally well-endowed women, neither of whom was his missus.

I'm waiting for a dancer. Her name's Omega—

"And mine's Giggles," I said.

—to finish her act.

"Finish stripping naked, Mike, puh-leese." I bent over the sink, started washing my face, and wondered if Omega was one of the basketball hotties.

Omega knows another dancer named Sandy Savoy—

"On second thought, call me Sticky Sundae."

—who's her ex-roommate and just quit working here.

*She's that razzle-dazzle blonde in those pictures of
Thompson at the Garden.*

"The one whose chest he was using as a face cushion,"
I said through a splash of cool water.

*If I'm lucky, I'll have a chance to meet with Savoy at
a club in Revere called the Sugar Shack, where she's
worked since the scandal broke,* Mike said. *We're driving
out there together—*

"Who's 'we'?"

Omega and I, that is—

"How sweet."

*—as soon as she's done with her last set, which she's
about midway through.*

"Not that you're paying attention."

Anyway, it looks like this is turning into a late night . . .

"Sure does."

I've got no idea when I'll get back to my hotel room . . .

"Uh-huh."

But I wanted to say hi while I had a chance—

"Hi backatcha, Mike."

—and that I've been thinking about you—

"Thanks, Mike," I said.

*—and will probably try you at home before we head
out.*

"Don't let me distract you," I said as Mike and the
grinding dance music went silent on my phone's speaker.

So much for worrying about a proclamation of love.
So much, too, for my being comfortable. Although my
*dis*comfort with Mike venturing out on dark, twisty roads
with the helpful and slowly-but-surely-revealing Omega
annoyed me, mainly because the feeling had caught me
by surprise. It wasn't as if he was out carousing. He was
a reporter doing his job, and that happened to be following a story that had made banner headlines in the *Boston
Globe* and grabbed the attention of the entire North
Shore. If the woman he was going to meet was half of
the juicy twosome in the Tommy Thompson photo it
would be a major coup for him and the *Anchor*.

And as for me . . . keep things open. That was my
motto. You could, in fact, call me open Sky. Which had

a certain ring to it, though it wasn't particularly slinky as a stage name.

I turned off the tap, soaked another cotton pad with witch hazel, whisked it over my face, and was applying some light moisture cream when the second voice mail started its playback.

Sky, honey, it's Betty.

Betty was my mother. Around when I was six or seven, my parents hooked up with a Jungian-Buddhist guru who recommended they address themselves to me by their first names and that I do the same to them. At our family-individuation session, he explained it had something to do with ego transcendence and removing psychic tyranny from the parent-child relationship. The guru fell out of favor with them after a few months, but the use of first names didn't.

I preferred the old tried-and-trues.

"Hi, Mom," I said to the cell phone. "What's up?"

Did you read my e-mail?

"Nope." I'd gotten the tub running, poured in some bath oil, and started to undress. "Haven't been on the computer."

Because if you read it, I hope you'll answer me. And if you haven't read it, you should when you get a chance.

Makes sense, I thought. "Care to say why?"

It has important news.

Now there was an explanation. Between Mike and Mom, I'd have to use every modern communications medium known to man tonight.

Okay, I'm hanging up, Mom said. *I feel foolish talking to an impersonal automated message bank. Please check your e-mail. Again, this is Betty.*

No kidding, I thought.

I eased into the steaming bathtub and soaked for a while. It was delightful and took the soreness out of me. When I got out, I added a few drops of liquid detergent to the draining water from a squeeze bottle on the shampoo rack. This helped prevent scum from forming on the sides of the tub.

Then it was into one of my oversized T-shirts—the

kind that almost reach your knees—and a pair of cat slippers. The slippers were Betty-Mom's creation. She'd hand-sewn and embroidered them after I adopted Skiball. Each slipper had half a cat on it. The right one had the cat's head, the left the tail. She'd used emerald green rhinestones for its eyes and stitched a pink ribbon scarf around the kitty's neck.

That's Betty-Mom. Weird but thoughtful.

My computer's on a desk in the bedroom, and I went straight over to it after finishing my bath and turned it on, yawning as I opened Betty-Mom's e-mail.

The yawn froze on my face and turned into a gasp. Then the gasp turned into a gulp. Her message read:

Dear Sky,

Big news! A wonderful doctor of psychoanalytical spirituality from Mumbai is holding a Laughter Yoga retreat for stress management in California! It's scheduled to coincide with the Christmas-Hanukkah-Kwanzaa winter solstice celebration, and Lou and I have signed up to attend! But here's the great part . . . are you sitting down for this?

Lou is already in San Francisco on business, and I'm flying in to join him from home. And since I have to take a connecting flight in Boston . . . I've decided to *visit you in Pigeon Cove* for a few days next week! Let's start making arrangements—I can't wait to meet your friend Chloe!

Couldn't wait to tell you! This is so EXCITING!!!!

Hugs and Kisses,
Betty

Lou, I probably needn't mention, is Dad.

I had no inkling—I mean none whatsoever—what Laughter Yoga might be. But I did know what a visit from Mom was. There wasn't a speck of confusion in my mind about that.

I sat there staring at the screen for a couple of minutes. I managed not to gasp again as I reread Mom's e-mail to confirm that it wasn't an optical illusion, but I did do some more gulping before I turned off the computer and went to bed.

Once under the blankets, I reached over and shut off the light. I heard Skiball jump down off the chair where she'd been snoozing and then felt her jump up onto my bed and settle in beside my legs. I told myself not to think about Mom's imminent touchdown in the Cove, and I succeeded. But then my mind turned to Mike instead. Why, I wondered, was it vital for him to hang around the Sugar Shack for Sandy Savoy's act rather than talk to her there *after* its grand finale?

Depositing that delightful question into my not-to-be-considered-while-trying-to-fall-asleep thought bin—which was filling much faster than I might have wished—I closed my eyes and listened to Skiball purr until I finally dozed off.

But sometime later I found myself lying on my back in the darkness, my eyes wide open. I'd been dreaming about Kyle Fipps falling from his stage hammock at the Art Association, and had awakened remembering Chloe's remark from when we were driving home.

I hate to be too negative under the circumstances . . . It does make me sound suspicious.

"Suspicious of what?" I asked the ceiling, repeating the exact same question I'd asked Chloe.

Like Chloe, the ceiling wouldn't say.

Chapter 5

The morning after the Art Association affair, I left the Fog Bell at quarter to seven, spent a while finishing the dishes and leftover tidying up at the exhibit hall, and then drove down to Lanesville, which has its own exit on the Grant Circle rotary. The owner of the town's largest manor, a man in his nineties named Austen Graffam, would be hosting a Christmas Eve reunion for about a hundred favorite relatives on his California redwood–sized family tree, and I'd totaled about four hours' worth of broken sleep to carry me through the job of getting his place sparkling clean for the festivities.

Austen was a dapper vintage gent who always answered his door wearing a turtleneck and checked sport coat. I liked giving him a hand, and normally found the drive through Lanesville enjoyable, as it took me onto the stone bridge that led across Mill Pond on Washington Street and then up and down some hilly, tree-lined streets to his riverfront home on Reef Knot Way. The rooms smelled of aged, polished wood and his hundreds of rare leather-bound books, and on clear days the sunlight flooded through the enormous upstairs windows so you could see the rocky breakwater out past the shore. Austen was very self-sufficient for his age and did most of his own shopping chores and errands in the warm weather, riding downtown on a motorized tricycle that he boasted could attain about ten miles an hour on battery power and rev to fifteen miles an hour when he pedaled.

Most days my trip to Lanesville took thirty minutes at the outside. But I'd given myself extra time, knowing it would be slow going in the rush-hour traffic heading down to Boston. Over half a foot of frozen precipitation had fallen overnight—and you will note I didn't say snow. At some point the flaky stuff had mixed with sleet and rain, and then turned back to snow, and then sleet again, making for three or four layers of slipperiness on the ostensibly plowed road.

It wasn't the driving conditions, however, that made me kind of wiggly as I approached the stone bridge that particular morning. Wiggliness, I should explain, falls short of a full-fledged case of the creeps. But it isn't fun, and may be accompanied by localized outbreaks of gooseflesh. Although I suppose my exhaustion played into it a little, I think it was mostly because you need to go past Addison Gilbert Hospital before crossing the bridge. That was where the EMS vehicle had delivered Kyle Fipps, who I assumed was in the process of being examined by the county coroner.

My spiffing-up of the Graffam manse took me until about two o'clock, but because of the bad weather I volunteered to buy some groceries for Austen afterward. When I got back I spent an extra few minutes politely begging off his grateful offers to stay for a smidgeon of Earl Grey, chocolate biscotti, a tale or three of his rascalish youth, and possibly a courtly pavane and galliard around his great room. He seemed disappointed, but brightened at the special holiday present I gave him. I'd made one for each of my longtime accounts.

"Sky, how fabulously inspired!" he said, looking over the gift

Actually the idea had come about less by inspiration than by accident, kind of like the discovery of penicillin. But I was okay with basking in Austen's praise, since my gift did have a high originality quotient.

It was about ten past three when I finally left his company, which put me in a bit of a rush. I wanted to be at the *Anchor* by three thirty to spend a couple of hours working on my Sky Writing column in the cubbyhole office I shared with Bev Snow, the gossip columnist. Since it barely had enough room for one person and a desk—providing the person was relatively slim and took his or her coat off before entering—Bev and I had worked out a schedule that gave me solo use of it a couple of afternoons a week. While I did a lot of writing on my computer at home, I found that the change of environment increased my productivity, maybe because it was easier to type without Skiball slapping her fuzzy tail across my keyboard.

The headquarters of the *Cape Ann Anchor* was two stories of rectangular concrete and glass off one of a pair of roundabouts on Route 128 in Gloucester. If you're driving from Lanesville, the Grant Circle rotary comes up first, a short distance past the Annisquam Bridge and the salt marsh alongside the river. Then there's the stretch of woods and bouldery ridge that's part of Dogtown Common and leads to Blackburn Circle. Going on to Pigeon Cove, you bear left inside the circle and continue northward on the main road for a few miles. A quick swing to the right off Blackburn into a curving drive will lead to the parking area out front of the newspaper offices.

I swung the Caliber into the lot, wound through a maze of plowed snowbanks, and took a spot near the entrance beside a scarlet Audi TT Roadster that drew me to it like a beacon. It was quite a dazzling eyeful— about fifty or sixty thousand dollars' worth of dazzle, I guessed. I didn't know anyone working at the *Anchor* who could afford anything like it except our owner and publisher, Boone Stevenson—though last I'd heard, Boone was off hot-air ballooning over the Mato Grosso do Sul in Brazil. This, I'd gathered, complemented the summer-long Arctic exploration cruise he'd taken a few months after I'd written my first column for the paper.

Boone wasn't what you would call hands-on. He'd inherited the paper from his father, and he left its daily operation to our editor, Gregg Connors. But who knew? Maybe his balloon had sprung a leak and he'd cut off his latest toot to stop by and say howdy to his employees.

I got out of the Caliber and admired the Audi for a minute, wishing I'd worn sunglasses to cut down on its bright red glare. Then I went around back to my cargo hatch, opened it, and reached inside for an extra one of my special client gifts. I'd felt it would be a cheery touch for the little kitchen that adjoined our employee lounge.

Pam DiGallucci is our receptionist at the paper, though the job title seems oxymoronic considering how unreceptive she is to everyone who passes through the door. "Rejectionist" might better describe her, but we stick with what the English language affords. Besides, most of us just call her the Digger. I know, it isn't as sultry a sobriquet as Omega. Or even Open Sky. But it is apropos—wait and see.

"Sky, you're here," she said with a puckery semblance of a smile.

"Yep, yep, here I am," I said, and tried blowing past her desk.

"It's such a cold, miserable day," the Digger said, looking at me through her huge red Dolce & Gabbana frames. "Snow should be banished to hell, don't you think?"

"Be the right place for it to melt." I kept moving.

The Digger's face followed me, her slabbed-on makeup giving it a plastery appearance. Back during my advertising days, I'd done a campaign for a famous European clothes designer who'd told me that French and English women in the 1800s would sip arsenic, or even eat arsenic wafers, to achieve pale, waifish complexions. I suspected Pam had a gigantic vat of the stuff at home for her daily immersion, and that she'd added gallons of formaldehyde and pickle brine to the formula. The result, however, was decidedly more Baby Jane Hudson than waifish.

"What's that you've got in your hand?" She was pointing at the extra gift I'd brought in from the Caliber.

"Just a little something," I said.

"What kind of little something?"

"A little something I brought for the kitchen upstairs."

"It looks like a bottle," she said.

"A bottle it is," I said. Another few feet and I'd round her desk, then safely zip into the corridor leading to our office area.

"I wouldn't be in such a hurry," the Digger said in a cryptic tone.

I paused for the slightest beat.

"Why not?"

She gave me a look to match her tone. Her eyebrows, waxed to pencil-thin points, spiked up above her D&Gs.

"I'd really love to see the bottle," she said. "It seems very interesting."

I sighed, paused, and raised it to let her have a look.

A few years into our marriage, my late husband, who'd been an accomplished chef, bought a bistro in downtown Manhattan called the Souper Bowl. Yes—give yourself a Mensa point—this was because his forte was gourmet soups. Whenever the sales reps from wine and liquor distributors stopped by to pitch their wares, they'd leave him samples in all sorts of fancy glass bottles and decanters. Fluted designs, spirals . . . every shape you can imagine. Paul would bring the prettiest bottles home—clear ones do it for me, so those were my keepers. When they were empty I would wash them out, put a few on display, and box up others, figuring I'd eventually find a practical use for some of them.

Then one day while I was washing the dishes, it struck me that the plastic bottles of dishwashing liquid I used were kind of clunky, not to mention unattractive, kitchen staples. They kept dropping from my fingers when I reached for them—whether because I'm a born klutz, or because I have small hands, or because I'm a small-handed klutz, I don't know. But in a burst of inspiration, I remember drying my hands, going to the closet, taking out one of the narrower decorative bottles I'd boxed away, bringing it to the sink, and then filling it with the contents of a plastic container of Palmolive Liquid—the original green type. The dish soap had been almost used up to begin with, leaving me with a load of room in the glass bottle, so I'd gotten a second, unopened container of Palmolive out of the sink cabinet—it was their red Spring Sensations Wild Berry Blossom, which I'd just bought for a change of pace—and topped off the bottle with it.

I had no idea the two varieties wouldn't mix—it honestly wasn't something I'd considered. When I poured them into the same bottle together I expected the different colored detergents to blend into a murky gray. But the green Palmolive stayed on the bottom and the red on top. Even when I tilted the bottle to pour from it, or gave it an experimental shake, the red and green would separate before too long. The green always settled to the bottom, I guessed because it was denser—but don't quote me on that in chemistry class.

What I knew for certain was that it was pretty. And that the bottle was much easier to handle than the plastic container.

After Paul died and I moved to the Cove, I'd realized there were all sorts of ornamental glass receptacles that could be used in place of bottles that contained expensive wine and spirits. Leaf-shaped maple syrup jars were just right, the notches between the lobes making excellent finger and thumb indentations. I also found decorative jars of chiles, vinegars, and infused oils at remainder shops after the holidays—some selling for as little as a dollar apiece—that worked beautifully. To seal them I would recycle natural corks that I saved from wine bottles. They looked nice and were pliant enough to fit different-sized bottle necks

So, there you have it, the origin of my special holiday gift. It was cheery. It was signature. It was perfectamundo and stylistically *pour moi*.

Not that the Digger looked impressed.

"So what's that inside the bottle?" She tapped her mouth with a lacquered and sharply manicured fingernail. "Colored water?"

I shook my head.

"It's soap," I said.

"Ah."

"Red and green dish soap."

"Ah." The Digger eyed the bottle. "So I take it this is another of your homemade items."

"Right. Any further questions or comments?"

"Just that red and green are Christmas colors," said the Digger.

"Nooo," I said.

"Yes," she said.

"Really? No kidding?"

"Really. No kidding." The Digger's hard-packed crust of makeup seemed impervious to my sarcasm. "And this is a public workplace."

She looked at me. I looked back at her.

"So what are you saying?" I asked.

"Only that we have a staff with diverse religious backgrounds. Besides the employees who may be agnostics or atheists. And it's possible those who don't celebrate Christmas will be offended."

"By a bottle of red and green dish soap."

"You never know."

I stood there a second.

"Are *you* offended?"

"Me?"

"You."

"Not personally, no," she said. "But I'm Catholic. Nonpracticing. Although still I enjoy certain traditions."

I stood there thinking. My parents had been through about a dozen spiritual transformations before I was twelve. I guess you could say they were early devotees of the Beatles. Especially George. Where he went, they went. Later on, they grew disillusioned with him and followed Dylan's lead toward happiness and fulfillment. But Bobbo never seemed to know which way he wanted to go for more than an album at a time, and always seemed crabby, and that confused them.

After a while Betty-Mom and Lou-Dad went on to follow in the cosmic footsteps of other sixties and seventies recording artists—well, unless they were tied to Satan worship. Thankfully that was one place my parents didn't venture, maybe because they'd never been metal fans. Also, they were not about to hurt cute, furry animals.

The point being that I grew up celebrating a hodge-podge of holidays. And that I hadn't considered that my red and green dish-soap bottle might have religious connotations. I just kind of thought it was fun and Christmassy in a seasonal way. Like *It's a Wonderful Life.* Or those *Frosty the Snowman* and *Rudolph the Red-Nosed Reindeer* TV specials. Or the annual *Ice Age* sequel. Call me naive, but it wasn't as if I'd put a manger scene inside.

I have to admit, though—the Digger suddenly had me wondering. Was it possible I was being insensitive to people's beliefs? That I'd insulted some of my clients with my dish-soap bottles? Austen Graffam had seemed appreciative of his . . . and so had the others . . . but maybe a bunch of them had covered up their feelings and just wanted to be polite. Who knew?

I looked at Pam's pickle puss. Give her a whiff of uncertainty and she'd eat you alive.

"I understand it's thrifty to make your own gifts, but you should reconsider creating divisions," she said. "A desk drawer might be the best place for that inappropriate creation until you can get it out of here and buy something we can all have the benefit of enjoying." She paused. "A box of inexpensive cookies might be preferable."

Zing! Double-zing! Now I was insensitive *and* cheap.

"Thanks for the tips," I said. And started turning back toward the corridor. "If you'll excuse me, though, I feel a need to go gag in the privacy of my office."

"You're sure of it."

I halted, still in the Digger's unyielding clutches.

"Of *what*?"

Her fingernail met her lower lip again. Tapped it. "I read a magazine article. Plus I've had my share of bad experiences. Four marriages, four ex-husbands. There are lessons to be learned."

I looked at her. Enough was enough.

"Did I miss something, or did you just completely not answer my question?" I said.

Tap, tap, tap.

"I may spend my days sitting right here," she said, "but I know what goes on back there."

Emphasizing the "back there" part with a backward nod toward the office suite.

There'd be no disputing that from me, let me tell you.

"Workplace romances lead to unhappy endings," she said, and forced a sigh. "Take it from one who knows."

I looked at her. *Aha,* I thought. This was about Mike and me . . . which, incidentally, and as promised, ought to explain why the Digger was called the Digger. Besides being a spreader of misery, Pam DiGallucci lived to dig into everyone else's business.

Not that Mike and I had gone out of our way to keep our relationship under wraps. But Pam had kept her claws out of it to that point. "Is there anything else you want to share with me?"

"The article on doomed office affairs," Pam said. Tap, tap. "I can bring it from home. Along with a few others on the same topic."

"That's so considerate," I said. "Bet you've got a file folder stuffed with 'em."

The Digger's finger stopped in mid-tap. "How did you *know*?" Blinking in surprise.

I didn't answer. I needed to reach a sane abuse-free zone, and sometimes silent flight is best.

I spun around and whooshed off into the hall before she could get her hooks into me again, my big herringbone overcoat flapping in my back draft.

In the office, I placed my controversial red and green dish-soap bottle on top of the credenza, hung up my coat, and then smoothed my outfit in front of the full-length mirror Bev and I had put up inside the door. I had on faded Levi's with a loose-fitting man's white shirt, a huge gray cardigan sweater, and a silky black scarf that I wore like a loosened necktie. Smart, comfy, and suitable for the housecleaning-pro-slash-newspaper-columnist.

After a minute I went to my desk and sat down. First

things first—I needed to quit worrying about the bottle for a while. Ditto for trying to make heads or tails of Pam's vampiric Dear Abby routine. As far as the bit about the articles, I thought, she'd probably improvised it on the spot. I mean, could it really be that she kept them in *files*?

I logged on to the computer. I'd been seeking a theme for my column, and as usual had wanted to let it come to me rather than feel for it. I'd sensed there was something worth saying about how a single night could encompass the tragedy of Kyle Fipps and the fantastical image of the Fog Bell shimmering like a box of precious gems in the snow. About how magic and loss could be so closely intertwined. The meaning I took from it was floating around somewhere in my head and heart, but hadn't yet articulated itself to me, which was okay. It would come when I relaxed, got clear of distractions, and put my fingers to the keyboard. This wasn't always easy, granted. Sometimes what I thought would be easy was longer, harder work than I expected, and sometimes the columns that I thought would be hard flew effortlessly from my fingers, as if I were writing in some kind of trance. But sooner or later the words would come. I'd learned to trust in that.

Of course, I *did* mention something about distractions, didn't I?

I was settling into my chair when I noticed the red LOAD PAPER light on the printer on its stand to my right. Bev was mostly a conscientious officemate, but filling the empty paper tray or bringing an extra pack or two of paper from the cabinet out in the hall was a notable exception to the rule. The trouble wasn't laziness—it just escaped her mind. Bev did all her proofreading onscreen and rarely bothered with printouts of her articles. But I didn't like to write without paper in the printer. Until I read my sentences in hard copy, I was never quite sure of their flow, and missed a bunch of typos and grammatical goofs.

I got up, stepped out into the hall, and turned toward

the paper cabinet against the wall near Mike's closed office door. I wondered if Mike was on his way home yet, and while I was wondering I tried to pull open the big steel cabinet's drawer. It stuck, though, and I had to pull again with added oomph before finally managing to wrestle it open.

That, I thought, would never do.

I took out a couple of reams of paper and, without closing the drawer, carried them to my office. Then I set them down next to the printer and went over to the metal Cleaning First-Aid Kit mounted on the wall to the immediate right of my desk. Once upon a time, before I'd picked it up at a local Goodwill for about fifty cents, the Cleaning First-Aid Kit had led another life as the sort of industrial Red Cross First-Aid Kit you'd see in businesses and schools back in the fifties. Its emergency medical provisions had been gone for decades, not that I'd have used Mercurochrome or aspirin that was older than I was. But the case itself was nifty—like a miniature metal valise with a lid that latched on top and opened conveniently downward, with two shelves for neat storage of emergency cleaning standbys.

I reached inside the well-stocked kit and took a small, wrapped generic soap bar from where it sat on the lower shelf, under my assortment of multipurpose brushes and flanked by a bottle of Goo Gone and a bar of Fels Naptha. Then I returned to the paper cabinet in the hall and rubbed the soap along the runners several times to get them good and greased, and to give myself another chance to stare at the outside of Mike's door and become annoyed at myself for it. I wanted to see him more than I cared to. I couldn't help it.

After I'd smeared a visible coating of soap on the runners, I gave the drawer a push and it glided smoothly into the cabinet. Phase One of my test was a go, leading me to, that's right, Phase Two—or pulling the drawer out.

I grabbed the handle, tugged.

Ever hear of something being too much of a go?

The drawer didn't just pull out, it came *all* the way out, gliding forward on its soap-greased runners like a hockey puck over ice.

"Whoops," I said as the front of the drawer banged into me.

No, hang on. That's downplaying things to spare myself a smidge of humiliation.

Actually, I screamed, *"Whooo-ooo-ooo-ooops!"* at the top of my lungs and flopped backward onto my rear end as the drawer skidded forward off the cheapo guards that were supposed to keep it from leaving the runners and doing what it did next—which was shoot out of the cabinet to hit the floor with a heavy, reverberating crash and pour an avalanche of paper reams over my sprawling legs.

Before I could recover, there was a second crash over to my right. I looked toward the noise from flat on my back and saw that Mike's office door had flown open and Mike was rushing into the hall to where I'd tumbled backward, a blond woman leaning her head out his door behind him.

"Sky!"

Mike came running over to me, knelt, and reached his hand out. "Sky, what happened, let me help, are you okay?"

I glanced up from the floor. The blonde who'd leaned out of Mike's office had followed him into the hall and was peering down at me from somewhere in the stratosphere. If I hadn't recognized her from newspaper photos, I'd have guessed she'd just arrived from Amazon Island.

Then a thought pinched my mind so hard I wanted to say ouch. Which I refrained from doing, since it would have been anticlimactic after *"Whooo-ooo-ooo-ooops."*

"What are *you* doing here?" I asked Mike.

He seemed at a loss. "What do you mean?"

"You aren't supposed to be back yet," I said. Deliberately ignoring his hand. "And I didn't see your car in the parking lot."

He kept looking at me but didn't say anything.

The stratospherically tall blonde did, however.

"I gave him a lift," she said. "That is, Michael and I drove in together."

"Together," I said. "You and *Michael*."

A nod.

"From his house."

"His house."

"Where we spent the night." The blonde smiled in his direction.

Still paying no attention to Mike's hand, I propped myself on my elbows, raised my head off the floor, and stared up at her.

"Snazzy red Audi you've got," I said.

Chapter 6

Call me Exhibit A. And Sandy Savoy Exhibit B. Shall we compare and contrast?

I had average, medium-brown eyes that were puffy from lack of sleep and that I'd recently found out needed stronger contacts.

Sandy Savoy's eyes were clear and blue as a summer sky, and big as, oh, let's all say "eternity" together.

I stood five feet five inches and weighed a hundred twenty-five, with a few pounds of extra winter cushioning around the hips that made my jeans feel a bit snug, and that you won't hear me mention again since I've already done it twice.

Sandy Savoy was five feet eleven inches and weighed about the same as I did—except about 10 percent of that weight was in her perfectly fitted, fifties-style, Audrey Hepburn–esque white ski pants, and the other 90 percent was up top in her chest, barely held in check by whatever feeble article of containment she'd worn under an ultra huggy pink sweater.

I once wrote a car ad that featured a running gazelle.

Sandy Savoy had the legs of a gazelle, albeit one that went darting around in soft and supple suede sock boots.

I had straight brown hair that fell just past my shoulders.

Sandy Savoy had silky blond extensions that went flowing down her back like a cascade of golden sunlight, setting off the stunningly blue eyes we've discussed.

Since I'm in control of this presentation, however, I think I'll downplay those eyes. And the *golden* part of that description. Emphasizing the word "extensions." Lovely to look at, yes. But expensive enough to pay a top salon's monthly overhead, and keep Sandy Savoy there for endless hours of high maintenance.

Okay, I was rebounding. Mike liked running his fingers through my hair, and I kind of liked it that that her artificial tresses screamed, "DO NOT TOUCH!"

And then I noticed that she'd parked a humongous Louis Vuitton monogram duffel on a chair next to the one I'd taken in Mike's office.

Our new terms of emphasis? Take your pick between "humungous" and the famous-designer brand name.

Rebound over.

I stared at Sandy Savoy's bag. And then stared some more. It must have cost about triple what she'd paid for the extensions. With its luggage tag, lock, and key, I was thinking that it was roomy enough inside to accommodate about a week's worth of outfit changes. And that it would barely qualify as carry-on aboard a plane.

"Maybe you should drink some of this, Sky," Mike said. As I continued to stare, he stood in front of his desk and hovered over me with a glass of water I didn't take. "From in here it sounded like you had quite a hard *spill*—"

"That wasn't me," I said, prying my eyes from the bag.

He gave me a puzzled, concerned look. Sandy Savoy, who was standing at full Amazonian height behind an empty chair on the far side of her purse, likewise seemed befuddled, though I wasn't sure she shared any part of his concern. I looked at her, trying to remember the name of Wonder Woman's ageless bombshell goddess of a mom.

It wasn't Betty—that much I knew.

"Sky," Mike said, "you do remember falling in the hall a minute ago, right?"

"Sure."

"Oh. I'm glad. " Mike looked relieved. "That you remember, I mean. Because your answer made me wonder if you'd blacked out or something—"

"I didn't clunk my head on the floor *that* hard," I said.

"Oh. I just wondered, because you said—"

"I meant it wasn't me you heard crashing down. It was the cabinet drawer."

"Oh. Right—"

"I'd have to be a great big fatso to make that kind of racket." *Rapunzel,* I thought. *No, wrong. She was the blonde imprisoned in the tower. And why am I being defensive about my weight?*

Mike stood looking at me. He was still holding out the water, and I still wasn't taking it. Instead I was suddenly recalling the name of the queen of Amazon Island. Or was it Paradise Island in the comic books?

"Hippolyta," I muttered under my breath.

"Excuse me?" Mike said.

"Never mind." I shrugged. "Now how about *my* question?"

"Yours?"

"The one I asked you while I hit the deck," I said. "You do remember it, right?"

Mike looked at me. His eyes, like mine, were brown. But unlike mine, they weren't average medium brown. They were a deep, dark, molasses color that could pull you in and make you feel warm and syrupy all over if you let them.

I wondered whether I had a right to sound so peeved. And why I felt that way toward Mike. It couldn't be jealousy, I told myself. I wasn't the jealous type. And besides, we were free birds. No commitment, no promises, no demands—that was how I'd wanted it. He wasn't obliged to report to me about his comings and goings. Strictly speaking, they weren't my business. Nor was whatever he was doing with Sandy Savoy and her pricey overnight bag. And besides, shouldn't I just be glad to see him? Wasn't a day early better than a day late?

"Michael came back to Pigeon Cove today because I insisted."

This was from Sandy Savoy.

I snapped my head around at her.

Not my business, I thought. *Not the jealous type. Nope, nope, nope.*

"You insisted," I repeated sharply.

She was nodding. "I told him I wouldn't tell him my story otherwise. Because if I do tell it, and that rotten phony denies the truth when it gets printed . . . which you can bet he will . . . then I intend to be right here in Pigeon Cove to tell him to deny it right to my face."

I sat there decoding that for a minute. The scary part was it made sense to me.

"By 'rotten phony,'" I said, "you mean—"

"Tommy Thompson," she said.

Which I'd already figured out. As I said, scary.

Mike looked over my head at Sandy.

"You don't have to discuss this right now," he said. "That is, if you want it kept in confidence."

"Sky's a friend of yours, isn't she?" she said.

"Well, yes."

"A close friend?"

He fidgeted with his collar. "Um, yes."

"And what I say is going to come out in your paper anyway," she said.

"True . . ."

The two of them exchanged glances. Across the air-space over my head, needless to say. Meanwhile, I sat there wondering if I should apologize for eavesdropping on their conversation about me.

"I trust you, Michael," Sandy said. "If you tell me Sky's your friend, which you do, I have no problem trusting her. Or with her being in the room when I tell you what I have to." Her hand came to rest on my shoulder from above. She had rings on every finger, including her thumb. "Besides, I think we need a woman journalist's view of things."

I looked up at her.

"Actually, I'm not a journalist," I said.

"You aren't?"

I shook my head.

"I write a column," I said. "Making me a columnist."

"There's a difference?"

I nodded.

Sandy Savoy's baby blues looked at me. Her rings twinkled. One of them had a sapphire the color of her eyes that was nestled in a crust sparkling with diamonds.

"As a columnist . . . what do you write about?" she asked.

I considered that.

"Living," I said. "With some cleaning tips thrown in."

Sandy patted me with her gemstone-encrusted fingers.

"That sounds wonderful. You're in, Sky," she said, and lowered her slinky length into the empty chair beyond the monster LV bag.

"Let's get going, Michael."

Mike went around his desk, sat, and reached into an inner pocket of his gray wool sport coat. The digital recorder he took out was about the size of a pack of Wrigley's gum. He set it on his desk and pushed it across his blotter so it would be closer to Sandy.

"All right," he said, turning it on. "We're on the record."

Sandy nodded. I waited, thinking that I found Sandy Savoy kind of likable. It wasn't her fault she was gorgeous.

"About your relationship with Tommy Thompson," Mike said. "Tell me how you'd characterize it, Sandy."

"I'd characterize my relationship with the phony—"

"This being Thompson, just so we're clear . . . ?"

"Yes, Tommy T. Thompson. The phony who's head of Thompson Accounting and the city council president of Pigeon Cove. The phony who claimed to love me and then did something I can't forgive."

Mike rapped his fingers on his desk. "Talk about that a little, if you don't mind."

"Which part? The I-love-you-Sandy? Or the can't-forgive?"

"For starters," Mike said, "I-love-you-Sandy."

I tried not to wince at the sound of that.

Sandy shrugged.

"We've been seeing each other for two years," she said.

"Seeing each other intimately?"

"Oh, you know it. Having every kind of intimacy you can imagine."

Mike cleared his throat.

"Okay . . ."

"Every kind and *then* some—that's how intimate we were, but I won't go into details. Though I want to add that we were completely exclusive for over a year and a half."

Sandy paused. Mike waited. While she paused, and he waited, a question occurred to me and I wondered if I ought to chime in with it. Then I decided that if I was in, I was in.

"Tommy Thompson's a married man," I said. "With a couple of children—"

Sandy held up three ringed fingers to correct me.

"He has a two-month-old," she said. "A baby girl."

"*Three* kids," I said, doing some quick math to account for the third. It didn't add up. "I guess that has me confused. If you've been exclusive as long as you say, but his daughter's two months old—"

"I meant exclusive, Tommy's relations with his wife notwithstanding," Sandy said. "I guess you've never been in mistress territory, Sky."

No, I thought, I hadn't. All at once I felt very naive.

"The phony and I had an arrangement," Sandy said. "He bought a very nice Back Bay condo where I could live, and where we could be together instead of sneaking around in hotel rooms. And then he offered to contribute to the maintenance payments."

"Contribute?" Mike asked.

"Yes," she said. "The whole monthly amount."

I tried not to let my jaw drop. A two-bedroomer in that neighborhood probably went for about half a million dollars, and I had no clue how much the maintenance would be.

"When he bought me . . . bought *us*, I should say . . . that unit, the phony promised he wouldn't see other women and asked me to give my word not to date other men," Sandy Savoy said.

"And you stuck to that arrangement?" Mike said,

"I did," Sandy said. And looked straight across the desk at Mike. "I only need one man at a time to satisfy me, Michael."

Such an old-fashioned homebody, I thought.

"How about Tommy? Did he hold up his end to your knowledge?" Mike asked her. "Aside from, ah, being with his wife?"

Sandy opened her mouth to answer, hesitated, and instead sat without saying a word for about thirty seconds.

"Once I thought so," she said at last. "But now I'm not sure." A shrug. "I suppose that makes me sound naive, doesn't it?" she asked, and then shrugged again.

It struck me that Sandy looked very sad at that moment. It also hit me that naiveté was more of a relative thing than I'd supposed. I felt kind of sorry for her, even considering the fact that her Amazonian—or was it Paradisian?—boobs heaved very prominently in Mike's direct line of sight whenever she shrugged.

I didn't think she meant to do it on purpose, and Mike pretended not to notice. Trust me, though—he'd have needed to be wearing a lead blindfold to avoid it.

"I'd like to get to talking about the Celtics game," he said. "According to Thompson, a close friend and client of his accounting firm give him his ticket as a holiday present. The client and another pal are supposed to meet him at the Garden. Tommy gets there first, finds his courtside seat, waits for the other guys to show. But they never do. It's a prank—he's been set up. Instead of his friends, two exotic dancers he's never seen before—you being one of them—arrive right before the opening tip and sit on either side of him. Before he realizes he's been tricked, you throw your arms around him and plant a kiss on his lips. But his friend hasn't counted on having your smooch get displayed on the Kiss-Cam. Or on a Gloucester newspaper photographer happening to be in the stands with a camera, and recognizing Tommy, and taking a picture that gets him in a whole lot of hot water." Mike looked at her. "Do I have it right?"

Sandy was nodding.

"That's the phony's version," she said. "Everybody's heard it on the news."

"And you dispute it."

I won't bother describing the Shrug again. Suffice it to say it was another total upper-body lollapalooza.

"Tommy's a married man and a politician," Sandy said. "If he wants to tell lies about our relationship to protect his reputation, I'm okay with it—that goes with the mistress territory I mentioned." She shot me a glance. "Do you have a sister, Sky? Older or younger?"

I shook my head no.

"Well, I'd still be willing to bet you understand," she said. "I have one. She's four years younger than me. And Tommy's mistake was dragging her into this."

"Your sister was the woman you were with?"

"She's the main reason I was at the game in the first place," Sandy said. "I earn a good living on the stage. I don't need to hire out for practical jokes. And no amount of money could make me sit through a Boston Celtics game anyway." She turned to Mike. "I went because Tommy's a basketball fan, and he asked me to go with him, and got that ticket for Jean as extra incentive."

"Jean being your sister," Mike said.

"Yes," Sandy said. "Jean Scupper. That's S-C-U-P-P-E-R, for your article."

Mike looked at her questioningly.

She looked back at him answeringly.

"My name's Becky," she said. "Rebecca Scupper. You didn't think I was a Sandy Savoy straight out of the womb, did you?"

Mike didn't say anything. He seemed embarrassed. The naiveté bug bites men and women in different places, I suppose.

"Jean is an Asian studies major at Bowdoin College up in Maine," Sandy said. "She's on the dean's list every year. You can check if you don't believe me."

"And I take it she doesn't share your loathing of the Celtics."

Sandy nodded.

"She'd come home for winter break and was excited about those courtside seats," she said. "Little did she know the kind of excitement she'd have in store."

"By that you mean . . ."

"Jean's never been crazy about my dancing," Sandy said. "She accepts it because she loves me. And because I tell her I enjoy it."

There's a certain look Mike gets when his attention is really locked in on you, and that's what I saw on his face. "Tell her?"

"Our father took a hike on us when we were young, and Mom serves hot lunches in a school cafeteria," Sandy said. "Do you have any clue what it costs to go to Bowdoin? The annual tuition is thirty-five thousand dollars a year. Add another ten thousand for a dorm room. Then the price of books and other everyday expenses. Even with grants and a partial scholarship, how do you think Jean could afford that?" She hesitated. "I don't mind dancing. If you've got it, you might as well use it—and *wow* them, you know? But ask me what I really enjoy, and I'd say it's being able to put my kid sister through school."

"So what you're saying is that Jean's the reason you're coming forward with your story."

"She's the whole reason," Sandy said. "Jean wants a career as a diplomatic interpreter. She's up for an internship at the United Nations next semester. But thanks to Tommy, the *Globe* called her a stripper—one of the 'topless twosome,' the caption read. The phony can say anything he wants about me. But what he said about her was selfish and unfair . . . and I won't let him ruin her chances."

Given how some ambassadors were rumored to spend their spare time, I was thinking the story probably would have increased those chances if it wasn't so public.

Mike had continued rapping his desk with his fingers.

"I need to ask you about the reports that Thompson was at Silk N' Lace the night after the game, throwing money onstage while you performed," he said. "He claims it's untrue . . . that he's never been to the club."

"It's just another lie, Michael. Where do you think we met? Whenever Tommy was in for a business trip he'd come watch me."

"And fling bills at you?" I asked, astounded.

"Sure, why not? It isn't as if he didn't do it when we were alone."

I hoped I didn't look too mortified. But they were consenting adults. What wowed them wowed them. On the flip side, Tommy Thompson had a family that probably wouldn't have been too wowed to learn he'd been tossing away money that could have gone toward something as unexciting as putting away for their future, since I got the distinct feeling the bills weren't returned to his pocket when the dance floor cleared. Which led me to wonder exactly how much of a bundle he earned as an accountant?

Meanwhile, Sandy had decided to elaborate.

"My terrace overlooks the water," she told me. "It's a fabulous backdrop. Blue as blue can be. And with all those boats moving by. I'd dance in front of it, and he'd pull out a roll of bills to rain me in green, and then we'd . . . well, you get the picture. It's very sexy—men love the fantasy. If you have a boyfriend, you might want to try something like it. He might be too shy to mention it on his own."

I shot Mike a look. *If you have a boyfriend*. Apparently, there was a thing or two *he* hadn't mentioned to Sandy. And I didn't see where shyness would have factored into it.

I told myself my next question for her had a purely objective purpose. I was *in*, right? A journalist. Sort of. For the moment. At Sandy's very own request.

"If you don't mind my asking . . . since Michael . . . *Mike* . . . is going to write your story . . . has it occurred to you that your having spent the night at his house might be seen as compromising?" I turned and gave him another pointed look. "Or am I off the mark wondering how it would be perceived?"

Mike scratched the back of his head. He has luxurious wavy black hair that I did not want to be noticing at that moment.

"It's an interesting question," he said.

"You think?"

"I suppose some people might get the wrong idea."

"Suspicious, narrow-minded creatures that they are," I agreed. "And I'd hate to see you make a mistake you'll come to regret."

Mike looked at me across his desk. My eyes didn't quite fire daggers back at him, but they weren't blowing kisses either.

"It was three o'clock in the morning when we reached Pigeon Cove—we couldn't exactly start knocking on the doors of B and Bs," he said. I wasn't sure if I was just imagining that his expression had turned sheepish. "Besides, this time of year it's impossible to find an available room at *any* hour. So I figured it made sense for Sandy to stay in my granny flat."

What did I say about daggers?

Mike owned a big, borderline fixer-upper in Gloucester that many locals had called the "funky house" before he bought it. The front third of it was late Colonial. The middle third was nineteen-forties boardinghouse. The rear was a wood-paneled nineteen-eighties addition that resembled the inside of a hunting lodge. It was the oddball mixture of styles that gave the place its funkiness.

The guest bedroom was in front. He'd done a whizbang job of restoring it. Exposing the woodwork, getting the fireplace in working order, sanding and polishing the floor. The connected parlor had been just as exactingly refurbished. The bathroom had a clawfoot tub with a solid brass showerhead and curtain rod.

"Granny flat" sounded cute, yessirree. But I couldn't remember ever hearing Mike use the term for that section of the house. A couple of times, in fact, we'd slept in it when I was helping him refurbish. The original wall trimmings and fireplace made it very romantic. And while Skiball had slipped in to join us on occasion, I can vouch that his granny hadn't.

"Sandy," he said, facing her, "we'll need to find you another place to stay. That is, if you intend to wait for Thompson's reaction to my piece . . ."

"I *absolutely* intend to, Michael."

He stared quietly into space for a second, looked back at me.

"I have a thought," he said.

"No!" I said.

"Sandy could stay at the Fog Bell," he said.

To which I said nothing for a second. Speechless as I was. Then I shook my head.

"Chloe doesn't take guests in the winter," I said.

"I know," he said. "I was hoping you could ask her to open up a room, though. As a favor."

I shook my head again. So fast it made me dizzy.

"I already did it once today," I said. "My mom's coming to visit."

"She is?" Mike looked at me with surprise. "I didn't know."

"Neither did I," I said. "But, lo and behold. She'll be here the day after tomorrow."

Mike looked at me.

"Hmm," he said. "I have to think."

"Mmm-hmm," I said, wishing he'd quit while we were still ahead.

"I don't guess we can impose on your mother to share her room . . ."

"No, it's too tiny," I said. "A tiny, tiny little room. I've got the only full-sized suite that's in any shape to—"

I broke off, foot in mouth.

Mike gave me another look. The quintuplet he drummed on the desk with his fingers had a very crisp, decisive beat.

"Sky, I've got it," he said.

"You do?"

"Sandy can stay with you."

"*Me?*"

"Right," Mike said. "What do you say?"

I looked at him, getting ready for another dizzying head shake.

"Wouldn't it also look bad if Sandy bunks at my place?" I said. "As far as using her as a source, I mean."

"How's that? You're not a *man*, Sky."

"No kidding, I'm not a man. But if I'm going to be working on the story too, we need to be consistent. It can't look like Sandy and I have a cozy relationship."

Which sounded like a good enough excuse for scrapping the idea. In my opinion, anyway.

Unfortunately Mike didn't seem persuaded.

"Our options are kind of limited right now," he said. "Sandy needs to be available to us. Better you put her up than me. The situation might not be ideal, but we'll just have to be clear about our reasons when the time comes."

A hand reached across the LV and alighted softly on my arm. Sandy Savoy was at the other end of it.

"I think it'd be wonderful staying with you, Sky," she said.

"You do?" I was repeating myself, I know.

She nodded again, smiling. "I've got a sense about these things."

A bunch of seconds ran together. And then a bunch more as I stared at Sandy in all her dazzling pinkness. Her smile looked very genuine.

"Okay," I said at last, figuring I'd wait till I was back in my office to kick myself. "You can come home with me."

Chapter 7

Five minutes after gaining a stripper with a grudge for an unwanted roommate, I was in the little kitchen off the employee lounge upstairs from the *Anchor*'s office suites about to insert a coffee pod into our new one-cup brewer. I still hadn't gotten around to the swift kick in the rear I'd promised myself—not because I was a procrastinator, but because I figured a strong dose of caffeine would give me the energy boost I needed to really make it sting.

Then I noticed the inner part of the splashguard was dirty. Not disgustingly so, but with enough residue to tell me nobody at the paper had bothered to rinse it under the tap in a while.

I opened the cabinet under the brewer and got out my bottle of white vinegar.

"Hey, yo, yo!"

No, this wasn't someone shouting out the title of an old Ramones song from the entry behind me. It was a greeting—and a pleasantly upbeat one.

Upbeat was good, I thought. Very good, in fact. I was definitely in the mood for upbeat with my French roast.

"Hey back at you, Bry," I said, and turned to look at him.

Stick-thin, spike-haired, and barely in his twenties, Bryan Dermond was our webmaster's intern and a sweet kid. Unfortunately, he also could have been a test subject for ongoing research into the effects of piercing-and-tattoo overkill on the human body . . . or on the human observer's sensibilities. Name a part of his face, and you'd find a stud, pin, or hoop in it. If there were additional piercings under his clothes I didn't want to know. The ones I could see, and the visible portions of the tattoos on his arms and neck, were chilling enough for me to ponder.

Bryan had glanced at the bottle in my hand.

"What's that?" he said.

"Vinegar," I said.

He flinched at the word. Either that or he felt a tweak from the beaded stickpin in his bottom lip.

"You make coffee with *vinegar*?"

I didn't really feel like explaining. But then I decided it might be a refreshing change of pace if someone at the office besides me cleaned the coffeemaker once in a while.

"No, Bry," I said in my best instructional tone. "What I was about to do is—"

I paused. The sleeve of his black hooded sweatshirt was rolled up his forearm and a new tattoo on his wrist—or circling his wrist, actually—had caught my eye. It was like an alphabet bracelet. But in bright green ink.

I tilted my head to see what the letters spelled out.

"Stay humble," I read aloud from the top of his wrist.

Bryan turned his arm so I could see what it said around the bottom.

"Or stumble," I finished.

Bryan grinned at me.

"Stay humble or stumble," he said. "Get it?"

"I got it, Bry," I said.

"Heavy duty, huh?" Bryan said. "It's my creed. Or my latest one, anyway. And it hardly even itches."

"Itches?"

"You know," Brian said. "When you get a new tat, they usually itch like crazy."

"Oh, right," I said.

"And then there's the post-tat gunk and crud that kinda seeps out of your skin—"

I tried not to draw away. "Never mind the details, Bry."

"Sorry, didn't realize you were squeamish." He was still holding his arm up on display. "So what do you think of it? The creed, that is?"

I groped for something nice to say. Then it came to me.

"Well," I said, "it's very affirmative."

Bryan's grin widened. "You really think so?"

"Sure do," I said sincerely.

He seemed pleased. "Thanks, Sky. Believe it or not, I sort of borrowed the saying from some book I found at the garbage dump."

Which suddenly made me wonder. Chloe had told me *her* weird words of wisdom came from a book she'd picked up in the same place.

"It wouldn't have been in the swap shop, would it?" I asked. "Something about sentence sermons in the title?"

Bryan nodded.

"*A Thousand and One Sentence Sermons*," he said. "How'd you know?"

"Just a guess," I said. "I'm curious, though . . . was there another copy besides the one you found?"

"Nah." Bryan shook his head. "Tell you the truth, I flipped through it, thought the rest of the sayings inside were pretty lame, and chucked it right back in the book pile."

"Oh."

"But I can see if it's still there for you. Next time I drive my trash over. If you want."

"No need," I said. And didn't bother adding I had a hunch somebody had already scavenged it.

A few seconds passed. Bryan stood waiting in the kitchen entrance.

"So," he said. "You gonna tell me?"

I looked blank for a second. And then remembered the bottle in my hand.

"I use this vinegar to clean the coffeemaker," I said. "It gets all the . . . uh . . . gunk and crud out from inside."

Maybe it was wishful thinking, but Bryan seemed interested.

"And that seriously works?"

"Seriously, Bry."

I turned toward the cabinet and reached for a stainless-steel pitcher I kept on a shelf, figuring I'd give Bryan a quick show-and-tell. You never knew. Help could come from unlikely quarters, and maybe I'd found some for keeping the grunginess out of the kitchen.

"I pour about six ounces of this vinegar into the coffeemaker's reservoir and turn it on like I'm brewing a cup," I said, holding the bottle in one hand and the pitcher in the other. "Once it runs all the way through the machine, I pour the vinegar into the pitcher." I paused. "You don't want to put it back in the bottle while it's hot."

Bryan was nodding. "Or the glass'll break, huh?"

"Got it," I said. "You need to wait till it's cool. Then you can bottle up the vinegar and reuse it."

"Awesome."

Bryan had kept his attention on me. It hadn't been my imagination, I realized. To my surprise, he was *genuinely* interested.

"You want an extra-special tip?" I said. "A Sky Taylor Grime Solvers exclusive?"

Bryan nodded some more.

"Vinegar's a fantastic disinfectant, and only a legal technicality keeps it from saying so on the label," I said. "The EPA wants disinfectants registered as pesticides, and you can't sell pesticides as food products. But the regular five percent vinegar solution you buy in stores kills almost all the bacteria, mold, and viruses hanging around the kitchen. Companies don't advertise it because *they* want vinegar stocked in the cooking aisles . . . that's where they make most of their sales."

"And the freakin' consumer loses out, huh? I mean, never mind that vinegar's *stinky,* it's cheap."

I nodded.

"No question," I said. "You can buy a half gallon of some generic brand for what? Two, three dollars? Pour just enough on a cleaning cloth to dampen it, and that's plenty for wiping off the outside of the coffeemaker, the fridge, countertops, faucets, cabinet doors and handles, even—"

I cut myself off. If there was such a thing as piercing and tat overkill, the same applied to cleaning hints. I didn't want to lose Bryan by going on too long.

Shows how smart I am.

Bryan suddenly looked bashful. He tried to hide it, and I tried to pretend he was being successful.

"Y'know," he said, "I read all your Sky Writing columns. Especially the cleaning tips."

"Really?" I said.

He nodded.

"Talk about dumps . . . which we were doing a minute ago, you remember . . ."

"I remember, Bry."

"Well, when I moved into my apartment, it was the *dumpiest* dump you'll ever see," he said. "This was, like, a month before you started writing for the paper. And then, after I started entering your content onto our Web site . . . that's one of my jobs here, you know . . ."

"I know, Bry. I've seen you at it."

"Oh, yeah. Right," he said. He scratched an ear with about six hoops in it. "Anyway, I've got this dump of dumps, and I meet this chick Krystal, who's the bomb of *bomb*s. And pretty soon it's like we're hanging out at my pad every other night, and she says I better make it presentable. But I don't have a lot to spend on cleaning stuff—not that I'm busted or anything. It's just, you know, cash flow problems."

I nodded. Boy, did I ever know.

"And then one day I'm working on getting your column online, and read what you say about how people waste money using too much scouring powder," Bryan went on. "How companies put those big holes on the top of the can because they *want* you to use too much and then have to buy more. And how I can tape half the holes with masking tape and get more bang for my buck. So I try it, and it *works*, and I'm saving all kinds of money."

Bryan shyly lowered his eyes to the studded black tops of his creepers.

"I guess you'd say I'm a fan," he said in a low voice. "I mean, I kind of *like* cleaning."

I looked at him.

"Bry," I said, "this bowls me over."

"You mean it?"

"I mean it."

Bryan looked up at me.

"You know your tip about getting candle wax off a rug? The one in your last column?"

"Sure. Scrape up what you can of the wax, put a brown paper bag over the spot where it dripped, then run a warm iron over the bag," I said. "The wax that's left melts onto the bag."

Bryan was nodding.

"Krystal's into candles big time. With her, it's aromatherapy this, votives that, soy candles, herb candles, beeswax . . . even the shape of the candle's supposed to be important. So a couple nights back she has some burning at my place and one of them drips all over the rug, and she gets really bummed—it's a whole guilt trip. But I brown-bag it, get my iron out, and in a couple of minutes, poof, the stain's gone. And Krystal looks at me like I'm a genius or something. She was *impressed*."

I smiled wholeheartedly. It felt like the first time I'd done it that entire day.

"Listen, how about I clean the coffeemaker?" he said. "Soon's I'm done, I'll brew your coffee and bring it to your office. Then tomorrow morning I'll come in early, clean the rest of the kitchen with that vinegar . . ."

I could not stop smiling.

"It's great of you to offer," I said. "But you don't have to—"

"Skyster," he said, "I totally *want* to do it."

I stood there speechless. From the moment Bryan walked into the room it had been one surprise after another.

"All right," I said after a minute. "When you put it that way, how can I refuse?"

Bryan grinned. It was one of those open, encompassing grins that involve the forehead, the eyebrows, the mouth, all of it. And though I felt it would have been a more appealing sight if he wasn't using his face as a pincushion, I was too grateful to let it distract me.

I walked from the kitchen into the lounge, and then took the stairs down to my office. I'd left the computer on, and its Da Vinci screen saver showed one of Leonardo's sketchbook flying machines launching into the air. I tapped a key and the flying machine was gone in a wink, replaced by a blank document page. It was a quarter to five and I hadn't written a single word.

I sat at the desk trying to think. This was easier said than done. The past twenty-four hours—less, really—had left me dizzy. First there had been Kyle on the hammock. Then Kyle falling *off* the hammock and getting wheeled out dead on a gurney with a sheet over his head. Then the messages from Mike at Silk N' Lace, and Betty-Mom, and Sandy Savoy . . .

It was right as I was getting around to asking myself "What next?" that the desk phone bleeped.

I picked it up and announced myself, figuring I'd be taking a message from somebody with some dish for Bev Snow. I didn't receive that many phone calls at the newspaper office.

But the call wasn't for Bev. It was my what-next arriving as the voice of Chief Alejandro Vega.

"Sky, I'm glad I got hold of you," he said while I sat there thinking I ought to scrap every emotion but surprise from my inventory. "I spoke to Chloe at the Fog Bell, and she told me you might be at the paper."

Aha, I thought.

"Look, I understand it's late, but I need to ask you some questions about last night," Vega said.

"Sure," I said. "Whatever I can tell you that might help."

"I don't mean over the phone," Vega said. "I'd appreciate it if you could stop by the station, Sky. So we can talk in person."

I stared at the computer monitor.

"Would tomorrow morning be okay?" I asked. "I need to get some work done—"

"Tonight would be better," Vega interrupted. "I can wait."

It was only then that I noticed the urgency in his tone.

"Chief Vega," I said, "what's going on?"

For a second he was so quiet in my earpiece I thought I'd lost the connection.

"Chief?" I said.

"Listen to me, Sky," he said. "I'm going to tell you because I consider you a friend. But this is off the record. There are certain things I need to sit on for now. Understood?"

I felt my grip tighten around the receiver. Now that I'd detected it, I really didn't like his tone.

"Yes," I said. "I understand."

"Kyle Fipps didn't die of natural causes," Vega said. "It's looking very much like he was murdered."

The telephone still in my hand, I reached for my mouse and turned off the computer. There was no chance I'd do any writing that afternoon.

All of a sudden it was the furthest thing from my mind.

Chapter 8

"Pong pong," I said.

"Cerbera odollam," Chief Vega said with a nod. "According to Maji."

No, we weren't citing Vedic sutras in their original, ancient tongue. That would've been more up Betty-Mom and Lou-Dad's alley.

The pong pong was a common tree throughout the Far East, and a very attractive one, as shown in the color photo Vega had slid into my hands. Green and lush, it had white blossoms that the text accompanying the picture—which had come out of his office printer—said gave way to large round fruits resembling green apples.

Also in the report e-mailed to Vega by Cape Ann's part-time coroner from his office at Addison Gilbert was the tree's botanical name, *Cerbera odollam.*

The coroner, I ought to mention, was Dr. Darpan Maji.

I should add that Vega was hinting Kyle Fipps had died from pong pong poisoning.

So now you have it. My equivalent of a Rosetta stone for translating what we'd just said to one another across his desk at the police station.

Of course, we'd talked about other things before that, and I had a notion more was coming.

"The fruit of the pong pong's got a single seed inside a big, hard shell," he said. "And the seed contains a toxin called cerberin."

"As in *Cerbera,*" I said. Was I or was I not *sharp*?

Vega was nodding at me. His office had the sort of gray metal desk, commercial-grade fabric chairs, and cluttered bulletin board you expect to see in a station house. A couple of spider plants hung by the window, and he had three small cactuses on the sill. The framed art print of Picasso's *Guernica* on the wall above his head made for a pleasing touch, though, as did a row of small oils on the wall to my right. Those, I thought, looked as if they were seasonal renderings of the Ipswich dunes painted by a Pigeon Cove artist. Of which there were naturally throngs.

"Cerberin's related to digoxin, a drug that's used to treat cardiovascular problems," Vega said. "Millions of people use it—it affects the electrical pulses going to the heart, and can help control arrhythmias, fibrillations, and other coronary abnormalities. But overdoses can be fatal . . . and easily mistaken for a heart attack. Unless you know that the person who OD'd was on the medication, or you have some other reason to look for signs of it in his system."

I considered that for a minute. Chloe's Court TV addiction had gotten me hooked on some of the true crime shows she watched, and digoxin did ring a bell for me.

"Wasn't there some famous murder case involving someone who used it—digoxin—on his victim?"

Vega nodded.

"Victims, plural," he said. "You're probably thinking of that male nurse who killed all those elderly patients in Pennsylvania and New Jersey—he admitted to committing forty homicides in about fifteen or sixteen years, and used digoxin and insulin as his drugs of choice. But there've been other murder convictions. A wife in Missouri who attempted to kill her husband . . . a California husband who killed his wife. And so forth." Vega paused, shrugged. "Sad to say, there's an even higher number of *accidental* digoxin fatalities. Those tend to be senior citizens who are prescribed the medication, don't have adequate home care, and are forgetful of the number of doses they've taken." Vega paused again. "Digoxin overdose is so common, relatively speaking, that

toxicologists have developed routine tests for it whenever there's any suspicion it might be the cause of
death."

I sat there without saying anything for a while, kind
of letting what he'd told me knock at the door of my
thoughts.

"Did Kyle have a heart condition?" I said. "I'm just
wondering if that was how the doctor knew to test for
pong pong poisoning."

Vega looked at me. I was hoping it wasn't because I'd
actually used the phrase "pong pong poisoning" aloud.

"The rest of this conversation stays between us for
now, Sky," he said after a second. His eyes were still on
mine. "I'm counting on you as a friend."

I waited another second or two and nodded.

"It's been less than twenty-four hours since Kyle died
and there's a lot we still don't know," he said. "But
while I can't share information we might have gotten
from his personal medical records, I'll go so far as to
say Maji didn't suspect Kyle had a preexisting cardiac
problem when he found cerberin in his bloodstream."

So there was nothing wrong with Kyle's ticker, I
thought. Or nothing for which a doctor would have prescribed digoxin.

"Also, these two drugs are similar in their clinical
effects—but their chemical markers aren't identical,"
Vega continued. "You use a different battery of tests to
detect them, and to distinguish a death that's a result of
cerberin toxicity from one that's the result of natural
heart failure. My understanding is that cerberin isn't prescribed in any form, or extracted from pong pong seeds
for pharmacological use. Not in this country, not in Asia,
not anywhere in the world. There've been so few cerberin fatalities in America, it's hard to find documentation
of a proven case."

I was quiet for a second. More questions had come
knocking at the door to my brain. This time, though, I
didn't intend to give the impression that the only one
home was a big dope.

"What made Dr. Maji think to test him for an overdose if it's such a rare cause of death?" I said. "I mean, if cerberin isn't used in medical drugs, how did it get into his system? Wouldn't he have had to eat the actual pong pong *seeds*?"

Vega gave me a small smile.

"Seems like a lot of questions for me to answer," he said. I nodded.

"As far as Maji, it probably isn't breaking news to you that he comes from India. A state called Kerala in the southwest."

Vega was right about this not being news. The *Anchor* had done a long human-interest piece on Dr. Maji, and I assumed he was referring to that.

"I know he was educated in India," I said. "And that he did some incredible work at clinics for helping women and kids at the bottom of the caste system."

Vega nodded. "Here's a statistic he shared with me about mortalities in Kerala—fifty percent of people who die from poisoning there are found to have eaten *Cerbera odollam* seeds. And the vast majority of *those* deaths are women. Some are tagged accidental, some suicides. Fewer are proven to be murders. But women's rights being what they are in India, the courts aren't known for their zeal in prosecuting a husband for the intentional poisoning of a wife or daughter. So we can assume a lot more intentional killings than the numbers show."

I thought about that. And then found myself remembering the conversation I'd had with Chloe while driving home the night before. She'd said something about recognizing that Paul was sick before we even told her and Oscar, and we talked about his weight loss. And then what was it she'd added?

I suppose that's why it occurred to me that Kyle looked very healthy tonight . . . it's odd, don't you think?

"Looking at Kyle, I always figured he was in great shape," I said. "I've seen him practically wear out the exercise machines at the Get Thinner gym all on his own. If he didn't have a history of heart problems, or maybe even if he did, Dr. Maji might've been on the lookout for something unusual. Guys Kyle's age, and in his condition, usually don't die out of the blue."

Vega nodded again.

"You won't hear me take issue with that reasoning," Vega said. "Now consider Maji's background and experience."

I already had.

"I'd guess they would make him familiar with signs of pong pong poi—" I caught myself. I was absolutely *not* going to repeat that phrase. "Death by pong pong," I said. Which didn't really sound that much better.

Vega looked at me.

"Another fair assumption," he said. "And here's some more info you could easily find out without my help—it's available from public sources. Mass spectrometry and liquid chromatography are two forensic procedures that can reveal cerberin's chemical fingerprints, so to speak, in the body. And thanks in part to Dr. Maji, Addison Gilbert has acquired state-of-the-art equipment for both those techniques."

I was quiet, my eyes in steady contact with Vega's across his desk. I might mention, incidentally, that his eyes were pale green. I might also mention that pale green eyes and a dark Latin complexion are a very striking and unusual combination. Not that I was noticing them too much at that very serious juncture.

"As for the last of your questions, I'll spare you another bit of research," he said. "With cases of deliberate poisoning in India, the *Cerbera* seeds are ground into a powder or paste and added to spicy foods. The combination of strong spices hides their taste."

I'd barely started to wonder about that when those lime-colored eyes I hadn't particularly been noticing broke away from mine and went to the picture of the pong pong tree in my hand.

"Mind if I take that from you?" Vega reached across his desk for the printout. "I want you to have a peek at something else."

I gave it back to him, and he returned it to his open

folder. Then he slipped a second sheet of paper from the folder, held it out for me to take, and waited as I looked it over.

It was a color fax of a caterer's brochure—and not just any caterer.

The logo atop the fax said "DeFelice's Creative Event Cuisine," the husband-and-wife team that had handled the Art Association's affair. In fact, they'd grabbed the corner on most of the town's major events. Understandably, too. Jim and Debra DeFelice had a reputation on the Cape for being imaginative, versatile, and reliable— they could plan any style of event, as the various buffet packages under their logo bore out. Jim was also a brazen Yankees fan in Red Sox country, which made him a man after my own pin-striped heart.

Running my eyes down the list, I saw half a dozen set menu choices—a traditional American buffet, a New England seafood buffet, a Chinese and sushi combo, something they called a Caribbean Jamboree, their Mexican Fiesta . . .

Toward the bottom of the page, one of the menu packages had been circled with a red highlighter pen, with green checks or double question marks alongside some of its individual selections.

I figured Vega had done the highlighting and checking. It also occurred to me that the Digger might have screamed secular insensitivity if she'd seen his pick of colors.

" 'Global Grab Bag,' " I said, reading the name of the circled menu package. Then I raised my eyes from the page to look at Vega. "That's the one the Art Association ordered for the party."

He nodded his head.

"Read the menu items," he said. "Then tell me if anything pops out at you about the ones I checked off or question marked."

Right away, I knew what he was getting at. High among the reasons I felt like a walking, talking yawn was that I'd been working the affair all night, and knew most of the buffet selections from scraping half-eaten leftovers off plates. Still, I gave them a scan.

The "Intercontinental Nibblers"—or hors d'oeuvres—list read:

Antipasto all'Italiana
Bavarian Ham and Cheese Strudel
Middle American Cheese Puffs
Japanese Sushi and Sashimi Combination ??
Keftedes (Greek meatballs)??
Kratong Tong (Thai pastry cups w/curry, spicy vegan filling)✓
Mini Chinese Egg Rolls
Mexican Quesadillas (vegan, three cheese, chicken, chorizo)✓
Quiche Lorraine Tarts Française
Southwest Chicken Crepes ✓
Imported Cheeses Garnished with Fresh Fruits and Accompanied by Assorted Wafers

The "Worldwide Belly Fillers"—or main course buffet—list read:

Bagara Baingan (Indian baby eggplant in spicy sauce) ✓
Creole Shrimp, Chicken, and Smoked Sausage Jambalaya ✓
Mama's Kosher Blintzes
Neapolitan Lasagna with Ricotta
New York Strip Steak with Brandied Mushrooms
Odang Goreng Sambal (Malaysian deep-fried shrimp with chile sauce) ✓
Ye Olde English Shepherd's Pie

At last I got to the "Universal Delights" dessert list, but didn't study it too closely. None of the offerings was marked in any way, and what I'd already seen confirmed my thoughts about Vega's reasoning process.

"I see three spicy appetizers, and three spicy main courses," I said.

Vega was nodding again.

"I put those question marks next to the Japanese combo because they're served with wasabe for optional dabbing. Also put them beside those Greek meatballs, because the DeFelices told me they jazz them up a little with different herbs." He gave a shrug. "That's five of eleven appetizers, three of seven main courses, and eight of eighteen menu items total—over forty percent of them, by my lousy math—that could've had pong pong seeds introduced into them and were heavily seasoned enough to cover the taste."

I looked at him.

"The DeFelices . . . You don't suspect *them* of poisoning Kyle, do you?"

"Speaking as a cop, I can't rule out anybody at this stage," Vega said. "But I know Jim and Debra, and to be honest they aren't really in my sights. They've been bending over backward to cooperate and are very distraught by this whole thing." A shrug. "Since they do all their own cooking and serving, there's no staff member to question."

"So you think a guest at the affair spiked Kyle's food," I said.

"I don't know what else would be likelier." Vega shrugged again, sighed. "Maji's still analyzing the contents of his stomach to see which foods he might have eaten, and what stage or stages of the digestive process they were in. That should provide a fairly accurate time of ingestion, tell us for sure whether the cerberin was in something he ate at the party, and hopefully what entry it was."

I sat there without speaking for almost a full minute. Kyle's death had been a shock all on its own. Finding out he'd been murdered . . . poisoned by someone at the holiday bash . . . it made my toes curl in my boots. Which was honestly kind of painful, being that my feet were still sore from the heels I'd worn the night before.

Then something occurred to me. Actually, it had occurred to me two or three dozen times since Vega phoned me at the *Anchor*. Obvious question that it was, though, it had kept being displaced by others that had come up during our conversation.

Now it had pushed itself back to the forefront of my mind. Making that the perfect moment to ask it.

"Chief Vega," I said, "I know Chloe and I were the ones to find Kyle dead . . . but I don't understand why you wanted to talk to *me* about all this."

Vega rubbed his chin. I'd come to recognize this as a sign of concentration. The harder his brain worked, the more he rubbed.

"I'd had a thought at the Art Association, and was about to bring it up to you right before the EMS team arrived," he said, proving me a marvelously shrewd observer of people's unconscious gestures. "Back in May . . . when you were caught up in that incident at the Millwood B and B . . ."

He paused. I could tell he was trying to choose his words with care, and I appreciated it. But it wasn't needed.

"The last time I stumbled across a murder victim, you mean," I said. "It must be habit-forming, what can I tell you?"

A smile threaded across his lips.

"Thanks for relieving me of being delicate," he said. "When that happened, you'd been cleaning outside the room where you eventually found the body. And you washed some stains off the wall that, well, turned out to be the killer's fingerprints."

The killer's bloody *fingerprints,* I thought. Although I hadn't realized what they were when I dabbed and blotted—not washed, if we're going to be precise—them off the rare flocked Italian wallpaper. Luckily my destruction of critical evidence hadn't hurt the prosecution's case against the killer, since he'd blabbed about the crime to me and Mike before trying to make us his next victims. But I still felt a kernel of guilt about it.

I looked at Vega.

"I thought they were stains from a cherry sundae," I said. "There was a couple staying in another room with some goopy kids."

He nodded.

"I know," he said. "But it's what got me thinking. This afternoon, when Maji called to tell me about the cerberin, I checked my notes and saw that Chloe Edwards had told me Kyle wouldn't have left his living art set to get anything to eat, but that it was possible one of the guests could have *brought* him something. As long as he stayed in character—"

"And you're wondering if I might've carried off a dish of poisoned food?" I said.

Vega hesitated. "It's just that you were cleaning up at the Art Association all night. And that I know you're very diligent."

I sat there in silence, remembering that I had removed a dish—at least one—from the Getaway Groves stage set.

All of a sudden, the kernel of guilt I'd been feeling over my previous obliteration of crime scene evidence was budding open into flowers that had a strong and uncoincidental resemblance to pong pong blossoms.

Huge, smelly pong pong blossoms.

"Ooowee," I said. "Ooowee, ooowee, *mama*!"

"What?"

"I did it again!" I said, my head sinking into my hand. "I can't believe I did it again!"

"Sky, I didn't want you to misunderstand me—"

"*Misunderstand* you? What's *not* to understand? It's like I've turned into . . . what? The Arch-Mistress of Evidence Disposal?"

"Sky, listen," I heard Vega say. "You've honestly got it wrong. My whole point was that your recollections of what you carried off—that is, if you have any—could be a significant help."

I stopped shaking my head and raised it a half inch off my hand.

"Help?" I said.

"Right," he said.

"How?" I said.

"For one thing," he said, "the evidence *wasn't* disposed of."

"It wasn't?"

"It was not."

My head continued elevating itself by slow degrees.

"What do you mean?"

"I mean that as soon as Maji called with his preliminary results, I contacted the Art Association to find out whether there'd been a trash pickup today," Vega said. "Luckily there hadn't. And there won't be. The garbage bags you left in the back room are already at the forensics lab—we got some help collecting it from the county sheriff's department."

I found myself looking up at Vega. Barely.

"I'd like you to go over your way of cleaning up dishes and food after the party," he said. "Just sort of summarize it for me."

I did. Starting with when I'd gone around the exhibit hall picking up, using the grocery bags as trash bucket liners for napkins and food scraps. Then explaining how I'd brought the dishes into the kitchen in stages, carrying a full tray of tableware and the trash bucket with each trip. Finally saying how I transferred the grocery bags from the bucket into heavy-duty garbage bags in the back storage room and then rinsed off the dishes and silverware, putting as much as I could in the dishwasher while leaving the rest in the sink overnight.

"This morning I had a job in Lanesville, but I stopped at the Art Association to finish washing the dishes before I drove out," I concluded. "When I think about it, I guess I noticed those Hefty bags were still in the storeroom."

Chief Vega was rubbing his chin again.

"Working back to when the affair was in full swing," he said, "do you specifically recall taking any dishes from Kyle's set?"

I gave an emphatic nod.

"That's why I got so disgusted at myself a minute ago," I said. "I remember one was left on a plant box and—" I broke off, visualizing it. "And you know what? It was a Villeroy and Boch Wonderful World design in yellow."

Vega gave me a questioning look.

"I've got a hunch that's significant," he said. "I just need you to tell me how." He paused. "Villeroy and Boch is an old dishware company, isn't it?"

I nodded yes. I'd gone from feeling guilty to feeling useful, and it excited me.

"Sorry . . . I didn't mean to leave you hanging," I said. "V and B is old *and* famous. The same family in Germany's been running it for two hundred and fifty years. They make all kinds of ceramics, but you're right, people mostly know them for dishes." I moved slightly forward in my chair. "Anyway, I knew Jim and Debra used Villeroy and Boch dinnerware because I complimented them on how pretty it looked. And they told me it was one of the modern lines. Wonderful World, like I said. It comes in different colors."

Vega grunted. "I suppose I wasn't paying close attention to the dishes when I got there," he said. "Or after I got there. But I'm thinking that I *did* see other colors besides yellow."

"You can mix and match when you order sets. That's what the DeFelices did," I said. "There were green plates, blue ones, orange ones . . . I noticed they used yellow at the table where they were serving Indian and Malaysian food. I thought that was pretty smart of them." I sat picturing the dish I'd taken from Kyle's plant box.

Vega waited.

"Turmeric's a main ingredient of curry powder," I said. "It's what gives Indian food some of its tang. And the yellowish orange color you see in a lot of it. My late husband owned a restaurant and made a chicken turmeric soup that was a variation on an Indian recipe. He never served it in white dishes, since the turmeric would leave a stain that was tough to get off. Even using a commercial dishwasher."

I leaned a little closer to the desk, slid the catering list Vega had given me back across to him, and watched his eyebrows go up as he examined it.

"There's one appetizer and two main courses that look to me like they might contain turmeric here," he said.

I nodded. "You could check with the DeFelices to know for sure. But I was thinking it might narrow things down. Especially if you could find out who brought Kyle his Indian food from the buffet table."

Vega looked up from the list, and smiled.

"Sky, you're a genius," he said.

I flapped my hand in the air.

"Cut it out," I said.

Vega's smile had broadened.

"I'm not kidding," he said. "When I asked to speak with you tonight, I never bargained for *this* kind of input."

It took me a second to realize he meant it. And then I was also smiling. Smiling and thinking I ought to say something appropriately modest. But felt too darned proud of myself, and didn't even have a convenient sentence sermon ready for claiming otherwise.

"Well," I said. "Glad I could help."

Vega sat smiling at me another second. Then he glanced at his watch.

"Listen, it's almost seven o'clock," he said. "I dragged you out here after work, so how about letting me treat you to dinner? Restaurant of your choice."

My heartbeat hadn't quickened. Had not. It just really, really felt like that.

"Thanks, but I have to get back to the Fog Bell—"

"I promise to have you home early," Vega said. "Won't even try talking you into coffee and dessert."

I sat there looking at him. He knew Mike pretty well, which meant he probably knew Mike and I were seriously involved. Sort of seriously, that was. Or did he? And why bother myself about it and assume he was being anything more than grateful?

"I appreciate the offer, but I can't," I said. "I have someone staying with me tonight . . . and my mom's coming to visit tomorrow—"

Vega spread his hands in a mild halting gesture.

"I understand," he said. "Some other time, then. As long as we agree I owe you one."

I looked at him and nodded but didn't say anything. The pitter-pattering in my chest was not only making me distracted and uncomfortable but aggravating me besides. I did not appreciate having my heart mess around. Even if I was imagining it.

Vega had pushed up from behind his desk.

"Come on," he said. "It's slippery out . . . I'll walk you to your car."

Strictly speaking, the Caliber wasn't a car, but I didn't nitpick. It *was* treacherous going outside—the temperature had risen just long enough during the day to melt a little of the snow on the street, leaving the pavement slick with ice after dark.

Out front where I'd parked, Vega held my elbow to steady me as I went around a frozen puddle to my driver's-side door. Then he thanked me again for my help, waited till I settled in behind the wheel, and closed the door behind me.

Waving good night to him through my window, I didn't notice for an instant how he was looking at me. And how his thick black lashes offset his sea green eyes under the streetlights.

Didn't, didn't, *did not*.

For an instant.

My imagination was quite the prankster.

Or so I tried to convince myself as I finally pried my gaze away from his and drove off.

Chapter 9

Take my word for it—driving is the fastest and most direct way to get to Pigeon Cove from Logan International in Boston, especially during non–rush hours. Once you're through the four- or five-mile knot of traffic arteries around the airport, it's an easy merge from Route 1 onto I-95, which takes you up to the Route 128 exit near Peabody for the stretch run to Cape Ann.

Total travel time home barring unforeseen delays? About an hour.

Betty-Mom's scheduled arrival from Syracuse was one p.m., which would have been perfect if I'd been picking her up in my Caliber. Even with holiday shoppers and travelers boosting the usual number of road warriors—this was a Wednesday exactly one week before Christmas—outbound traffic from the city tends to be sparse until around four thirty or five o'clock, and I'd known that would keep my teeth-grinding down to an acceptable level as I sat behind the wheel.

Notice I said *if* I'd been picking her up in my Caliber.

That's because I didn't drive Betty-Mom from the airport, Betty-Mom having refused to let me drive her. As a dedicated guardian of our ecosystem, she'd felt that the passenger jet bearing her through the sky would already burn an unconscionable amount of refined fossil fuel, and did not want my oversized vehicle greedily consuming yet more natural resources—and spouting pollutants into the atmosphere—during the final leg of her transport to the Cove. Certainly not with an alternate

means of transportation available to her. In fact, Betty-
Mom wouldn't think to inconvenience me. No need to
meet her at all, she said when we'd been planning for
her visit over the phone.

Betty-Mom had gone ahead and found directions from
Logan using public transportation. She would take the
T—that's Bostonian shorthand for MBTA, or the subway
system—from the airport to the State Street station, switch
to another train there, and ride it to North Station. At
North Station, she would transfer to the Newburyport/
Pigeon Cove commuter rail and ride that up to the station behind the Whistle Stop Mall in a part of town
we call the South End. At which point she'd agreed to
grudgingly relax her environmental restrictions so I
could meet her in my obscene gas guzzler and cart her
the short remaining distance to the Fog Bell.

Total travel time for Betty-Mom's determinedly con-
servationist route? Around three hours with a pocketful
of fully charged New Age karmic trinkets. And a whole
lot of optimism.

Still, I'd known better than to argue about driving her.
She was too stubborn, and had been a card-carrying eco-
watchdog for too many decades. It would have been a
total waste of breath explaining that the public route
was far less convenient than it looked on her Internet-
derived map. Or telling her that the map didn't clearly
show that she'd have to take a shuttle bus from the
arrivals terminal to the Blue Line T. Or pointing out
that once she stepped off the Orange Line at North Station, she would need to haul herself and her suitcase of
hippified clothing along the platform, up a bunch of
stairs, and then across the street to the grubby commuter
rail waiting area under the Boston Garden.

I also didn't tell her that you could always identify
the tourists emerging from the subway by how they'd
frantically bump into each other in the middle of the
street, waving maps around in a panic while trying to
find the railway station before they missed their connections.

Betty-Mom was two years shy of her sixtieth birthday.

Betty-Mom had arthritis in both knees that growled at her all winter long. But she did not like making concessions to age or admitting to any physical slippage. If Betty-Mom was willful enough to take the train and rail from Logan, then I was determined to meet her right there *at* the airport.

That morning the temperature was about twelve degrees outside, with a windchill of minus four owing to an Arctic cold front that had roared in overnight like an irate polar bear. At a quarter to nine I'd treaded quietly past the living room sofa where Sandy Savoy lay dead asleep with her blond-tressed Amazonian head buried under a quilt—with my adorable little Skiball, who'd hopped off her customary spot on my pillow in the middle of the night, fickly snuggled against her side. Loath to disturb their cozy arrangement, I'd slipped out the door without a peep, gone downstairs for a quick cup of coffee with Chloe, then driven my Caliber into the parking lot off Railroad Avenue and waited for the 9:07 to Boston in the frigid wind blasting over the platform. That would bring me into North Station around a quarter past ten, providing all kinds of leeway for foul-ups on the T that might prolong my trek to the airport.

As it turned out, I got there with about forty minutes to spare. At first the prospect of sitting around the terminal lounge for a while didn't bother me. With Betty-Mom's advent to the Cove looming over my immediate future, I figured I ought to relax and soak in every moment of calm, cool collectedness that I possibly could.

Still, there's just so much soaking you can take, and forty minutes' worth would have been plenty. Beyond that it gets monotonous and wearing. Double the wait in a hard plastic chair and it will knock an increasing-number of vertebrae out of whack and cut off the circulation to your legs—as I began to find out when I checked one of the arrival and departure monitors, and learned that Betty-Mom's flight would be coming in more than an hour late.

This depicts the not-so-bad part of my afternoon and evening. The worst of it started after her plane finally

hit the runway at a quarter past two, delayed for reasons
she'd make sure nobody ever forgot. Or that *I* certainly
wouldn't, being that the details of her misadventure were
drilled into my head throughout the entire ride home—
which did not begin until four o'clock, since very few
trains run to the Cove during off-peak hours and we'd
missed the 2:20 out of North Station.

"The landing gear bay was frozen shut, Sky!" Betty-
Mom was saying in her loudest voice. For the twelfth
time.

I should explain that it was now about ten minutes to
five and, after an hour on the train, we were coming up
on Manchester-by-the-Sea, three stops from Pigeon
Cove.

"Have you ever heard of that happening before? In
your whole *life*? Frozen shut with ice! Ho-ho-hahaha!
Ho-ho-hahaha!"

Betty-Mom, I might further explain, wasn't laughing
because anything was funny. As she'd done for most of
the trip, she was practicing her Maha Deependra laughter yoga techniques. Each round would start with her
clapping her hands in rhythm to the "ho's" and "ha's"—
a one-two, one-two-three beat, sort of like your basic
cha-cha. After a little warming up, she would throw her
hands in the air and whoop freely away.

This apparently was supposed to reduce her stress
level. As far as I could tell, though, its main effect was
to drastically increase mine. The only reason I hadn't
already curled into a fetal ball and died of embarrassment was because we were alone aboard the car. It
was the one thing that stacked up on the plus side of
taking an off-peak train to the Cove—there generally
weren't many passengers.

Still, I was tempted to run screaming to the front of
the train and fling myself out onto the tracks in its direct
path. Which was to say, Maha Deependra's laughing
techniques were about to drive me off the deep end.
Ho-ho-hahaha.

I turned to look out my window. Sunset had long since
come and gone, but the high-pressure front from up

north had settled in over the coast, and the passing scenery was revealed to me in a bath of cold starlight.

As the train approached Manchester Station from the south, the tracks ran along the lip of the shore with the ocean opening out to the left, and then crossed the town harbor at the lower end of Ashland Avenue. Most of the marina's pleasure boats were berthed indoors for the winter months, and there was very little movement in the water except for floating chunks of ice with crowds of gulls hitching rides on them, staying very close together as they were carried along with the current.

"I realize you had a lousy experience, Mom," I said without turning from the window. "But thank heaven it turned out okay—"

"Sky, do you know what would have happened if the pilot *hadn't* gotten his wheels down in time?"

"No, Mom," I said. "I don't."

"We'd have had to make a belly landing! That's what!" Mom clapped her hands and laughed again. She was getting loose: *"Ha-ha-hoooooo-hoooooo-haaah!"*

I stared out at the birds and wondered if they felt cold. They didn't look it. The birds looked still and serene. And none of them were even laughing.

"Mom," I said, "you had a scare. It's over. You need to try and let these things go."

"I *am* trying," she said. "Can't you see?"

"I can, Mom," I said. "I mean, not to put down the laughter yoga—I'm sure it's fantastic. But it just seems to me that you might want to save it for your private time."

She didn't answer.

"What's wrong?" I said, turning to her.

"You're making fun of me," she said.

"No," I said, "I'm not."

"Yes," she said, "you are."

Betty-Mom gave me one of those combination wounded-and-dirty looks through her round John Lennon glasses. It was the sort of look mothers had honed to perfection over the ages, causing their overmatched children to helplessly wilt away.

One-two, ha-ha-ha, I thought. *I hate you into nonbliss-ful eternity, Maha Deependra.*

I returned to staring out my window. The train pulled into the station, pulled out, rolling through snow-blanketed wetlands and then over the track along Lily Pond on the east side of the reservoir dike.

After a while I heard the door between our car and the one in front of us rattle open, and turned from my window as a portly ticket taker appeared at the head of the aisle.

"West Gloucester, Gloucester, Rockport last stop," he announced.

Betty-Mom reached into the pocket of her fleece coat for a rail schedule she'd gotten at North Station, glanced down at it a second, then looked up at him. Trouble, I realized, was a-brewing

"We're going to Pigeon Cove," she said, confused. "Doesn't it come up before Rockport?"

"Yup," said the ticket taker. "That'd be what makes Rockport the last stop."

Betty-Mom looked at him some more.

"But you skipped it."

"Skipped what?"

"Skipped Pigeon Cove," Betty-Mom said. "In your announcement."

The ticket taker looked at her.

"Wasn't it you who just told *me* it's the stop before Rockport?"

"Yes—"

"And isn't that a schedule you're holding there in your hand?" The ticket taker poked a spatula-shaped chin at it.

"Yes, but—"

"I bet you see 'Pigeon Cove' listed clear as day," he said. "Besides which, why should I have to tell where it is on the line if you already know? Which you said you do?"

Betty-Mom looked at him again.

"That wasn't my point," she said sharply.

"Well, it's mine, ma'am, case closed," the ticket taker said, and walked down the aisle past our seats.

Betty-Mom's head spun toward me, a thick gray cloud of curls shaking around her face. Her confusion had turned to angry consternation.

"What was *his* problem?" she said

"The map flap," I said.

"The *what*?"

"The Great Pigeon Cove–Gloucester Map Flap." I expanded, and sighed. "When the Cove's chamber of commerce ordered next summer's tourist brochures, somebody accidentally forgot to mark Gloucester on the map. But because it wasn't noticed till after they were printed up, the chamber didn't want to go to the expense of doing them over for that single correction, and decided stick with the Gloucesterless brochure." I shrugged. "The ticket guy's probably a Gloucesterman. And nine out of ten are convinced their town was left off the map on purpose."

Betty-Mom looked at me.

"Explain, Sky," she said. "You've told me Pigeon Cove is a very nice town."

"It is," I said.

"If you consider nice another way of saying *filthy rich and full of snobs*," the ticket man said over his shoulder from down the aisle.

I sighed again. I didn't know all that many filthy rich people in Pigeon Cove. Sure, we had our share of well-heeled families. So did Gloucester. So did many other places. And like people with money everywhere else, some of them were snobs and some weren't. But I'd learned that both towns had more men and women struggling to make ends meet—and in too many cases hanging on by their fingernails. Things definitely had been rougher on Gloucester when the local fishing industry collapsed back in the nineties, the Cove's tourist trade having buffered it against some of the economic fallout. But the flourishing business of its B&Bs, shops, and art galleries hadn't done much for the out-of-work—

or sporadically working—fisherman and their families. I'd helped Chloe with her holiday clothing and toy drives, seen the needful faces in South End trailer parks and Gloucester's low-income areas, and their expressions had all looked the same to me. While the Great Map Flap just seemed petty and stupid on the surface, I was bothered by the bonehead preconceptions and hostilities underlying the bad-blood feud, by the energy wasted in perpetuating it—and at that particular moment by the ticket taker's unwarranted rudeness.

I'd decided I ought to say something to him about it when I realized he'd moved off into the car to our rear.

"I'm writing a letter of complaint to the railroad," Betty-Mom said, as if reading my thoughts.

"I wouldn't blame you," I said.

"There was no reason for him to treat us that way," she said.

"No, there wasn't."

Betty-Mom looked at me. I looked at her.

"Maha Deependra time?" I said.

"If you don't mind," she said.

I told her I didn't. Then I closed my eyes, leaned back against my headrest, and listened to her clap her hands and laugh like a maniac, tapping my toes to the cha-cha-esque beat until the train lurched into the Pigeon Cove station ten minutes later.

On her way out the door, Betty-Mom reached into a coat pocket and pulled out a cold-weather hood.

"You see this?" she said, displaying it to me. "It's like a balaclava but different. Lou said it's called Under Armour—imagine, you can wear it around your neck or pull it over your head."

"That's fascinating, Mom." We were on the frigid platform now. "You should put it on."

"I'm worried it will make my hair look funny," she said. "In case we run into your friends Chloe and Oscar."

I watched the wild explosion of curls flapping around her head in the wind and almost bit my tongue.

The Fog Bell was a mile or so from the railroad sta-

tion, and we got there right around five thirty. Chloe
didn't seem to be home—her VW was out of the garage,
and as usual she hadn't bothered lowering the door—
but I saw Sandy Savoy's red Audi parked alongside the
house on Carriage Lane and pulled in behind it.

"Is that Chloe's car?" Betty-Mom asked. "I didn't picture her driving anything so *flamboyant*."

"She doesn't," I said, shaking my head. Amid the
day's hectic rushing around, I'd forgotten to mention my
temporary roommate to her. "It belongs to, ah, another
guest . . . I'll tell you about her later."

Entering the house, I heard Oscar firing away on his
clarinet and decided to postpone Betty-Mom's introduc-
tion to him. When Oscar was practicing, he did not react
well to interruptions like knocks at the door. It wasn't
that he was impolite. Just distracted—in fact, I think
he'd have let in a bandit in a gorilla mask. Or a gorilla
in a bandit's mask, for that matter. Whether or not he
seemed to recognize you from under the brim of his
beat-up old workman's cap, or had any idea if Chloe
was home, he would fling open the door, holler her name
in the general direction of the ceiling, and then scurry
back to his studio with his instrument tucked under his
arm.

"So," Betty-Mom said as we went upstairs to the second floor. "This is where you've been living."

I nodded, pointed out my door. Hers was three rooms
down at the far end of the hall. "I'll show you around
once you're—"

I'd been about to say "settled in."

Before I could finish, though, she stopped, reached for
my doorknob, turned it, and pushed.

"Mom, my door's—"

I'd been about to say "locked."

Home or not, I always kept my door locked.

But I'd once again forgotten about Sandy Savoy.

Mistake.

Big, *big* mistake.

"I can't wait to see your place!" Mom said as the door
swung inward.

When you open my door from the hallway, you're looking straight into my living room. I keep it sparely but comfortably decorated and like to think it gives a welcoming first impression.

I wasn't positive what the sight of Sandy Savoy standing stark naked in the middle of the room did for that impression. Though Betty-Mom's wide-eyed, slack-jawed stare told me absolutely it did *something*.

"Hi!" Sandy said, facing us in all her bounteous, larger-than-life glory. She smiled and held up a loofah sponge. "You caught me right when I was about to exfoliate . . . we women should never settle for anything less than perfection!"

I looked at her. Took a long, long breath. Then looked at my mother.

"Mom, this is Sandy Savoy," I said. "Sandy, my mother, Betty."

Sandy flounced over to the door and put out her hand.

"I'm a friend of Michael Ennis," she said. "He and I have a special relationship—but I guess Sky's already told you."

Wrong, I thought.

Betty-Mom was staring at me. "Relationship?"

"Mom—"

"With Mike Ennis the reporter?"

I squirmed. "Mom—"

"But I thought you and Mike were . . . that he was *your* special friend."

Sandy smiled her perfect white smile and shrugged her bare shoulders.

"That's how it goes with people, doesn't it?" she said, still extending her hand toward Betty-Mom. "One day you're strangers, and the next you're quite the threesome!"

I wanted to explain. I tried to get the words out of my mouth. But my squirminess left me tongue-tied a second too long.

And then, the eruption: "HAHAHAHA! HAHAHA-HAHA! HAHAHAHAHAHA . . ."

This time Betty-Mom wasn't clapping her hands. Nor did I hear a single *ho-ho* mixed in.

I'm not the type to jump to conclusions. I really am not.

But there was no way—I mean no possible way—I could interpret that as a sign of good things to come.

Chapter 10

"I tell you, Sky, it feels like we haven't spent any time together at all lately," Mike Ennis said. He reached for the first of his two eggnog custard donuts and took a bite.

"That's because we haven't," I said, restating the obvious. "Besides at the *Anchor* the other day."

Mike nodded. "And seeing each other at the office isn't exactly the sort of time I meant."

I looked across the table at him and sipped my coffee. It was black, strong, and best of all, piping hot. Coupled with a welcome flood of sunlight pouring through the storefront window to my right, it did a lot to take the chill out of my bones.

This was Thursday morning and we were having breakfast at Beatrice's Bake Shop and Café on Main Street—or simply Bea's, as it was known to townies. The place was very tiny and had started out as strictly a bakery. But Bea Coones had decided to add a coffeemaker and three small, round tables up front near the window for eat-in service, figuring she would make the most of her busy location catercorner to City Hall.

Certainly that location was the reason I'd picked Bea's as the spot to meet Mike. After returning from the airport with Betty-Mom, I'd found a message on my answering machine from a woman named Corinne Blodgett at City Hall, who had phoned about my bid for the cleaning contract. She'd introduced herself as an alderwoman from the Personnel Committee and asked that I meet her at nine thirty the following morning or call her first thing to set up a later appointment.

The timing couldn't have been lousier. Betty-Mom had been so exhausted from her trip the night before that she'd gone to bed without even meeting Chloe and Oscar, and I'd planned to spend the morning getting her settled in. But while the message didn't mention why the alderwoman wanted to see me, or give any hint about my prospects for landing the job, I hadn't even considered putting her off. The gig was too important to me, and I was not going to chance blowing it.

When Mike called to ask me out for breakfast, an eight o'clock at Bea's had seemed just right.

Now I drank some more coffee, studying my blueberry muffin. Bea's muffins were very fresh and tasty, but I'd been spoiled. For our daily coffee klatches, Chloe kept her homemade muffins in the oven until we were ready to eat, and then served them wrapped in cloth napkins to keep them warm.

"I guess it's that we both got so busy," Mike said, picking up where he'd left off a minute ago. "Me with the Thompson story, and my trip to Boston on account of it. And you with everything you've been up to—your mom coming to visit, and before that what happened to Kyle Fipps at the Art Association party. And of course those new developments that I heard came out of the coroner's exam."

I noticed Mike hadn't mentioned his foisting Sandy Savoy on me, which I had a teensy suspicion would put the kibosh on our intimate nights at my place for the foreseeable future, being that I found having a stripper exfoliate outside my bedroom door an instant passion-douser. And also being that I wasn't ready to rumble in a merry threesome, contrary to whatever visions Sandy's unfortunate choice of words to Betty-Mom might have conjured in her warped mind—she and Lou-Dad really had participated in one too many love-ins back in their commune days.

I avoided commenting, though. I'd missed Mike. Missed him constantly from the minute he'd left for Boston.

Okay, almost constantly. There were my heart palpitations over Chief Vega outside the police station. But they'd been . . . well, I didn't know what they'd been about. Except I'd been overtired that night. And had a lot on my mind. Whatever I'd felt, or thought I'd felt, it could be chalked up to a minor electrical misfire.

No, I'd looked forward to seeing Mike too much to let myself get annoyed over his omission.

I was about to reach for my muffin when I noticed him glancing out the bakery's window.

"Speak of the devil," he said with interest. "There's our esteemed city council president."

I looked over my shoulder and saw Tommy Thompson coming briskly up the street in our direction, bundled in a long tweed overcoat and muffler, and carrying a hard-shell briefcase in his gloved hand.

"He's early to the races," I said.

"Always," Mike said. "Every morning at five thirty Tommy parks his car at his accounting office down the block, stays there a couple of hours, then hustles over to conduct his public duties. That's six days a week, with your occasional Sunday thrown in for good measure."

"Really?" I said. "I thought City Hall's closed on Sundays."

Mike shrugged.

"Not if you have the keys to the citadel," he said. "As does Lord Tommy."

I looked at Mike.

"Somebody here's been paying close attention to his routine," I said quietly. "Are you trying to figure out how he can do all he does here in town and still find time to carouse at Boston strip clubs?"

Mike grinned slyly.

"Maybe," he said. "Or could be I'm just stalking him to glean the secret of his forever young appearance."

I smiled. Thompson was a good-looking man—I'd always kind of thought he resembled the actor Robert Wagner. Not the dashing playboy-cum-rogue *It Takes a Thief* Robert Wagner, or the sophisticated middle-aged *Switch* or *Hart to Hart* Robert Wagner, but the slightly-

overweight-yet-still-handsome-and-polished latter-day version who'd played Number Two in those *Austin Powers*
flicks . . . and then unfortunately become a TV shill for
some financial outfit trying to sell senior citizens on reverse mortgages. I guessed he was pushing sixty, making
him easily twice Sandy Savoy's age. And while I had no
issue with anyone being involved with an older guy, I
did happen to disagree with it when he was married to
another woman and sneaking around behind her back.

Passing the bakery, Thompson turned into the cross-
walk a couple of doors down, then quickstepped to the
opposite side of the street and up the shoveled cobble-
stone path leading through City Hall's snow-covered
courtyard, where, every Saturday at noon for the whole
month of December, a Santa would wait to give kids
free horse-and-wagon rides around town.

The building was one of those neoclassical types you
see all across coastal New England, and though Santa
and his buggy weren't out front this morning, there was
a fanciful charm about how it looked in its holiday
trappings—the entry door flanked on either side by a
giant Christmas tree and menorah, its colonnades and
windows hung with garlands, mistletoe, and candy canes,
its high belfry wearing a king-sized red bow. Cast in
bronze at Paul Revere's Boston foundry back in 1802,
the bell in that tower was one of the Cove's historic
treasures and had clanged in the New Year for the past
two centuries, with the traditional bell ringer honors falling to the duly elected president of the city council. For
over a decade, none other than Tommy Thompson had
held that position.

"Well, nobody can ever claim he isn't energetic," I
said, watching him briskly climb the broad limestone
stairs.

Mike nodded and bit into his donut, a look of supreme
gratification spreading over his face. Bea's seasonal spe-
cialty, the eggnog custard donuts generally disappeared
from her shelves by nine a.m. If you weren't on the list
of customers who preordered massive quantities every
year, you needed to get to the bakery right when she

opened her doors to line up for them—and the daily limit was two per person.

"So," he said, recovering from his donut ecstasy. "What were we talking about a minute ago?"

"Us being busy," I said. Then I dropped my voice. "And why the new onyx silk negligee I bought while you were in Boston hasn't left its box."

Mike looked at me.

"Onyx silk?"

"And lace," I said. "With side slits."

Mike looked at me some more.

"Want to come over for dinner later?" he said. "You can bring along Skiball and that box."

"And what about Mom?" I said. "Or do we forget she's here on a short visit?"

Mike snapped his fingers in an aw-shucks gesture.

"Foiled," he said. "I was hoping to sneak my idea past the censors, but guess we're on hold. Although Sandy *could* keep her company tonight."

I laughed. "You're kidding me, right?"

Mike shrugged, gave a little smile.

"Half," he said. "Maybe."

I sat there a moment and pictured Mom and Sandy harmoniously buffing themselves to feminine perfection with matching loofahs.

"Quite a twosome," I mumbled under my breath.

"Hmm?"

"Just remembering their first close encounter—I'll have to tell you about it once I've recovered from the trauma to my psyche," I said, raising my coffee cup to my lips. "You know, Mike, forbidden PJ parties aside . . . Mom's only in town a few days before heading off to California, but I think it'd be great if you could meet her."

"Sure," Mike said. He gulped down the rest of his donut, started on the second. "And by the way . . . while we're on the subject . . . I've been wondering how things are coming along at your place. With Sandy."

I looked at him over the rim of my coffee cup. How sweet of him to be concerned.

"Getting there," I said, giving Mike's question exactly two more syllables than I got in answer to mine. Call me a numskull, but I was under the impression the subject had been my mother's visit. In fact, I'd expected a different response. Say, *I'd love to meet her, Sky.*

Or something.

I lowered my cup to the table, broke off a chunk of muffin, and took my time dunking it.

"She's easy to like," Mike elaborated. "Sandy, that is."

I ate in silence. *You know, Sky, since your mother's only here for a few days, let's not put it off. We can make it tonight. Maybe go to my uncle Alex's restaurant in Gloucester. Don't worry about the logistics—I'll take care of our reservations. Pick the two of you up at seven sharp.*

"Sandy seems very credible to me," Mike said. "You've got to respect how she's been taking care of her sister. And her willingness to confront Thompson when push comes to shove."

I stopped eating my piece of muffin and stared across the table at him.

Mike sat there looking back at me for a while. Sat some more. Cleared his throat.

"You know, I'm thinking we can talk about Sandy another time," he said finally. "About your interview . . . does it look as if you're getting the contract?"

My expression was frozen.

"Who knows?" I said through a mouthful of semi-chewed muffin.

"Ah, right. I was just curious . . ."

"Guess I'll find out soon enough."

"Right."

"Or not."

Mike made another throat-clearing sound. "Rolling on along," he said, "have you heard anything recently from your friend Jessie Barton?"

I didn't utter a word, or take my eyes off his for about thirty seconds. Then I slowly finished what was left in my mouth, wiped my hands on my napkin, folded it, and put it on my empty dish.

"Okay," I said. "You better tell me what's going on."

He looked at me without saying anything.

"Talk, Mike," I said. "You've asked me about Jessie maybe once or twice since she left town. And not for months. What's with your sudden interest in her now?"

Mike sat for a few more ticks of silence. Then he took a long, deep breath.

"Sandy's told me some things on and off the record," he said. "But as a reporter I can't share them with you. That's why I was hoping she'd mentioned them on her own. If she had it would be another story."

I crossed my arms on the table and bent forward.

"You're the reason Sandy Savoy is staying in my home," I said in a near whisper. "The reason I let her into it. But I won't live with secrets. Not for you or anyone."

"This isn't about what I want, Sky. I've got an ethical obligation—"

"I heard you the first time," I interrupted. "But we both write for the *Anchor*, and that makes us colleagues."

I sat there waiting, my face so close to Mike's that our noses almost touched.

"I'm a news reporter," he said. "There's a distinction between what we do."

I shook my head slightly.

"Mike, starting this very moment, on *this* story, we need to be partners," I said. "I'm either in or out. It's up to you."

Our gazes held. Then Mike cut his eyes toward the people at the other tables, turned to where Beatrice Coones was gabbing to a regular over a pastry case, and finally brought his attention back to me.

"You have time for a stroll?" he asked, motioning his head toward the door.

I checked my watch, saw it was barely eight thirty, and nodded.

"Loads," I said.

Mike reached around to undrape his coat from the back of his chair.

"Let's get going," he said. "I want to talk where we can have some privacy."

A minute later we got up, brought our empties over to the counter, and left.

Outside, we turned right past the Second Read used bookshop and Griffin's Art and Drafting Supplies, heading down to where Broadway converged with the long, narrow curve of Gull Wing wharf. There we passed between rows of shingled stores and galleries, including Jessie's conspicuously bare shopfront and Drecksel's Diner next door, at last winding up by the old slatted wooden benches that faced the quays.

I pulled my scarf up around my collar as Mike motioned to one of the benches and we sat with the harbor opening out in front of us.

"The night Sandy and I drove here, she told me a lot about her relationship with Thompson," Mike said after a few seconds passed. "Everybody's got a dream, and I believe Tommy was hers. He claimed he and his wife had been leading separate lives for years. Their arrangement was social, political, financial . . . you can mix and match. But when his term as town council president ended, he promised the charade would end too. That he'd file for divorce."

"The usual cheater's package of lies," I said. "You think Sandy believed them?"

"I think she willingly accepted them."

"That isn't the same, Mike," I said.

He shrugged his shoulders beside me. "She was in love with Thompson. I'm convinced of it. His lies kept the dream within reach for her."

A frosty gust blew over us from across the water, and I tucked my chin deeper into my scarf.

"After the photo of Sandy and Thompson hit the newspapers, it must have been wake-up time," I said. "Her bubble burst, didn't it?"

"With a loud pop," Mike said. "Tommy started to pretend she didn't exist. He wouldn't see her, phone her, or accept her calls. On the one occasion she managed to get through on Tommy's cell phone before he blocked her number, he blew his stack and told her never to contact him again. Calling her foul names, even threatening her."

I looked at Mike. "Threatening her how?"

"I don't know. Sandy had plenty to say about him when we met at the club where she dances. But driving up from Boston she was coiled tight. The reason we got to the office so late that next day was because she was back to being relaxed and talkative at my house, and I didn't want to stop her." Mike shrugged. "I have a sense she's covering up two pieces of information for every one she gives me."

I smiled wanly at a passing thought.

Mike gave me a look.

"What is it?" he said.

"Nothing," I said. "It's just that from the way Sandy struts around my apartment, you wouldn't think she knows how to cover up any part of herself."

Mike raised his eyebrows.

"No," he said.

"Yes," I said. "If you're in doubt go ahead and ask my mom."

He opened his mouth, closed it, and then looked at me with subdued amusement.

We sat quietly. The wind blew hard from over the water. Far out past the harbor lighthouse, a little white shrimp boat was coming in, and I watched it for about a minute. New England shrimp was a cold-water bounty, and the shrimpers would be out all night under the harshest conditions, dragging their nets for the winter harvest. After they dropped anchor, you'd see them on the deck drying the nets in their watch caps and slickers before moving the catch into vans or covered pickup trucks. The local shrimp weren't very large, and it was rough competing at the marketplace with the big, plump warm-water catch shipped in from Florida or the tropics. It was one of the reasons the local industry had hit hard times. Shoppers didn't realize the small shrimp were the tastiest, and that the meat was usually peeled and cleaned when you bought it, making them a pound-for-pound bargain.

Whenever I had a chance, I liked to drive to the waterfront and buy directly from the shrimpers as they came off their boats. It meant I'd have to do the cleaning myself, but they often threw something extra onto the scale to make up for the weight I would have to throw away with the shells.

I turned to Mike, saw that his face was back to being serious. Mine must have looked the same.

"Tell me where Jessie Barton fits into this whole thing," I said.

Mike looked at me.

"For now I can only talk about where she *might* fit in," he said. "A few months back, Sandy felt Tommy had changed toward her. He'd seemed kind of distant, and missed a few dates when she'd expected him to show at her condo. She didn't completely buy his explanations and thought maybe he'd patched up his relationship with his wife."

He paused.

"And?" I said with a hand gesture.

"And then once when Tommy was at her place, she came out of the shower, and noticed he was in the bedroom with her door closed, and went up to the door and heard him having an argument with someone on his cell phone," Mike said. "Sandy guessed it was another woman because of his tone. Then she heard him call her a bitch and some fouler things, and knew it for sure. Right before he got off the line, she also heard him shouting about a key."

"Shouting what?"

"I wish I knew." Mike said. He shrugged. "It was a quick call, and Sandy came in toward the end—she figured Tommy probably tried to sneak it in while she was cleaning up. And keep in mind that she was listening through a door. What she remembers clearly is him telling the woman to keep her mouth shut or she'd regret it when he got back to the Cove."

My eyes had been gradually widening as I listened.

"This ugly conversation," I said. "It wasn't between Tommy and his wife, was it?"

Mike shook his head.

"Her name is Angela," he said. "This was someone else."

I didn't need long to consider that.

"Jessie," I said.

Mike nodded. "He used her name twice, when he wasn't using unrepeatable terms to describe her."

I felt my body tense.

"You said this was a few months ago," I said. "Did Sandy tell you *which* month?"

"No," Mike said. "The closest she could put it was around the end of the summer. She remembered the weather starting to get cool."

I was silent. Again, I didn't have to do much thinking. Jessie Barton had left town around the middle of September.

I turned my head, gazed down the Wing at Jessie's vacant August Moon boutique, and noticed that Bill Drecksel had stepped outside his diner alongside it for a smoke, not bothering to throw on a jacket over his grease-splattered cook's apron. I hadn't known he was a smoker—the cigarette seemed out of place sticking from under his walrus mustache. But then, I hadn't really known too much about him except that he made the lousiest coffee on all of Cape Ann and had been partners with Kyle Fipps on the Getaway Groves project.

And that he and Jessie had been close friends.

A sudden shiver ran through me in the blowing wind.

"You okay?" Mike said from over my shoulder.

I nodded. "Yep," I said. My eyes had returned to the empty boutique window. "Just cold."

I felt Mike put his hand over mine on the bench between us.

"That's better," I said. Turning to face him, our hands resting together on the bench. "But there's room for improvement."

He moved closer. I felt his other hand reach across my body and come to rest on my waist.

"How's that?" he said. His voice was husky.

"Getting warmer," I said.

He kissed me twice on the cheek, and then behind my ear, and then softly on the neck just above the line of my scarf. I shivered again, this time not from the cold, and slipped my hand over his face and tilted it so our mouths came together.

"Perfect," I said. As our lips parted I heard a gasp that might have come from either or both of us, I couldn't tell.

"Good thing you have that appointment," he said after a while.

"A public smooch in December?" I said. "You must be feeling a sugar rush from those custard donuts."

Mike looked at me. We were both a little breathless. "Actually," he said, "it happened when you mentioned that onyx silk negligee."

I gave him a wink.

"With lace and side slits," I reminded him.

Chapter 11

A short, plump woman in her fifties with a sprayed pouf of margarine-colored hair and more than a smidge too much blush on her cheeks, Corinne Blodgett turned out to be the assistant vice chairman of the Personnel Committee, as she told me when I got to her office at City Hall, which was grouped with several others behind a transomed door on the third floor marked SUITE 308.

"I'm very pleased you could come on such brief notice," she said, extending her hand with a courteous smile. "I should say, *we're* pleased, Ms. Taylor."

"No trouble. I appreciated your call," I said. "And 'Sky's' fine, by the way."

Corinne stood smiling in her doorway.

"Sky," she said. "Such a pretty name. Is it short for something?"

I shook my head.

"Just Sky like the sky above our heads," I said.

"How special!"

"Thanks," I said. "I'm always glad my parents didn't decide to make it Ground or Water. Or worse, Groundwater."

Corinne didn't double over laughing and slap her knees, but instead continued to smile politely. It made me doubt whether my quip had registered on her joke-o-meter.

We stood in the doorway some more. Corinne Blodgett's smile likewise remained in stationary between her burgundy cheeks.

"Well, I've been eager to tell you our committee's had a chance to review and discuss your bid proposal in full," she said. "We were impressed by your wonderful client referrals. So many of them! And all offering such high praise."

I smiled back at her now, wondering when she was going to move us over to her desk.

"On a personal note, I want to say hurray, hoorah for developing a female-owned-and-run business that's grown and flourished in our town," she said. "It's exceptional considering you've lived here a relatively short time and started out with no professional cleaning background."

We kept smiling at each other in the entrance. A peek over Corinne's shoulder at her wall clock told me it was two minutes and counting since her receptionist had deposited me there.

"I don't believe I'm out of line mentioning that Noel Lawless sent an unsolicited testimonial on your behalf to the committee—it was received soon after your bid appeared in the *Anchor*'s public notice section," she said. Her voice dropped to a confidential tone. "As a Double-Xer, I strongly value Noel's opinions."

This surprised me in more ways than one. The Double-X Club's name referred to the sex chromosomes that determine female gender and not a love of smutty movies among its women-only membership. As far as I could tell, the group was dedicated in the short term to finding reasons to hate and complain about males, with the broad, long-range goal of purging the human race of them at all costs—even if it meant the total extinction of the species. Interacting with guys on anything but a confrontational basis was a major violation of club dictates, since it could lead to the natural mating urge, a random, repulsive pairing of X and Y chromosomes, and the birth of deceptively adorable baby boys who would grow up to be overtly malevolent, full-sized men.

Noel was the club's founder and chief man basher, and her angry no-makeup look set the bar for the typical Double-Xer. The odd thing was that Corinne didn't fit that profile—she clearly made an effort to keep herself fixed up, and didn't have permanent scowl lines around her mouth. And compounding that bit of oddness was learning Noel had put in a good word for me. She'd never, ever spoken to me or acknowledged my existence, having pegged me from day one as a traitor to my sex who'd once been happily married to a man and still had a lot of loathsome male friends.

So now I owed Noel Lawless. Whether or not I won my bid. It was something to ponder.

Meanwhile, Corinne hadn't yet shown any inclination to budge from the door. I glanced at her clock again and saw we'd reached the three-minute mark standing in that spot.

"Well, I shouldn't keep you in suspense," she said, pausing to keep me in suspense. But her smile had widened, and I took that as an encouraging sign.

"Congratulations, Sky," she said. "Our committee has decided to approve your bid."

I almost gulped. No, that's not true. I did gulp. Loudly. But I tried not to let my knees buckle. Door, *shmore*, I was in! The contract paid about sixteen thousand a year. Tack that onto what I earned from my existing clientele and the money I got for the Sky Writing column, and I would at long last be able to cobble together a respectable income.

"This is great," I said, hardly able to see Corinne through the merry little dollar signs dancing in a line across my vision. "I can't tell you how excited I am that you've chosen me."

Corinne smiled.

"Tentatively chosen you," she said. "Pending your interview with the city council president."

I gulped again. A very quiet gulp this time. Those dancing dollar signs had gone still before my eyes.

"Tommy Thompson?" I said

"That's right," Corinne said. She was of course still smiling at me. "You see, the Personnel Committee can approve bids, but Mr. Thompson needs to consider our recommendations before they're actually *awarded*."

I looked at her, unsure what to make of this latest development. My dancing dollar signs had drooped over and filed out of the Sky Taylor Conga Ballroom, shuffling their little feet, taking my approximation of Corinne's smiley face with them.

"I guess I should ask what's next," I said.

She finally stepped from her office entrance now, sort of guiding me along by the arm as she backed us out into the hall.

"Mr. Thompson is expecting you in his office," she said. "Once you're back out in the main corridor, make a right and go straight to Suite 315. It's the last office before you get to the stairs." She lowered her voice again. "I saw those photos of Tommy in the paper. It's a disgrace, but don't let that put you off. Election Day isn't far off. Our time will come."

I didn't know what to say to that, and figured the smartest thing was to stay quiet.

"Well, good luck!" Corinne walked me past her receptionist's desk. "I hope to see you cleaning my office soon!"

And with those words of sisterhood and empowerment, Noel Lawless's embedded Double-X mole in the town government put a chubby hand on my back and nudged me on my way.

Suite 315 didn't bear much resemblance to the Personnel Committee's humdrum digs, the most noticeable difference being that it wasn't split up into small, separate offices. There was a formal anteroom with lounge chairs, a matching sofa, and carefully polished cherry furniture. Three of its four walls were decorated with framed etchings of horses with riders in their saddles. Beyond the reception desk, a single large wooden door had a shiny brass plaque engraved with Tommy Thompson's name and title. A stainless-steel watercooler near the door was the only fixture that didn't have an old-fashioned feel about it. Well, okay, aside from the receptionist, a pixie blonde who looked like an *American Idol* runner up to me, don't ask why.

I went over to her desk and told her who I was. Then

she reached for her phone, punched the intercom button on the console, announced me, and cradled the receiver.

"Mr. Thompson's on a call," she said with a sparkly smile. "He'll be right with you."

I sat down to wait, my coat draped across my lap. I wondered about the chances of finding myself in Tommy Thompson's office on the same morning I had learned he'd been threatening Sandy Savoy—and another woman who might very well be my friend Jessie, someone whose sudden departure from the Cove had bothered me for months. Then I wondered about the chances of Sandy's overhearing him as he made those threats to her over the phone, and then telling Mike about it at a Boston strip club, and then winding up as my roommate.

It was fluky how all those threads had come together. If you spoke to either of my parents about it, you'd probably get a very Zen explanation about how everything that happens to us is interconnected and coincidental at the same time. These days Chloe might have some pithy sentence sermon on hand to make her feelings about it clear. The same for Bryan at the *Anchor*, although he'd probably ink the sermon across his forehead at a tattoo parlor.

As for me, I wasn't biting. Sure, I tried to keep an open mind. But I was determinedly levelheaded and refused to go pulling metaphysical threads out of the air.

With time to kill in the reception room, I decided to give myself a quick once-over instead. The interview with Tommy Thompson had been a big fat curveball thrown into my morning plans, but fortunately I'd dressed okay for it. Or thought I had. I'd worn a caramel brown pleated skirt, matching opaque stockings and boots, and a bright emerald green sweater with one of my mother's huge gold holiday safety pins on the shoulder. The pin wasn't exactly glam, but it accented the color of the sweater and was very cute. Besides, Betty-Mom had insisted that her dangling handmade ornaments—a red Christmas bell, a blue Star of David, a dove, a reindeer, a poinsettia, a gift-wrapped box, and a tiny yellow peace sign—were filled with love power, and, levelheaded or not, I'd found the sentiment so sweet that I would've probably worn the thing if it had lint balls hanging from it.

After a few moments, my wardrobe check was almost finished and I was feeling pretty satisfied.

This, naturally, was when I saw the salt stains on my left boot. Egads.

I crinkled my forehead. Considering that Mike and I had strolled from Main Street to the Wing and back after we left Bea's, and that there was rock salt sprinkled all over the pavement and walkways outside, I guessed the stains could have come from anywhere. But figuring out where they came from wasn't my problem.

Bottom line, they had to go.

I stood up, went over to the watercooler, pulled a plastic cup from the dispenser, and filled it about a third of the way to the top. Then I returned to my seat, took four or five facial tissues from the pack in my handbag, and bunched them into a couple of wads, dipping one into the water. I would've preferred using paper napkins—they hold together better and you don't need to use as many of them. But with eyesore emergencies you sometimes have to make do using whatever is available.

With the dampened wad, I wiped my boot off till I couldn't see any more streaks of white. Then I moved on to the second stage of the procedure.

For years I'd carried around little tubes of Vaseline to keep my lips from chapping in the winter. But my current lip-saver of choice was cocoa butter, and I knew it would work as well as the Vaseline to lubricate the boot and protect its leather from drying out.

I fished around in my purse again, took out my cocoa butter stick, and rubbed some on the dry wad of tissues I'd set aside. Finally I applied it to the area that had gotten salt on it, worked it in with the tissues, and then did a quick buff to bring back the shine.

And that was that. The salt removal operation was a cinch, and no more than a minute or two had passed between its launch and accomplishment.

Which was perfect timing, since I'd no sooner gotten up to toss the tissues and paper cup in the wastebasket by the cooler than Tommy Thompson appeared in his doorway.

"Good morning," he said to me, coming around the reception desk. "Sorry I made you wait."

Tommy had been a little excessive in slapping on his cologne—kind of like Corinne Blodgett with her blush— and its scent wafted out into the anteroom ahead of him. But whatever the brand, it was expensive stuff, and didn't make my throat grab at my tonsils. If you've ever been crushed against a guy wearing Brut or Aqua Velva on a New York subway car, you know that terrible feeling.

We shook hands. Besides the cologne, Tommy had on a brown tweed hacking jacket that coordinated niftily with the equestrian prints on the walls, a navy blue turtleneck shirt, a silk pocket square the same color as the shirt, tobacco-colored trousers, and black cordovan English paddock boots that zipped up the front. Presumably he had a riding crop somewhere to go along with the ensemble—maybe in his desk drawer—in the event he was struck by the impulse to climb atop his steed for an invigorating gallop through the town center. I should mention that he was also sporting a gold Cartier tank watch with an alligator band that must have cost in the neighborhood of three thousand dollars. Since the city council job paid only a token salary, I guessed his accounting firm had been flourishing.

I got a good look at the watch, mainly because he wore it on his left wrist and had let that hand gently settle over mine as we shook.

"So," he said. "I'm very happy to meet you, Ms. Taylor."

I nodded.

"Same here," I said. "And please call me Sky."

Thompson smiled but didn't comment on my name. This was good. It spared me from any more attempts at self-deprecating humor that were bound to land with a clunk.

He stood there in the anteroom for a few seconds, his eyes in steady contact with my eyes. The two-handed handshake seemed too touchy and familiar for someone who'd never met me before—not that it was blatantly inappropriate. But it lasted longer than necessary, I supposed because he was waiting for me to swoon at his XY suavity.

"Why don't we step into my office?" he said, and nodded toward his door. "We have a lot to talk about."

I stepped in, Tommy hanging back to let me enter first. Inside, I noticed a case full of trophies for horse riding and showing competitions, and yet another piece of equestrian art on the wall to my right. Not a print like those in the reception area, but a large canvas of red-jacketed riders gathering for a foxhunt.

Tommy saw me admiring it as he followed me through the door.

"It's an original George Stubbs," he said. "Are you acquainted with his work?"

"The name rings a bell," I said. "But that's about all. It's really striking, though."

"Yes, it is." Tommy smiled, looking directly at me and not the painting. *Argh.* "Stubbs was an eighteenth-century British artist whose themes were sporting and animals. I have several of his oils in my collection." He closed his door and gestured me toward a chair in front of his desk. "Please make yourself comfortable, Sky."

I sat. Tommy sat opposite me. His desk was the size of an ocean liner—one that had beached up on a braided Early American oval rug in the middle of the floor.

"I've assessed your proposal for the cleaning contract, and the Personnel Committee's recommendation that it be granted to you," Tommy said. He broke his urbane pose long enough to pull a file folder from his top desk drawer and set it down on his blotter. I could read my name on its tab. "I just have a few questions, if you don't mind."

I nodded. "Sure," I said. "That's why I'm here."

He placed both hands flat on the folder and smiled again. I still wouldn't have described his smile-look combo as outright flirtatious—it seemed much more about him thinking he was smooth and charming, and being impressed with himself for it, than about him trying to send me any messages. But I admit to being a little relieved we had that HMS *Titanic* of a desk between us.

"Looking at your résumé, I noticed that you have a broad range of clients."

"I try to keep busy," I said.

"And you work alone, yes?"

"That's right."

"And do you intend to reduce your number of clients should you be awarded the contract?"

"I don't take on more than I can handle," I said. "If that's what you're asking me."

Tommy lifted his hands from the folder, pressed his fingertips together in front of him, right about level with his blue silk pocket hanky. His nails were predictably well manicured.

"Here at City Hall we have more than a dozen office suites on three floors. And that excludes the main council chamber and auditorium," he said. "This building is larger than what you might be accustomed to, and my concern is over your ability to assess the demanding workload it would present." He paused. "I trust you'll take it in context when I say you're a physically slight woman."

I fought the urge to clench my teeth. True, I wouldn't win any tractor pull contests. But my size had never been a problem when it came to my work.

"I'm very realistic about what I can and can't do," I said. "If I need to make adjustments, I'll make them."

"And that would mean . . . ?"

"It depends on what comes up," I said. "All I can tell you is that City Hall will be a priority for me. I'll know as I go along whether I need to hire help, cut back on my other obligations, or whatever."

Tommy looked at me, continuing to form an igloo with his fingers.

"You're very confident. I like that," he said with a

faint smile he clearly thought was engaging. "No wonder the committee was so keen on you."

I didn't say anything. I didn't like him commenting on what he liked about me. It made me imagine him telling Sandy Savoy—and my friend Jessie, assuming she really was the woman Sandy overheard him arguing with on the phone—what he'd liked about them. And that made me dislike his comment a whole lot more. Was this the guy who'd broken both their hearts? It started me wondering if the gleam of his gold Cartier watch could have blinded them to his condescending smile . . . and then I realized that wasn't what I *ought* to have been wondering. Though I didn't want to think it, I knew its gleam wouldn't blind any woman who'd lived her life outside a paper bag. The only thing it might have done was make that smile easier to take, or maybe overlook, depending on what she might want out of their relationship.

Tommy sat eyeing me in silence for a minute or so. Then he straightened in his chair and put his hands back on the folder.

"All right, Sky. I'm going to provisionally award you the contract," he said. "It's not altogether unusual for us to hire on a trial basis, and that's what I'm prepared to offer. The contractual language would guarantee you ninety days as our exclusive cleaning service. After that you'd be subject to a review. Should everything work out to our mutual liking, as I hope it does, we would extend the arrangement to a full year."

I sat a minute looking reserved. Provisionally. Tentatively. It hadn't taken me long that morning to find out that Pigeon Cove's government representatives—XX's and XY's alike—shared a knack for slipping vague excuse-me words into their sentences.

I figured Tommy could tell I wasn't satisfied, but tried not to show him the extent of my disappointment. I knew I'd met the requirements for the job. So did the Personnel Committee—they wouldn't have given me their okay otherwise. And I hadn't heard anything about a three-month tryout before. There'd been no mention of it in the bid posting when I'd read it in the newspaper, or in the documents that came with my application. No ambiguity about the offer being for a full year's contract. Tommy's conditions had caught me by surprise, and I had a feeling he'd come up with them on the spot because of whatever personal doubts he had about me. Maybe because I wasn't built like the horses in his pictures. I didn't know.

Still, I realized it wouldn't pay to get hung up on the negative aspects of the deal. Ninety days was ninety days. I was getting a shot. That was the important thing.

Tommy was looking at me. "Well, Sky," he said. "Do I trust we have an agreement?"

"Yes, and thank you," I said. "You won't regret it."

He gave me one of his smiles and extended a hand across his desk. I shook it quickly, pulling away before he could bring his other hand into the action again.

"On behalf of the city council, I'm pleased to have you aboard," he said, getting up to show me out of his office.

On my behalf, I was pleased to be leaving it.

Chapter 12

It was about eleven thirty in the morning when I got to Drecksel's Diner on the Wing, having walked over to do some nosing around about Jessie Barton after leaving City Hall. As I entered I saw Bill helping the Beaufort sisters—who were his only regulars, as far as anyone knew—at the end of the counter farthest from the door. A downward arrow on an overhead sign marked this as the take-out section.

I sat toward the front of the counter and waited. The place was empty except for the four of us, so I had my pick of stools.

"We'd like a cup of noodle soup," Abigail Beaufort said. Bundled in a long gray coat, she guardedly clutched a purse under her arm.

Beulah nodded in agreement beside her. She wore a shorter blue coat with a floral peasant skirt spilling shapelessly out from underneath it. Since Abigail was usually their spokesperson, I sort of figured she was the elder of the sisters, but it was hard to tell. The best estimates I'd heard about their ages put them at somewhere between forty and a thousand. From their pasty, shriveled appearance, you had to wonder if they'd used some of their substantial inheritance to convert the bedrooms of their old home on Plum Street into dehydrating chambers.

Drecksel had stood regarding them a second from behind the counter. Now he gave his walrus mustache a tug, turned around, and made a show of looking up at the menu board.

"Hmmm, yup, thought so," he said.

"Excuse me?" Abigail said.

"I said I thought I put *chicken* noodle soup up there. Not noodle soup."

Abigail frowned at the back of his bald head. When she did, her lips pinched more tightly together on one side than the other.

"You know the soup I mean," she said.

"And you know the soup *I* mean, so why can't you or your sister ever call it what it is?" Bill said. "When you call it noodle soup, it could mean beef noodle, vegetable noodle, or any kind of noodle soup under the sun."

"The problem, Mr. Drecksel, is that if we call it anything but noodle soup, you give us more soup and less noodles. And we do like our noodles."

"Yeah, yeah. And maybe I got a lot of selections to remember, and like it when my customers help me out by ordering the right way."

Abigail's lips grew more crooked, screwing up one side of her face.

"You don't need to be testy with me," she said. "There are other restaurants in town."

"Go ahead and try 'em. I want to see who else'll put up with you two." Bill chortled. He gave me a slyly mischievous wink, and then turned to her again.

"Okay, you want chicken noodle. That right?"

Abigail produced a sigh.

"Yes," she said. "A two-dollar and twenty-five-cent cup, not a three-dollar bowl. Just so you understand."

"Sure. I know you wouldn't want to spend an extra seventy-five cents to get twice as much."

"We don't overeat. It's unhealthy and wasteful," Abigail said. She gave Bill a needling look. "As a piece of advice, you might consider putting similar restrictions on yourself, Mr. Drecksel. To quote a wonderful book we'd been reading at the dump before some selfish individual stole off with it, 'People call it middle age because that's where it shows most.' "

Overhearing her, I wanted to scratch my head. Book? At the dump? It couldn't have been the one I thought it was. Or could it? Had everybody in town laid hands on it but me?

As I sat refusing to further contemplate anything that downright bizarre, Drecksel glowered across the counter at Abigail. The truth was he had put on some weight, making his apron bulge out around the waistline.

"Anything else you care to tell me while you're at it?" he said.

She exchanged glances with her sister, who gave her a little nod. "Please scoop from the bottom so we get enough noodles for both of us."

"And?"

"Last time, Beulah and I felt the noodle soup wasn't hot enough," she said. "If it's not piping hot, could you put it in the microwave for a couple of minutes?"

"And?"

"We'd like an extra take-out container," Abigail said. "Since we're going to share."

Drecksel inflated his cheeks, shook his head, and let the breath escape through his puckered mouth, ruffling up the hairs of his bushy mustache as it spouted out. Then he grabbed a ladle and went over to the soup warmer behind his counter. A few moments later he returned to the take-out area and packed the soup and extra container in a paper bag, stuffing in some napkins before he rolled down its top. I hadn't seen him detour to nuke the soup and guessed it must have been satisfactorily piping.

"That'll be two thirty-one with tax," he said, holding out the bag. "But for you big spenders I'll let the penny slide."

Beulah silently took the bag from him. Meanwhile, Abigail had allowed maybe a half inch of airspace between the purse and her side, opening it barely wide enough to let her hand creep into it and then resurface with her change purse—one of those old oval plastic types you squeezed open to get the coins out.

"Your portion comes to one fifteen," she said to Beulah, shaking change into her palm.

Beulah nodded.

"Just add it to what I owe you for our toothpaste," she said.

"If you keep floating your debts they'll become unmanageable."

"I know. I'll pay you back in full when we get home."

And then they were headed toward the door, leaving a scattered assortment of quarters, dimes, and nickels behind on the take-out counter.

Bill watched them walk down the street through his storefront window.

"Merry Christmas and Happy New Year to you too, ladies," he grumbled aloud. Then he scooped up the change and tossed it into his pants pocket. "No sense wasting electricity to use the register."

I had to smile at that as he came over to me.

"Long time no see, Sky," he said. "How ya been?"

"Good," I said. "You?"

Bill seesawed his hand in the air. "Hangin' in there," he said. "Want a cup of coffee?"

"No, thanks, Bill."

"You sure? I put up a fresh pot maybe ten minutes ago. And I ain't forgotten that one I promised you on the house."

I shook my head.

"I'm cutting down on the caffeine," I lied. Nobody knew what gave Drecksel's Special Blend its inimitably revolting taste. I'd heard a café chain in Boston shipped him its stale overstock at a bargain-basement rate, but that alone wouldn't have accounted for it. My own theory was that there had to be multiple secret additives. Pencil shavings, say, mixed in with some broken tips, and possibly high-urea potting soil. With mud-puddle water crucial to the brewing process.

Bill shrugged.

"Whenever you want it, it's on me," he said. "So what'll you have to eat? A triple-decker club sandwich maybe? I got in some tasty cold cuts the other day."

I hesitated.

"To be honest, I kind of came to talk," I said.

"Oh," Bill said. "Humph."

He looked dejected, and I understood why. During Pigeon Cove's annual warm-weather tourist boom, he would have a fairly constant stream of unwary day-trippers coming through the door. That seasonal trade pretty much carried him through the winters, when there weren't many people around besides the locals, and the Beaufort sisters were among the few, if not only, patrons he could rely on to stop by for a bite. Somehow, I doubted their business did much to help pay his over-head.

"Well," he said, "what's on your mind?"

I looked at him.

"Jessie Barton," I said, getting right to the point.

Surprise flashed across Bill's face. But then he straightened up and struck a defensive posture.

"Sorry," he said. "It comes to Jessie, I have nothing to talk about."

"Bill, listen—"

"Nope, stop right there," he said with a slicing gesture. "I mean it."

"She was your best friend in town."

"That was before she took off," Bill said. "But now she's gone." He paused, his eyes turning downward for an instant. "Never even said good-bye to me. Guess maybe we weren't such good friends after all."

"Do you ever wonder *why* she left like that?"

Bill shrugged his chunky shoulders. "What's the difference I do or don't?"

"The difference is that maybe she didn't really want to leave," I said. "That she might have been running away from something."

He looked at me and stepped closer to the counter, his stomach pressing against its inner edge. He couldn't hide his eager curiosity.

"You hear from her lately?" he said.

"I guess you could say so," I said. "She sends me electronic postcards on the computer. Singing jack-o'-lanterns and goblins on Halloween. A gobbling Thanks-giving turkey. Last week I got elves dancing in the snow."

Bill grunted.

"That it?"

"That's it. They all come with cheerful hi-how-are-yous that don't tell me anything about how she's doing."

Another grunt. "Sounds like the cards I get in my mailbox. 'Cept nothing on 'em sings, gobbles, or dances."

I looked at him in the quiet of his empty diner. I'd known before dropping by the restaurant that I'd have to be open with Bill—at least as open as I could be without breaking any of Mike's confidences.

"Bill," I said, "I need to ask . . . was Jessie having an affair with Tommy Thompson?"

He didn't say anything for almost a minute. Then he opened his mouth, closed it, and waited another long moment to speak.

"We flap our gums, what's the use?" he said at last. "It won't bring her back here."

"I don't know for sure that it will," I said. "I think there's a chance it might, though."

Bill looked at me. "You just said you ain't talked to Jessie since she went away."

"Not to her, no," I said. "But there's someone who claims to have overheard Tommy Thompson making threats to a woman that might've been Jessie."

"Huh?"

"You heard me, Bill."

He shook his head. "Ah, c'mon. That ain't no kind of gossip to repeat."

"It's more than gossip. Trust me."

"You going let me know how it came your way?"

"I would if I could," I said. "All I can say is that if I didn't think it had a very good chance of being the truth, I'd never have shared it with you. Or with anyone else."

He looked at me, smoothing a hand over his bald dome.

"Those threats," he said. "How long ago was it your someone heard 'em?"

"I asked the same question," I said. "It was late summer or early fall."

Bill shook his head.

"Jeez," he said. "That's right about when Jessie closed up shop."

"Right about," I said with a nod.

Bill stopped shaking his head and looked me again.

"I ever tell you I think Thompson's a sleazebag?" he said.

I didn't say anything. It was a rhetorical question. Bill and I had never discussed Tommy Thompson before.

"I hate wastin' my Special Blend, but he walks in the door right now, I'll pour that whole pot I brewed up over his head," he said then. "And that's for reasons got to do with me as much as the miserable way the SOB treated Jessie."

I looked at him, letting myself absorb that. There it was, I thought. Sandy's Jessie . . . the one Tommy had been talking to on the phone . . . was our Jessie. Unless I was willing to believe Thompson had been involved with two women with the same name. And I wasn't. Not any more than I thought Sandy was lying about the threats.

"How so, Bill?" I said. "I need to know."

"Where should I start? With the *me* part or the Jessie part?"

"Start wherever you want," I said. I'd been around Bill often enough to figure that once his verbal faucets started running, they wouldn't stop gushing till he'd gotten everything out. "I'm in no hurry."

He tugged at his mustache and sighed.

"With Jessie, it's an easy story," he said. "Thompson's a real sweet-talker. He tells Jessie she's the woman of his dreams. He even promises her a condo at Getaway Groves once it gets built. Says that someday he'll leave his wife and they'll live there happily ever after."

Two condos, for two mistresses, I thought. Or two mistresses that I knew of. It seemed Tommy had a pattern going when it came to his love nests.

"Do you think he was leading her on?" I asked.

"Not about the condo . . . I know because he asked if I could set aside one of my luxury ocean-view units,"

Bill said. "Much as Tommy Thompson loves his money, though, ain't no way he'd ever let some judge give Angela half of it."

"So you don't believe he really planned on filing for divorce."

"He was definitely full of it."

"But he'd convinced Jessie?"

Bill shook his head no. "She might've acted like it, but she's got too much in the smarts department to be fooled deep down inside. Thompson's a politician. And politicians don't get divorces unless they're caught with their pants down." He paused. "A woman's messing around with a married guy, she knows he'll toss any kind of bull at his wife to cover for it. Friend of mine or not, I figured Jessie couldn't gripe too much when the wind blew it back in her direction."

I have to admit, it surprised me to hear that from Bill Drecksel's mouth. He'd never struck me as having a particularly keen sense of right and wrong—for a slew of reasons. There were the cheap, drecky ingredients he passed off as edible to his customers. There was Jessie's admission to me that he'd paid her fifty dollars a week to refer tourists shopping at her store to his restaurant, something I'd thought pretty shifty of them both. And there was the way he and Kyle Fipps had wheedled the town government into approving their Getaway Groves project over the objection of most town residents, who'd fought to have the waterfront acreage where it was being built declared off-limits to developers.

The fact was that I'd always considered Bill a bit of a huckster who wasn't that different from the sort of person he'd accused Thompson of being. But here he'd said something I found very admirable. I supposed it went to show you could never know what to expect.

"What *did* bug you about Thompson's relationship with Jessie," I asked after a second, "if it wasn't his deceitfulness?"

"I already told you. How he treated her. How she was supposed to sit around and wait for him to call her. How it got so she'd have to be ready for him exactly when he wanted. Tommy'd say 'jump' and she'd jump." He snapped his fingers. "Just like that."

"The woman you're talking about isn't the Jessie I know," I said. "She's always been so independent."

Bill shrugged.

"Hey, she fell in love," he said. "You go gaga over somebody, I hear it can make you do funny things. And Tommy, he's the type wants them done his way."

I thought about him pulling out his file back in his office. And about his changing the terms of my contract without explanation.

Just like that.

"Bill," I said, "do you think there was some kind of problem between the two of them before she left?"

"Not that I noticed," he answered. "But from the way Jessie cut out without a word, I ain't sure she'd have let me in on it if there was."

I chewed my bottom lip.

"Does anything else come to mind?" I said.

"As far as Thompson and Jessie, no." Bill hesitated a beat. "But it ain't only wives and girlfriends that can't trust the crumb. There's a whole lot about him that makes me sick, I can tell you from personal experience."

"Go ahead," I said.

"Huh?"

"Tell me," I said.

He hesitated again. Shook his head.

"Nah, forget it," he said with a wave of his hand. "Won't do no good."

I didn't want Bill to stop talking. It seemed to me there might be something in his story. But I had a hunch some simple reverse psychology might be in order.

"Okay," I said.

"Okay?"

"Whatever it is, I guess it can't be too important."

He looked offended.

"Why's that?" he said.

"Because if it was important, you'd want to tell me," I said. "Maybe some other time."

I started getting up.

"Hey, c'mon, don't go running off!" Bill said. He motioned me down with both hands. "Wait a sec, willya?"

I settled slowly back onto the stool. As I said, "simple." When you dealt with Bill, that was usually the operative term.

"Women," he mumbled, shaking his head. "Sheesh."

"Hmmm?"

"Nothing," he said. "Look, Thompson and me, we kinda got mixed up together business-wise."

"Oh?" I said.

Bill nodded.

"With the Getaway Groves project," he said. "It was Fippsie's idea from the start."

Fippsie? I thought. "You mean Kyle Fipps?"

"May he rest in peace." Bill's eyes rolled heavenward. "I heard you're the one who found him dead in that hammock."

I nodded. Of course, it was actually Chloe who'd found Kyle. And he was out of the hammock and on the field turf before either of us knew he was dead. But I didn't want to get caught up in the details. I'd had no inkling Thompson had any involvement in the condo project, and that information had gotten my mind working.

"He look peaceful to you?" Bill said. "Fippsie, that is."

"Very," I said a little distantly.

"Didn't seem like he was in pain or nothing beforehand, huh?"

"Not at all." I tried to focus. "At first, I thought he was asleep."

Bill looked consoled.

"That's good," he said. "I was hopin' it wasn't too bad for him. A guy Fippsie's age . . . you never figure he's gonna kick."

No, I thought, *you don't.* But you also wouldn't figure on him getting poisoned by the pong pong.

"Heard he was pushin' the Groves to the end," Bill waxed on. "Put on a helluva show at the Christmas exhibit."

"It was very realistic," I said for lack of anything better to add.

Bill nodded.

"The condos were my brainstorm, y'know," Bill said. "It came on like a bolt one night when me an' Fippsie were plopped down drunk in some Gloucester bar like a couple'a boozehounds." He scratched his head. "Whatever the hell a boozehound is."

I didn't say anything. I already had enough to spin my wheels about.

"Anyway, Fippsie jumped right on board with me," Bill resumed after a second. "Been like that since we were kids. I had all the moves, he had all the money. He went in as my silent backer. Talked his dad, Oren—he owns the real estate company where Kyle worked—into helping us get the plots of land we needed. And find the right builders. The units, they're gonna be fabulous. I mean fabulous! Fippsie, he looked forward to seein' 'em go up as much as I did."

"And Tommy?" I said. "When did he join your partnership?"

Bill let out a derisive guffaw.

"Tommy wasn't no partner," he said. "More like our piggybank. Or maybe a safety deposit box."

"How's that?"

"You know Fippsie an' his wife was goin' through a bad divorce, right?"

I nodded. They'd been legally separated for a while. And even before Kyle moved out of their home, everybody had guessed his marriage was on the rocks. It probably started when he'd gotten into flexing his gluteus maximus muscles around the gym as a sign of his emancipation from married life. The gossip had spread from there.

"If there's ever been a woman who could drive a man out of his house it's Lina—Lina the Leech, I call her," Bill went on. "She ain't nothin' like Thompson's wife, Angie, who I feel sorry for, bein' she's a real nice lady and didn't deserve to be humiliated by that picture in the paper of him with those two strippers . . . especially that big blond Viking. I mean, you get a load of her?"

I looked at him.

"I saw the picture," I said.

"She's gotta be the most gorgeous babe I ever saw in my *life*!" Bill said. "If I was a gal, and she came anywhere within ten feet of my guy, I'd know I was in trouble."

I kept looking at him.

"I think maybe it would depend on the guy," I said.

He flipped a hand in dismissal. "Aw, c'mon, Sky, you take it from me. Ain't a woman in the world can compete with that hottie. No way, nohow."

I cleared my throat.

"Bill, seriously, I'm getting a headache trying to keep these broken marriages straight," I said. "You were just about to tell me how Tommy Thompson became involved with Getaway Groves . . ."

He nodded.

"Uh-huh," he said. "And it started with Kyle worryin' that Lina would throw a wrench into things."

"In what way?"

"He'd set up a bank account to pay the builders. With her divorce lawyers filin' petitions left and right, he figured she'd try to get her hands on it. And that even if she couldn't, some judge might freeze the account for years till they finally worked out a settlement." Bill shrugged. "Fippsie and Thompson was pretty good friends. Had their offices a couple doors apart on Main Street. So Fippsie went to him and asked if there was a way to keep Lina's shysters away from that money. And Tommy told him the easiest thing was to sock it away in third-party escrow. Being Tommy has a law degree himself, he offered to do it as a favor."

"Under his name?"

"The Thompson Corporation's name," Bill said, nodding. "Same difference."

I considered that. "And did some trouble develop between them?"

Bill was tugging his mustache again.

"Thompson's a rotten lying rat," he said.

Which left no doubt about his feelings toward Tommy but wasn't an answer to my question.

"So I take it Kyle and Tommy's arrangement had its rough spots," I said, thinking I'd feel him out a little more gently.

Bill looked at me. I didn't have to be an FBI interrogator to see he'd become edgy all of a sudden—his mustache tugging had gotten so fast and furious he was yanking out one hair after another. As they sprinkled from his thumb and forefinger, I was thinking that a food dish in front of me would've made for a pretty repulsive landing pad, and was gladder than ever I hadn't ordered anything to eat.

"I guess that's a decent way to put it," he said. "I ain't exactly sure what happened between them."

I found that hard to believe. "Kyle didn't tell you?"

Bill kept plucking away at his whiskers.

"Sure he did," he said. "But money was his end of things. Bein' the big-picture man, I didn't keep close tabs on that end of it."

I wasn't totally buying that either.

"What about now?" I shrugged. "I mean, with Kyle gone, wouldn't you need to get more hands-on?"

Bill eyed me cagily. "I thought you was interested in Thompson and Jessie. How's any of this connected to her?"

"I don't know it is," I said. "But I've learned that sometimes things can come together in ways we don't expect."

Bill scrutinized me some more. Pluck, pluck, pluck.

"Listen," he said after a moment. "Maybe you oughta be talking to Ed Gallagher. He runs the construction outfit we hired to build the units. They're down in Beverly."

"Is there a company name I can look up?"

Bill nodded. "An easy one to remember. Gallagher Brothers, it's called. Eddie being the oldest of three."

"And you think he'll talk to me."

"That's up to him. Got the same treatment Fippsie

did, so you might not have to twist his arm." Bill shrugged. "Me, I have ta start getting ready for the lunch crowd."

I looked at him. Since the soonest his next lunch crowd would be walking through the door was Memorial Day weekend, I figured that one was really reaching. But I also felt I'd gotten all I could out of him—more than I could sort out, in fact. And besides, I didn't want to be responsible for his mustache getting any thinner.

"Okay, Bill," I said. "Thanks a bundle. You've been a help."

He nodded again.

"You get in touch with Jess, send her my regards," he said.

"I promise I will," I said.

As I rose from my stool, I noticed Bill had stayed put behind the counter . . . and that he'd stopped de-whiskering himself.

"While you're at it," he said slowly, "tell her I miss her somethin' awful."

I hesitated.

"I promise I'll do that, too," I said, and gave him a smile before finally turning toward the door.

Chapter 13

"You know, Sky, when you think about it, the universe is out of this world," Betty-Mom said from the passenger seat of my Caliber.

I glanced over at her, my gloved hands on the steering wheel. It was around nine o'clock in the morning a day after my interview at City Hall, and we were driving from the Fog Bell toward the Fontaine Culture Club on Myrtle Lane.

"That a fact?" I said crankily. Besides being so cold my teeth were chattering, I'd woken up in the pitch-darkness at around four a.m. when Sandy Savoy, who'd been out all night without explanation, came home and got Skiball started in on a yelling fit.

Betty-Mom nodded. "Sometimes we need to toss aside our cares," she said. "Take a broader view of the things around us."

"Uh-huh." I nodded my head toward the heater, which she'd turned off about two minutes after we'd started to roll. "Would you mind putting that back on?"

Betty-Mom didn't move.

"The dry heat's bad for your nasal passages," she said. "It makes them into breeding colonies for bacteria, and that's how you get sinusitis."

I looked over at her again.

"I'm freezing," I said. "That's how you get pneumonia."

Betty-Mom sat there without budging.

"This is December," she said. "December comes around in the winter. And winter's a cold time of year."

"Thanks for helping me figure that out," I said.

"Don't get wise. I'm still your mother."

"I'm just trying to understand your position," I said. "Are we all supposed to ditch our modern heating systems and air conditioners?"

Mom puckered her brow.

"There's nothing wrong with being a little cold in the winter. The same as you'd expect to be a little *warm* in June," she said. "If people dressed according to the weather, they'd be fine."

I caught the implied criticism on its way by me. Besides my leather gloves and black felt roll-up hat, I was wearing a warm black balmacaan over a ribbed wine-colored turtleneck sweater, dark blue Paige jeans with embroidered back pockets, and black ankle boots. Contrary-wise, and true to her earthy form, Betty-Mom had on a fleece jacket, faux-fur mittens, and hiking boots, making her look like a mountaineer or a trapper, I wasn't sure which. But in her mind, warm equaled clunky.

"Mom, seriously, the windshield's fogging up," I said. It wasn't an exaggeration; my breath was really clouding it. "At least put on the defroster."

Betty-Mom reached for the dash controls.

"Why didn't you tell me you couldn't see? Not being able to see when you're on the road is dangerous."

"I kind of didn't think I'd have to explain not wanting to be frozen stiff."

She sighed, gave me a look of disapproval.

"When a lump of salt dissolves in the ocean, it gives up its saltness and becomes the ocean," she said. "*That's* all I'm trying to explain to you."

I felt an inner wince.

"This is the worst," I said. "My absolute worst fear's come true."

"What are you talking about?"

"Did Chloe show you that lame-o book of hers?"

"What book?"

"The one she took home from the dump after the whole town seems to have browsed through it. Except me, thankfully. Since it's rotting everybody's minds with those sentence sermons."

"Sky, I don't know what you're talking about."

"Come on, Mom. Spill the beans."

"There are no beans," Betty-Mom said. "And Chloe hasn't shown me any books."

"Then where'd you get that mumbo jumbo about the salt and the ocean?"

Betty-Mom took off her mitten, reached a hand into her coat pocket, and pulled out a small paperback with a plain brown cover and some gold print across the front.

"It came from in here, and I resent your attitude," she said, waving it at me. "This is my book. I've owned it for ages. The title's *Mukteshwari: Aphorisms,* by Swami Muktananda. A nice young Hare Krishna man gave it to Lou and me after we'd left a consciousness-raising clinic up the block from the Exploratorium in San Francisco. I believe he was right outside on the steps."

I took a deep breath. *Calm*, I told myself. *Be calm.*

"I'm grateful for the clarification," I said. "That's a whole different story."

"You're very welcome," Betty-Mom huffed, putting the book back in her pocket. "Though I could still do without your sarcastic attitude."

"Sky Taylor? Sarcastic?" I took a hand off the wheel and pointed to myself. "Not me, Mom. You've got the wrong person. I was named after the blue sky above the field where my parents were fooling around when they conceived me in a hippie commune. I've got too much flower power charging my genes to cop an attitude."

Betty-Mom swiveled her head around to face me.

"Sky, you're ranting."

"I am not."

"Yes, you are," Betty-Mom insisted. "I don't understand what's made you so upset."

I shook my head. *Calm, calm. You can do it—*

"I'm not ranting or upset," I ranted, upset. "I mean, I'm just glad I found out you weren't quoting some mail-order minister, or Maha Deependra the laughing man, but the Swami Muktananda. So in the future I know which cosmic quack's to blame—maybe the near future, right before I have a mental and emotional breakdown!''

Betty-Mom kept looking at me. I acted oblivious and turned onto Pennington Way, which would eventually hook up with Myrtle Lane. Both were countrified two-lane roads bordered on either side by tall snow-frocked pines.

"Sky," Betty-Mom said after a while, "what's the matter?"

"I told you—"

"Never mind all that," she said. "I'm your mother. I love you. If something's wrong, I should know."

I drove between the pine trees. The shadows of their overhanging branches made it hard to see too far past the front of my hood, and provided a convenient reason to keep ignoring Betty-Mom's steady attention.

"Sky—"

"Shh," I said. "Can't talk. I'm watching the road."

"You can talk and watch at the same time."

"No, I can't. Safety first, that's my rule . . ."

Betty-Mom chopped her hand in the air. "Tell me what's bothering you. Let's have it."

Let's have it? You knew Betty-Mom was serious when she started sounding like Joe Friday.

I felt myself about to cave, and shrugged.

"A lot's been going on around town," I said finally. "A few months back my friend Jessie Barton leaves the Cove, no explanation offered. Then I stumble on Kyle Fipps's body after a Christmas gala. Then my boyfriend, Mike, brings a gorgeous Amazon stripper home from Boston, and before I know it she's rooming with me, coming and going at all hours when she isn't walking around my place stark naked. Meanwhile, Mike can't stop talking about her in the little time we're alone together. Also meanwhile, I find out that not only was she having an affair with Tommy Thompson, the married head of our city council, but Jessie was, too. And that he made threats of some sort to *both* of them, and that maybe his threats are the reason Jessie took off." I sighed. "Next, Tommy winds up being the man who hires me for a job I've been after for months. And finally, bringing things full circle, I'm told that Tommy and the dead guy at the Christmas bash were hooked up in a business deal because the dead guy was getting divorced and wanted to keep his soon-to-be-ex-wife from laying her hands on his money, and Tommy's a legal accountant who knew how to arrange that for him. But the deal went sour. Just like the dead guy's marriage. And this all happened before the dead guy died."

I drove on. Betty-Mom was still looking at me from the passenger seat.

"The dead man . . . Kyle, that's his name, right?"

I nodded.

"Didn't he die from natural causes?" Betty-Mom asked.

I was quiet. The coroner's report hadn't been made public. Until that happened, I had to keep my promise to Chief Vega.

Betty-Mom adjusted the round wire rims on her nose.

"Kyle didn't die from natural causes," she said.

I stayed quiet, trembled a little.

Betty-Mom watched me through those John Lennon glasses. After a long moment she leaned forward, switched the blower from the DEFROST to its HEATER setting, and then turned it up to high, adjusting the vents to blow in my direction.

"There," she said. "Feel any warmer now?"

"Much," I said.

"Because I wouldn't want to see you freeze stiff."

I gave her a look. "Thanks, Mom. That's very supportive of you."

She smiled and patted me on the arm.

"Sky," she said, "would our visit to the dance studio this morning happen to have any connection to what you've told me?"

I nodded. I couldn't talk about Kyle's poisoning. Or *suspected* poisoning. But there were some things floating around in my mind that hadn't come from Chief Vega. And I could talk about them.

"Finch and her husband bought a waterfront townhouse at Getaway Groves," I said. "She mentioned it to me at the Art Association, and then made some comment or other about being friends with the Fippses."

"And?"

"I want to see what else she might have to say about them," I said. "It's no more complicated than that."

I swung carefully into a turn and followed the road as it curved along under the pines for another quarter mile. Then I saw a woodburned sign for the Culture Club ahead on my right. I knew the gravel drive leading up to the studio would be just past the sign.

Meanwhile, Betty-Mom had settled back into her seat.

"When you were a little girl, you always loved puzzles," she said. "Remember that M. C. Escher jigsaw Lou and I gave you for your birthday?"

I remembered, picturing it in my head. Called *House of Stairs*, the puzzle had played tricks with perspective in typical Escher fashion. Adapted from one of his black-and-white engravings, it showed a parade of six-legged reptile thingies on a staircase that led up and down into forever at impossible angles.

"I must've been ten years old," I said.

"Eight," Betty-Mom said. "And the jigsaw was really meant for adults. It had two thousand pieces."

"That many, huh?"

Betty-Mom nodded.

"You'd do your homework and head right over to that puzzle table in your room," she said. "We couldn't tear you away from it for weeks. Not till you finished putting it together. And then afterward, it always stayed your favorite. I can still hear you explain why to us."

That part I hadn't recalled. "I told you?"

Another Betty-Mom nod. "You said the picture was like a puzzle all on its own, and gave you something new to try and figure out whenever you looked at it. For you that was even more fun than putting the pieces together."

I shot Betty-Mom a quick glance

"You know what that means?" I said.

She shook her head.

"Weird parents, weird kid," I said.

We smiled at one another, and then I was tapping my brakes to slow the Caliber. We'd almost come up on the wooden sign.

"So," Betty-Mom said, "what's our plan?"

I shrugged. Strictly speaking, I wasn't sure I had a plan. It was more like wanting to poke the bushes around Finch and see what, ah, fluttered up. When I had last cleaned her studios a week or so ago, she'd been in a panic about the big jade plant in her foyer being infested with aphids. While she had desperately wanted to avoid losing the plant, she was convinced that spraying it with chemical pesticide would throw the club's feng shui totally out of whack. I hadn't had any alternative suggestions for her—not right then. But over breakfast that morning at the Fog Bell, I'd listened to Chloe and Betty-Mom talk about their own houseplants, recalled Finch's aphid problem, and asked Betty-Mom if she might have any home preparations for getting rid of the disgusting little buggers. Not the least bit to my surprise, it turned out that she did know of one. She was as into natural remedies as I was into cleaning. Which was to say, she was a bona fide fanatic.

"I'd just love to get Finch loose and talking," I said after a minute. "I've got a feeling she can throw some light on Lina's relationship with Kyle. How much, I don't know. But I'm curious to find out." I shot Betty-Mom a glance. "Stick to discussing your aphid concoction with her. I'll handle the rest."

Betty-Mom was nodding. I drove on for a few yards past the sign and then turned from the road into Finch's unpaved drive.

"Ready?" I said, bumping uphill.

Betty-Mom grabbed the paper bag between our seats.

"Yes, Detective Taylor," she said with a conspiratorial wink.

See what I mean about her sounding like the guy from *Dragnet*?

Its entry recessed under an overhanging gabled roof, the Fontaine Culture Club was a one-story brick-fronted building with arched windows and all kinds of bright, open space inside. Visible from the foyer between stately columns, and crowned with a high, vaulted ceiling, the huge master studio opened onto an elegant garden of flowers and shrubs that rambled off behind huge French doors at the rear. The entire right wall of the studio was mirrored, a ballet bar running the length of the room in front of it.

Betty-Mom and I arrived right when Finch had been expecting us, and she answered the bell seconds after we stepped onto the porch.

"Bonjour, amis!" she said through the door. Then she motioned us into the foyer and hugged me, air-kissing both cheeks. "Sky, *mon petit!*"

"Hi, Finch." I tilted my head toward Betty-Mom and started to introduce her. "This is my—"

"Shush! Shush!" Finch clapped her hands to cut me short, gave Betty-Mom a flitting smile. *"C'est la mére!"*

"Pardon me?"

I cleared my throat. Betty-Mom seemed befuddled, and I was afraid her befuddlement might trigger a bout of laughing yoga. It was something I preferred she didn't act out in front of spectators.

"Um, yes, Finch. As I was saying, this is my mother, Betty," I broke in. "Betty, Finch."

Betty-Mom turned to me.

"Sky, why didn't you say Finch was French?"

"Because I'm quite American," Finch interjected before I could answer. Her ginger-colored hair gathered and clipped into a calculatedly improvised updo, she was wearing a black turtleneck leotard, a black lace midriff top, striped gray and fuchsia leg warmers, and pink ballet slippers.

Betty-Mom looked at her through her circle rims.

"If you're American," she said, "why are you speaking French?"

Another smile darted across Finch's lips. "Morning evokes our most subtle thoughts and feelings, wouldn't you agree?"

"I think mornings are wonderful," Betty-Mom said.

She was holding her paper bag against her side. "But I still don't see what that has to do with you talking to us in French."

"*Cheri*, it has everything to do with it," Finch said. "If a morning moment is subtlety, then *française* must be its very expression." She turned her feet outward, put her hands on her narrow hips, and did a quick plié.

Betty-Mom watched her with a blank stare. I supposed she was trying to figure out how Finch's dance move related to her remarks. Maybe she would've known not to bother if I'd given her advance notice of Finch's unbearable pretentiousness, but I hadn't, no more than I'd tipped Finch to Betty-Mom's incomparable nuttiness. Once you stepped into that quicksand, there was no getting free of it. The important thing was just to prevent them from distracting each other.

"How about giving my mother a peek at your jade plant, Finch?" I said. "You'll want to get around to it before your students show up for rehearsal."

Finch nodded, turned lightly on her feet, and took a gliding step toward the studio.

"Come, Betty." She motioned for her to follow. "Before the infestation worsens."

The patient was in a large terra-cotta wall planter near the division between the foyer and the main practice studio. As we stopped in front of it, I could hear classical music playing softly from speakers mounted somewhere out of sight. Finch's adult class was putting on a Christmas weekend recital of Tchaikovsky's *Nutcracker*, and I recognized it as something from the ballet.

She paused to listen, closed her eyes, and took a long, deep breath, expanding her chest as she slowly lifted her arms over her head. This, I knew, was meant to demonstrate that she was filling herself with melody—as opposed to showing us that she was just plain full of herself, which was kind of what I got out of it.

"The Sugar Plum Fairy and a celebration of dances!" Finch said, exhaling. "The Waltz of Flowers! The Mirliton! Le Pas de Deux! I do so live for this time of year!"

"Finch," I said, thinking a nudge toward reality was in order. "The jade plant, remember?"

"Shush, shush, shush—let me draw on inspiration!" she said. *"Fouetté!"*

She spun on one leg, whipping her other leg out around her body.

Betty-Mom looked at me.

"Not bad," she said.

"No, not at all," I said. "She's actually pretty graceful."

Finch turned back toward the planter, having finished her move with the toes of her left foot touching her right knee.

"These aphids are vile," she said, lowering her pink-slippered foot. "A plant has nowhere to run and hide, Betty. We must be their champions. *Comprendez vous?*"

Betty-Mom nodded.

"I think so," she said. "They can't cure themselves without our help."

They stood facing each other, both of them nodding. Then Finch bent over the jade plant.

"I want the horrid things gone . . . Is it possible without a feng shui disruption?"

Betty-Mom joined her in examining the plant's fleshy oval leaves. Then she opened her paper bag and took out a cleaner-type plastic spray bottle she'd borrowed from me. It was filled to the halfway line with a pale amber liquid.

"I brought my remedy," she said. "A good spritzing should take care of the problem."

Finch eyed the bottle with skepticism. "You're sure it contains nothing *toxique*?"

Betty-Mom paused a second.

"Finch, there's no elegant way to say 'toxic,' " she said. "Also, you don't need to insult me—I prepared the remedy especially for you and came all the way here with it."

Finch looked at her. Having grown up in Betty-Mom's house, I'd seen her assertive side often enough. But most people weren't prepared for it—her spacey ways lulled them into complacency.

I waited, holding my breath. Between Finch's flamboyant preening and Betty-Mom's hippie-earth-mother routine, I was thinking it might add up to a clash of two mighty and opposite-but-equal forces.

Goes to show what I knew.

"My apologies," Finch said after a moment. She sounded genuinely chastened. "I am a rude and unappreciative creature."

Betty-Mom gave her one of her reassuring arm pats.

"Oh, come on, don't make a big deal out of it," she said. "Just trust me and pay attention."

And that was that. Conflict resolved.

As Finch and Betty-Mom turned back to the jade plant together, it suddenly hit me that I'd been watching the two of them bond. In some ways, this was an even more fearsome notion than having them stay at odds.

"The solution's mostly weak tea," Betty-Mom said now. She was once again holding the spray bottle on exhibit. "I prepare a couple of cups, then add two drops of ammonia, a drop of Listerine, and one drop of dishwashing liquid." She smiled at Finch. "You want I should show you how it's used?"

"Please do," Finch said.

Betty-Mom put her hand on the trigger and sprayed.

"The thing is to make sure the whole plant gets coated," she said. "That means the top and bottom sides of the leaves, the stems, and the main trunk all the way down to the soil." She paused. "You have to be careful to keep the plant out of bright sunlight until it's dry, since there's a chance it might burn. And I don't recommend using this on outdoor plants or garden vegetables—it can kill some of the natural predators that keep aphids in check."

Finch was paying careful attention.

"Betty, you have impressed me," she said.

"Why . . . thank you!" Betty-Mom said, and slapped her on the shoulder. "And *merci beaucoup* too!"

They both giggled. It was a happy scene, granted. They seemed to be having fun together. But I'd been hoping to get some information, and was anxious to steer Finch along a track that might provide a morsel or two.

"Finch, I'm glad my mother could help, but we really ought to be hustling over to the Art Association," I said.

Betty-Mom looked at me.

"We should?" she said.

"I know I mentioned it before," I said, and gave her a look. "Remember?"

She hesitated, slow on the uptake. A good liar she'd never be. "I honestly don't."

"*Think*, Mom." I stared at her. "What were we talking about on the way over here?"

Betty-Mom crinkled her brow, finally hopping aboard my Bee Ess Express. "Oh, right, I understand."

"What is it you're doing over at the association?" Finch asked.

"The DeFelices asked me to pack away the dishes they used at the holiday party," I said. "They serve their food on Villeroy and Boch dinnerware, and have been putting sheets of newspaper between the plates when they box them up. To keep them from rattling around and breaking, you know. But when we were getting ready for the affair, I noticed that the newsprint kind of smudged the china and suggested they use inexpensive washcloths instead. So they bought some, and had them delivered there, and now I need to start putting the dishes into cartons. I've kind of stalled until today—it's taken me a while to get over what happened to Kyle Fipps."

Finch looked at me. I hadn't made up the part about the newsprint rubbing off on the dishes, or the part about my noticing it, or Jim and Debra ordering the washcloths. Where I'd fudged was claiming I was ready to pack anything away for them. That would have to wait until Chief Vega gave us the go-ahead, and he hadn't done so yet. In fact, I hadn't heard from him since he'd called me down to the station, and I was under the assumption that he was holding the dishes for possible forensic testing . . . even though I'd washed them before we spoke.

But that was all irrelevant. The whole purpose of my bringing up the Art Association, and the dishes, had been to change the topic of conversation. I'd wanted an excuse to get Finch talking about Kyle.

Now she spun around, leaped about three feet off the floor, and went flying sideways into the studio, her arms outflung, her legs bent so far upward that her toes pointed straight at the ceiling.

"Pas de Chat!" she shouted out to us, alighting near the ballet bar. "Thank you for coming to my plant's rescue, *mes amis.* I won't keep you any longer."

That wasn't the response I'd wanted. Finch was obviously going to need some additional coaxing.

I followed her into the studio

"You were close to Kyle and Lina, weren't you?" I asked.

Finch ignored the question and began to flex, holding on to the oak bar with one hand for balance.

"Shush," she said. "I need to concentrate on my exercises."

I didn't believe her. It was pretty clear she'd already done them from the way she'd been whirling through the air.

"It must've been rough for you to hear about Kyle," I said.

"Why do you ask?"

I shrugged.

"Chloe and I didn't know him very well, and finding him was hard enough on us," I said. "I guess I've been imagining how his friends have dealt with it. And his wife, of course."

Finch paused in midstretch, her right arm straight above her head. If I sounded convincing, it was because I'd told her the truth. I had been trying to imagine it. I just hadn't explained my reasons.

"It was crushing," she said after a moment. "For me, that is. You would have to ask Lina how she feels."

I looked at her. "I knew they were separated," I said. "I've been hearing some stuff about him and Lina that doesn't make it sound like they split on good terms. But I wasn't sure how much to believe."

Finch slowly brought her right arm down, reversed her position, and raised her left arm.

"Kyle was a dear, thoughtful man of refinement. And a consummate talent. Oh, how he could act! Oh, how he sang to make the heart weep! And oh, how he danced, his movements so sublime I would feel them in my own limbs," Finch said. She'd gotten emotional. "Were you aware I was his dance instructor for years before I became his real estate client? Or socialized with the Fippses as a couple?"

I shook my head.

"He never mentioned it," I said. "I knew he wanted to act professionally, though. He told me he'd auditioned for a Broadway show."

"Many more than one," Finch said. "You've heard of *Starlight and Kisses*? And *The Woodland Princess*?"

"Sure," I said. "They were both big smashes."

"Among the longest-running ever on the Great White Way," Finch said. "Lina's brother Renault was their chief choreographer . . . and in the case of *Princess*, the co-producer. For those of us versed in the fine art of dance, Renault Metcalf is a legend. He studied under Maurice Hines, Alvin Ailey, Luigi . . . all modern greats. And he had badly wanted Kyle in his productions."

"That's kind of mind-boggling," I said. "If Renault was so high on him, what got in the way of things?"

Finch's eyes beaded in on me.

"Again, you may want to ask his wife," she said, sounding resentful.

I wondered if I was reading her tone correctly. "Are you telling me Lina didn't want him in her brother's show?"

Finch's face closed up around her emotions like a Venus flytrap leaf.

"I don't know," she said. "Now, *petit*, you have dishes

to pack at the Art Association. And I must complete my workout."

I considered pressing Finch some more. But then I decided against it. I'd been excused.

"Thank you for your plant remedy. *C'est magnifique!*" she called to Betty-Mom, peering at her around a ceiling column. "I hope you'll forgive me for not seeing you to the door."

Betty smiled. "I understand, it's chilly over there," she said. "I wouldn't want your muscles to cramp on our account."

"Exactement, Betty! *Joyeux Noel!"*

"An uplifting spiritual journey to one and all this holiday season!" Betty-Mom replied, and gave her a sweeping wave good-bye.

Clenching my teeth, I snagged hold of Betty-Mom's coat sleeve, hauled her outside to the Caliber, and a couple of minutes later was steering us downhill toward the road.

"Finch seems to be a nice person," Betty-Mom said. "A little high-strung, maybe. And I wish she'd stop making with the French."

I shrugged.

"I would've had an easier time putting up with her airs if she'd told me more about Kyle," I said. "She didn't exactly spill her guts."

Betty-Mom glanced over at me. "Solving a puzzle takes patience," she said. "I don't need to remind you, of all people."

I supposed she didn't.

"I want to pay a visit to somebody else," I said. "Feel like coming along?"

"I wish I could," Betty-Mom said. She checked her wristwatch. "But I need you to drop me off at the Fog Bell for that laughing yoga session."

I almost jerked from my seat. My jaw had barely unclamped, and now this. "What laughing yoga session?"

Betty-Mom looked at me as if I'd teleported down from outer space.

"We're holding it in about an hour. Didn't you hear us chatting over breakfast?"

"Obviously not," I said. "Who's 'us'?"

"Chloe, Sandy, and me," Betty-Mom said. She made a thoughtful face. "Now that I think about it, we discussed it right before you came downstairs . . . You took a while to get ready this morning."

I didn't bother to explain that it was because Sandy had beaten me to the shower, and I'd had to twiddle my thumbs waiting for her to come out.

"Let me get this straight," I said. "You're telling me Chloe's gotten into Maha Deependra."

"I wouldn't put it that way," Betty-Mom said. "It's more like she's curious."

"And Sandy Savoy?"

"The same. It must be taxing to dance naked in front of strange, lonely men, and I suggested the Maha's system might reduce her stress," Betty-Mom said. "You're welcome to join our meditation group if you change your mind about that visit."

Unbelievable, I thought, reaching the bottom of the drive. Three days she'd been in town, and already my mother was recruiting devotees for her latest whacked-out guru. My best friend among them.

I turned onto Myrtle Lane in the direction of town.

"That's okay," I said. "Think I'll pass."

"Are you sure? It might do you some good."

"Maybe another time."

She gave me a small shrug, looking vaguely injured, and then began to inspect her hair for split ends. It was a habit she'd always had when trying to seem indifferent.

"Sure, I won't insist. You're a grown woman," she said. "So, where are you hustling off to?"

"Grace's Greenhouses," I said.

She looked at me. "What's there besides plants and flowers?"

"Not what. Who," I said. "Grace Blossom owns the place. And before you ask, I have no idea which came first . . . the name or her horticultural license."

Betty-Mom plucked off a strand of flyaway gray frizz. "Is Grace another friend of the Fippses?"

I remembered what Chloe had told me on our way home the night of Kyle's death.

"Of Lina's, at least," I said, nodding. "They kind of grew up together."

Betty-Mom was quiet as I reached the intersection with Pennington.

"I can understand why you're interested in all of this, Sky," she said after a while. "But shouldn't what you're doing be left to the police?"

I had to admit that was a fair question.

"Grace is one of my clients, and I promised I'd take care of some cleaning for her when I had a chance," I said. "So it isn't as though I don't have a legit reason for stopping by."

"A reason or an excuse?"

"A little of both," I said honestly. "You mentioned yourself how I couldn't stay away from my puzzle table once I started putting the pieces together." I shrugged. "Guess I still can't."

Betty-Mom looked at me for another long minute. She seemed to want to say something more, but then just nodded and sat quietly for the rest of the drive.

After delivering her to the inn for her Maha meet, I drove on toward Grace's. It was on a large piece of land at the South End, not too far from Rollie Evers's storeroom units, where Abe Monahan had once kept his secondhand books boxed away. The flower and garden center was in front facing the parking lot, with several greenhouses and wide outdoor show areas in the back. In the spring and summer they would teem with growing things, and there was even a big pond full of lilies, lotus, and other plants for water gardening. This time of year the pond was frozen over, and the rest of the area—or as much of it as Grace could manage to keep clear of snow—became a Christmas tree forest that drew customers from all over Cape Ann.

I found Grace behind two long folding cafeteria tables

set up in an L shape at the end of the store's main aisle. The tables were crowded with huge wintry arrangements of bare branches that she'd covered top to bottom with spray frost and decorated with pinecones, ornamental robins, and sprigs of berried holly and yew.

As I made my way toward her, she was stringing clear little twinkle lights through the six-foot-tall branches, pieces of which had been trimmed off and scattered all over the floor. I did my light-footed best to step around them, carrying a paper leaf bag I'd brought in from the Caliber.

"Sky, how are you?"

"Hiya, Grace. I'm okay," I said. "Things look busy around here."

"Crazy busy." She angled her head so we could see each other through the white thicket of branches between us. "I've got half a dozen orders to finish today and no help. My regular assistant called in sick, and it's my part-time girl's day off, and she can't get hold of a babysitter."

"Doesn't sound good," I said.

She shrugged. A slender woman with short brown hair, she was wearing a florist's apron over an olive green zip sweater and Levi's.

"It's never good to be short-staffed this close to the holidays," she said.

I gave her a look of commiseration.

"Listen, Grace, I'm useless at doing arrangements," I said, "but you might find it easier to work if I pick up some of these branches lying all over the place." I showed her the leaf bag. "I have about an hour to spare right now."

"And came equipped."

"Always."

Grace smiled. "Great," she said. "It's still a little early for most of my customers to drop by, so they won't get in your way."

I nodded, took off my cap, and stuffed it into a pocket of my balmacaan. Then I hung the coat in Grace's supply room and was ready to go.

My job was simple. I needed to collect the branches and toss them in the leaf bag I'd bought at the hardware store, a fifty-pound capacity, heavy-duty type that stood on its own and was much handier to use than those flimsy lightweight bags that were constantly tipping over on their sides. I started near the end of the L that was farthest from Grace, trying to stay out from underfoot while I figured out how to deftly broach the subject of the Fippses to her.

As it turned out, she was in a talkative mood and provided the lead-in herself.

"So, Sky," she said. "Have any special plans for the holiday?"

It was a surprise to realize I didn't. The week before, I might have taken it for granted that Mike would be my date at Chloe and Oscar's annual Christmas party—and that we'd celebrate New Year's together. But he hadn't mentioned anything about either one.

"Nothing firm," I said. "My mother's in town for a few days, but it's just a stopover—she'll be heading off to meet my dad in California." I knelt to clear a jumble of branches from under the table. "Guess I'll know before too long whether cooling out at home's in the cards." I picked up a branch, reached around to my leaf bag, and chucked it in. "You?"

Grace moved an arrangement to one side of the table. It couldn't have been easy. The branches were taller than she was, and the clay pot they were in was filled with sand to keep them steady and upright.

"New Year's Eve is a lock . . . I'll probably head out to the bell-ringing at City Hall," she said. "Local yokel that I am, I've been doing it since I was a kid. Though the ceremony must be way too small-towny for you, huh?"

I shrugged.

"It's a nice tradition," I said. "Guess I'd appreciate it more if somebody besides Tommy Thompson was doing the honors."

Grace paused. "What's wrong with him?"

The look on her face made me remember Thompson had plenty of friends and supporters in the Cove.

"Nothing really," I said. "Just not my type."

Grace kept looking down at me. "I don't believe all those rumors about him and that dancer from Boston. He denies them, you know."

"I'm not sure how much that means," I said with a shrug. "Tommy's married, a politician . . . It would hurt him if the stories turned out to be true."

Grace was shaking her head.

"You're too suspicious, Sky," she said. "Maybe the attitude's a holdover from your time in New York, but you should take my advice and let it go. If you want to be content here, that is."

I wasn't sure how to answer that, and decided it was probably best not to say anything. Grace's defensiveness was a slightly uncomfortable reminder that I was still a relative newcomer in town. It made me want to change the subject. Or at least get back to our original one.

I picked up some more clippings.

"Any plans for Christmas?" I said after a minute.

Grace sort of laughed to herself.

"Hoping to find a wonderful surprise under my tree," she said. "I'm inviting Lina Fipps over on Christmas Day. I figure we'll have a quiet dinner, relax . . . She could use a boost."

I know. It was barely ten seconds since I'd gotten my foot out of my mouth. But how could I resist that opening?

"It's hard when you lose somebody who's been a big part of your life," I said. "Suppose that's true even when you've wound up on bad terms with the person. Like Lina did with Kyle, that is"

Grace was quiet. The tabletop blocked her from sight, but I could hear her working on an arrangement.

"Lina loved Kyle," she said after a bit. "I can understand why most people in town wouldn't believe it. Having been friends with her since she was little Lina Metcalf next door, I've experienced her worst. Don't think for a second I haven't." Grace rattled some branches. "Lina's very competitive. She's always wanted everything for herself, especially attention. Growing up,

I had to learn how to stand up to her—to *not* let her take what belonged to me. But sometimes she gets a bad rap."

"How so?"

"Kyle was so much Lina's opposite, everyone made her out to be the villain," Grace said. "I won't declare she was the perfect wife, Sky. But that old cliché about there being two sides to every story might be worth bearing in mind."

"It sounds as if you feel Kyle deserved a share of the blame for their marriage coming apart."

Again I heard branches shaking around.

"I liked Kyle," Grace said. "Same as everyone else, I saw the part of him that was outgoing and friendly. But Lina lived under the same roof as him. Only she knew the Kyle Fipps that existed behind closed doors. And she'd felt neglected for years. I think toward the end, rightly or wrongly, she came to believe he'd married her for her family connections."

"You mean her brother the Broadway choreographer."

"Renault," Grace said. "You've heard about him?"

"Just recently," I said. As in, oh, about an hour before. "He was supposed to be very impressed with Kyle's talent."

"According to some people," Grace said.

"There's another side to that story too?"

A beat of silence.

"Kyle's funeral is tomorrow. It seems awful and gossipy to say anything negative on that score. And I'd hate to spill anything I was told in confidence," she said. I heard her poking around for something on the table. "I need to go and get another box of lights, Sky. Be right back."

Listening to her walk off toward the stockroom, I took the opportunity to see how much of a mess I had left to tackle. By my eyeball estimate, I wasn't quite two-thirds done. I'd bagged up the branch segments that had been scattered on the floor around me, but another pile was waiting a few feet away, under the table.

Still ducked down between the table legs, I shuffled over to them and found myself walled in on either side by about a dozen humongous arrangements. They looked pretty much finished, and I assumed Grace had hefted them onto the floor to clear room in her workspace.

I knelt there gathering branches together. The remark Grace had made about Kyle's theatrical abilities had been a major teaser, and, her reluctance notwithstanding, I was hoping she'd share something more with me when she got back.

A couple of minutes passed. I wondered if I should have offered her a hand with the extra lights. In fact, I felt cruddy because I hadn't. I'd assumed the boxes didn't weigh a whole lot, but with all the lugging Grace had to do with those monster arrangements, I was sure she would have appreciated it.

Well, I thought, *maybe it isn't too late.*

Then again, maybe it was. I'd just started to crawl out from under the table when I heard her approaching.

"Hey, Grace, stop right where you are," I said, unable to see her through the branches to my left and right. "I was so busy talking about Lina and Kyle, I didn't think to ask whether you needed help."

Finally emerging into the aisle, I got to my feet and let out a sudden gasp. It was the kind that sounded like I'd inhaled through a harmonica. And an off-key one, at that.

Standing there face-to-face with me, looking as stunned as I felt, was Lina Fipps.

"*What* was that you were saying about Kyle and me?" she said, her voice full of outrage. Her dark blond hair was so tightly pulled back from her bony features it looked in danger of coming out by the roots. The hairdo seemed to accentuate her anger—that and the bright red coat she was wearing with an old-fashioned fox stole complete with head, legs, and bushy tail.

Momentarily dropping my gaze from her livid face to the poor creature draped over her neck, I wouldn't have doubted she'd run it over for sport on her way to Grace's store.

"I asked you something," she said, staring at me. Her hands were balled into fists at her sides. "I expect an answer."

I looked at her mutely. Then, out of the corner of my eye, I saw Grace wheeling a dolly full of string lights from the stockroom.

"What's going on?" she said, looking from one of us to the other.

I wished I'd known how to say "a big-time screwup" in French.

As Finch might have attested, things always sounded better that way.

Chapter 14

"So, what was the outcome of the showdown between you and Lina?" Mike said, perched on the corner of his desk.

I looked at him. After leaving Grace's, I'd been on my way home to meet Chloe and Betty-Mom for lunch when he texted me on my cell phone. Was I planning to be at the *Anchor* in the next few hours, by any chance? He was finishing his leadoff piece on the Tommy Thompson scandal and wanted the three of us to go over some things together.

Yep, yup, you heard it right. I said three of us. As in threesome. Sandy Savoy also having been asked to join in. And please keep your twisted pervo orgy-person mind to yourself. I'd gotten enough of that from my mother, who, back in the days of waving her freak flag high, had probably soaked up more firsthand recollections about *those* kinds of threesomes than I would ever want to hear.

But back to Mike's request. Though I hadn't figured on heading over to the paper, and was reluctant to cancel out on lunch, I thought I'd turned up some important info in the last day or two. Which was why I had told him I would reshuffle my other plans and meet them to compare notes.

And so there I was in his office forty minutes and a whopping Betty-Mom-induced guilt trip later, having about finished summarizing, more or less, my various encounters with Bill Drecksel, Finch Fontaine, Grace Blossom, and Lina Fipps . . .

I say more or less, incidentally, because I couldn't mention anything about Kyle's murder, or suspected murder, to Sandy. While I was thinking I might be ready to discuss some of that with Mike in private—assuming we ever had another private moment during our lifetimes, which by no means seemed certain—the explanation I had given her about my nosing around was the same one I offered Bill. Namely that it was related to Jessie Barton's affair with Tommy Thompson.

"I wouldn't exactly call it a showdown," I said now, answering Mike's question about that last and decidedly accidental *hi how'd'ya do.* "More like a one-sided staring contest. With Lina being the reigning champ."

Sandy shook her head sympathetically.

"Don't let it bug you, Sky. I can't count the times I've gotten the stink eye from a boyfriend's wife or fiancée." She glided her palms down the front of her clingy red Diane von Furstenburg wrap. "I mean, check me out! Can *I* help it if a married guy sees all this and decides to roam? It isn't like I slap a billboard across my chest to get attention."

Speaking of which, I suddenly noticed Mike noticing Sandy's guided tour of her extreme curves. A second later Mike noticed me noticing him, coughed into his hand, and glanced down at the floor.

Give me credit. I didn't even glare at Sandy à la Lina Fipps. Instead, I just bit my lip trying to recover from her latest assault on tastefulness. She'd been trying to be supportive, after all.

"Anyway," I said, "I don't know what else to tell you about that run-in. Besides that it happened, there isn't much *to* tell."

Mike quit studying the nap of his carpet and looked at me. "How'd you manage to explain yourself to Lina? As far as why you were snooping around about her and Kyle?"

"I didn't," I said with a shrug. "I sort of mumbled a few words to her, I guess. Asked how she was doing. Or something."

"And then you left?"

"Beat it out of there in a hurry," I said. "I was pretty flustered by her, uh—"

"Stink eye," Sandy said.

"Right," I said. "That."

Mike rubbed the back of his neck a minute. "You know what I'm thinking here?" he said. "I'm thinking I need to talk to this Ed Gallagher about his dealings with Tommy."

Which made sense except for one teensy-weensy detail.

"You mean 'we,' " I said.

"We?"

"Need to talk to Gallagher, yes," I said. "He's my lead. And you've already established we're working this story as a team."

Mike looked at me. "I'm not sure that's exactly what I—"

" 'You're in, Sky.' Wasn't it right in this office that I heard those words the other day? Or am I not recalling them correctly?"

"You're recalling them fine. The thing is, it wasn't me who said them . . ."

"A minor technicality. You went ahead and turned on the tape recorder," I said. And paused. "What is it, Mike?"

"What's *what*?"

"The problem," I said. "You having second thoughts about trusting me?"

He looked at me again. I looked back at him. And *this* time he very definitely got stink-eyed.

"No," he said, combing his fingers back through his hair. "No, I'm not. You're absolutely right. Better two heads than one—"

"Make that three," Sandy said.

Silence. I heard a loud gulp from Mike. Or maybe it was me gulping, I'm not positive. What I know is we both turned in Sandy's direction fast enough to give ourselves whiplash.

"Three?" Mike said.

"Three," she said, and nodded firmly. "I'm going too."

We all sat there staring at each other. Talk about thick silences, this was pure goopy molasses.

"Sandy, listen," Mike said after a minute. "Three won't work. It's one thing for Sky and me to walk into Gallagher's office with a bunch of questions. But unless we want to put him off, it really isn't a good idea for *all* of us to go traipsing in there."

She shook her head.

"Wrong," she said. "You both have your reasons for wanting to look into Tommy's affairs. A condo project. Sky's friend Jessie. And that's fine. But I have reasons of my own. The same reasons I had for telling you my story. And the same ones that brought me to Pigeon Cove."

Mike looked at her. "I understand, Sandy. I really do. But—"

"But nothing," Sandy said. "Please, Michael, will you quit making a fuss about having two beautiful women keep you company? I've never put a man off in my *life*."

She got up, swept her coat from the chair beside her, and shrugged into its sleeves. It was a full-length shearling with fur trim and a long shawl collar.

"Faux?" I asked.

"I'd rather be tortured to death," she said.

And with that she hooked an arm through mine and swept me through the door, Mike following close behind us.

As we hustled past the Digger's busily inquisitive, Dolce & Gabbana-ed eyes into the lobby, I have to admit I really didn't mind Sandy tagging along. For sure, the threesome thing was getting ridiculous. And it definitely wouldn't have broken my heart to learn that PETA had put out a fifty-state bounty on her fur-pelted bod. But I kind of admired her brassiness, and had been sold on her case for joining the party.

Out in front of the building's entrance, Mike stopped and motioned toward his Mini Cooper.

"My car's over there," he said, and took a half step forward into the parking lot.

Sandy stayed put, her hands deep in her pockets.

"You're joking, right?"

He didn't say anything.

"You're not joking." She made a face. "Michael, you're a doll. But that's not a car, it's a little toy icebox," she said. "Let's take my Audi."

I glanced around and saw the snazzy red Roadster over to our left. Actually, I would have had to be blind to miss it among the other vehicles in the aisle.

"Remote starter, huh?" I said, noticing the exhaust coming from its tailpipe. "Sweet."

Sandy nodded and brought a hand out of her pocket, holding the doohickey up for me to see.

"It's nice and toasty inside," she said. "C'mon, Sky. You won't believe all the legroom. The ride's positively erotic."

Positively erotic?

Whatever. I'd taken a ride or two of that sort before, but the turn-on was always my company rather than the car's interior. Although I can't say it wasn't delicious to climb aboard, spread out on the front seat, and move around to my heart's content while feeling the buttery-soft leather upholstery press against my body . . .

Ahem. Well. Okay. On second thought, maybe I could see myself surrendering to the charms of *that* blazing-hot bad boy.

It took us about half an hour to drive down to Beverly. The town has a very suburban feel, probably because it *is* a suburb, and a large one, complete with shopping malls, plexes, and comfortably middle-class teenagers trying to look inner-city tough in Red Sox do-rags. Not twenty miles from Boston, it sits well outside the land of Faerie that encompasses the Cove and some of the other small coastal towns farther north across the Annisquam Bridge—all of whose combined populations just about equal Beverly's head count of forty thousand.

A flat, wide cinder-block building with a large lumber and equipment yard in back, Gallagher Brothers General Contracting was on Cabot Street out past the downtown area. We could tell once we reached it that finding a place to leave the Roadster would be a problem—the plows and snow removal crews hadn't kept pace with the past week's heavy accumulations, and everywhere we looked spaces were either occupied or piled under.

"You two go on ahead," Sandy said, pulling up beside a parked car. "I'll cruise around till I find something."

"No rush," Mike said from the backseat. "Catch you inside." And then he lunged for his door handle.

I joined him out on the sidewalk a minute later.

"You could've tried not to look so relieved," I said.

"Huh?"

"You know what I mean," I said. "How come you were so anxious to shake her?"

Mike watched Sandy slide back into traffic, then looked at me.

"It was that obvious?" he said.

"I'd say the giveaway was when you practically dove out of the car while it was still moving."

He sighed.

"Look, Sky, I understand why she wanted to come along. But I'd still rather not have three of us walk in there and make Gallagher skittish." He nodded toward the entrance. "C'mon, follow my lead," he said. "People tend to be guarded around the press, but I've got a way of working through their defenses."

As we went inside, I noticed that the motto under the company name read, BUILDING THE FUTURE OF THE NORTH SHORE. It reminded me of the "Pigeon Cove's Growth and Expansion" et cetera theme the Art Association had chosen for its holiday party . . . not that I thought this signified anything, besides possibly that local development was on a lot of people's minds. And, I supposed, that enough of them were willing to pay the price for it.

The receptionist, a plain, neatly dressed woman in her thirties, looked up from a copy of *Glamour* magazine as we approached her desk.

"Good afternoon," she said. "Can I help you?"

Mike showed her his press credential.

"I'm Mike Ennis with the *Cape Ann Anchor*," he said.

"I was hoping to chat with Ed Gallagher for a few minutes."

She studied the credential. "You're a reporter?"

"That's right."

Just as Mike had predicted, her features clamped up with suspicion.

"I'm not sure Mr. Gallagher's in," she said. "And if he is, I don't know that he's available. It's very hectic around here."

"Would you mind checking?" Mike said.

She looked at him, stone-faced. "This would be with regard to . . . ?"

"I'd rather tell him directly," he said.

She sat there being leery of us.

"If you don't mind," Mike persisted, nodding toward her speakerphone. "I'd really appreciate it."

The receptionist glanced in my direction without lifting a finger to press the intercom button.

"And you are . . . ?"

"My colleague, Sky Taylor," Mike said. "Sorry, I should've introduced you."

But before I could get too annoyed that he'd jumped in before I could introduce *myself*—something of which I've been capable since I was eight or so—the receptionist snapped upright in her chair, a huge grin appearing on her face.

"Omigod!" she said. "You're *the* Sky Taylor? The writer who writes Sky Writing?"

I nodded after deciphering that.

"This is such a thrill . . . I *love* your column!"

"Thanks."

"Love it! It's like you're talking to me personally! And your cleaning tips are the best!"

"Gee, thanks again. I'm really flattered."

The receptionist kept beaming at me, reached a hand across her desk.

"My name's Ellen," she said as I shook it. "Ellen Tyler. Eddie's my brother-in-law. For *you*, I'll buzz him right this second!"

She actually took about three seconds, but I wasn't

about to split hairs. I was too busy looking pleased with myself for Mike's benefit.

"Ed, Sky Taylor from the *Anchor* is here to see you!" she said into the intercom. "Sky's with a gentleman named . . ." She looked at Mike questioningly. "Mark, was it . . . ?"

"Mike Ennis," I reminded her. Pleased, and doubly pleased.

How shall I describe Ed Gallagher? A dishy hunk of man seems uninspired, though it does cover it. Especially, I suppose, if I sketch in details like his solid-as-brick six-foot frame, broad shoulders, ruggedly handsome face, and sandy brown hair, all packaged in corresponding workman's regalia—jeans and a flannel shirt.

He came in a side door and shook our hands, his firm grip convincing me that even his knuckles had muscles.

"You caught me right in the nick," he said, glancing from one of us to the other. "I was just getting set to head out to a building site."

"This won't take long," Mike said. "Is there a place we can talk?"

"Sure." Gallagher looked at him. "This about anything in particular?"

"Getaway Groves," Mike said.

Gallagher looked at him briefly, a question on his face. Then he turned toward the reception desk. "El, why don't you take five?" he said.

His sister-in-law was back to looking wary.

"Are you sure?"

"Yeah. You can maybe head over to that Chinese restaurant, grab us some takeout for lunch."

Ellen seemed about to say something, but instead just got up and left through the same door Ed had used to enter. As she did, he motioned Mike and me over toward some contoured swivel chairs against the wall.

"So," he said when the three of us were seated. "You doing some kind of piece on the Groves?"

"That's part of it," Mike said.

"And the other?"

"Tommy Thompson."

Gallagher raised an eyebrow. "Why him?" he said.

Mike shrugged. "He's involved in the project, right? Financially, I mean."

Gallagher shrugged. "I guess you could say."

Mike looked at him. "Is it true he opened an escrow account for its principal investors?" he said.

"Who told you that?"

"I can't give the source," Mike said. "But we've heard the money was set aside to pay for construction, and that some problem or other might've developed with the arrangement."

Gallagher hesitated.

"From what I saw in the paper, Thompson's got troubles with a whole different kind of arrangement," he said.

Mike and I didn't have to be geniuses to understand he was talking about the juicy Garden photo.

"That's no secret," Mike said. "But we'd specifically like to discuss the condo development . . ."

Gallagher looked at me.

"I thought you wrote—what's it called?—human-interest stories," he said. "El reads them first thing every week when the paper comes out. She says they can be funny and sad and give her a lift all at once."

I tried not to bask too much.

"I'm just helping out with this piece," I said. "Though it's nice to hear I'm hitting my marks."

Gallagher knitted his hands together on his lap and studied them.

"Ed . . ." Mike said, and paused. "It's okay if I call you Ed, right?"

"That's my name."

"Ed, what can you tell us about Thompson's involvement with Getaway Groves? Financial, political, whatever."

Gallagher continued to stare at the backs of his hands.

"Far as the political end goes, you don't need my help," he said. "Go back to when Pigeon Cove's city council approved the condo project. That's all on the record, isn't it?"

Mike nodded. "The town Web site's got the minutes, agendas, and votes for every council session they've held in the past hundred years."

"Like I said, you ought to take a look at 'em," Gallagher said. "Meanwhile, here's a question. You see any construction on the units lately?"

"No," Mike said.

"Know the last time you did?"

Mike shook his head.

Gallagher brought his eyes up to mine. "How about you?"

I tried to remember. "My best guess would be back in the fall."

Gallagher unmeshed his fingers and gave me a thumbs-up. "You win the grand prize," he said. "It was the end of September. Three months ago."

Right around when Jessie Barton left town, I thought. For whatever that was worth.

"How come you stopped building?" Mike said.

Gallagher looked at him for a long moment. "Wasn't because of bad weather," he said.

"Is that the best you can do for us?"

"Yeah, it is."

We were all quiet.

After a minute, Mike said, "What about that escrow fund?"

"What about it?"

"Same thing I asked to start out," Mike said. "Did Bill Drecksel and Kyle Fipps have Thompson establish one for them?"

Gallagher sat for a while without saying anything, lost in thought. Then he shrugged.

"I can't get into their money arrangements," he said. "You'd need to talk to Drecksel. Or better yet, Tommy Thompson. Say there was a fund, he'd be the person to know its ins and outs."

"But you got paid through Thompson," Mike said. "He'd have signed the checks—isn't that right?"

Gallagher sat looking thoughtful again.

"I don't see how I can say anything about that," he

replied finally. "Like I told you, Thompson's the man to—"

"He won't help us," Mike said. "I think you know that's why we're here talking to you."

Gallagher hesitated.

"You have to understand," he said. "I'm a middle-sized contractor. Almost a hundred percent of my jobs are local. How I compete with bigger guys from outside the area is to be hands-on. I don't use foremen, project managers, and so forth. It keeps my costs down and lets me stay competitive." He paused again, looked at Mike. "But that isn't enough. Things don't work that easy. I need to stay in good with the people making decisions around this place. And you look at who's on top of that heap, you're going to see Tommy Thompson."

While Gallagher was talking, I'd felt a blast of cold against my neck as the entrance to the street opened behind me. Now he glanced over my shoulder and suddenly rotated his chair in its direction.

His eyes gaped open.

"Hey," he said, "you're— What're *you* doing here?"

I had a suspicion about who it was and spun my own chair around to check it out.

Sure enough.

There inside the door stood Sandy Savoy, her shearling coat open to display her figure-huggy Von Furst.

"I'm with them," Sandy said, nodding toward me and Mike.

"You are?" Gallagher said.

"I am," Sandy said. "Part of the team."

"Team?"

"Yes."

"What team?"

"Haven't you been talking about Tommy Thompson?"

"Well, yeah . . ."

"The team that's investigating him," Sandy said.

Ouch. It struck me that Mike and I should have prepared Ed Gallagher—and ourselves—for her eventual grand entrance. As much as anyone could prepare. After all, we'd known she was going to find a spot for the Audi sooner or later.

Now Gallagher turned to Mike. Well, okay, that's not exactly what he did. First he took about five thumps of the heart I could practically hear through his chest to soak up Sandy's Viking chick entirely. *Then* he turned to Mike.

"I don't get it," he said. "She's one of those lap girls in that picture of Thompson at the Celtics game. From when he had that practical joke played on him."

Ouch, ouch, ouch. Mike sat there trying to regroup while I bit my lip and Sandy looked hurt and indignant.

"I'm a dancer, not a lap girl," she said. "And the other woman in that photo was my sister, who's a college student. And it was a *date*, not a practical joke!"

"It was?"

"Tommy Thompson was my fiancé. Sort of. If he hadn't been married to someone else."

Gallagher faced her again.

"Hey, I'm sorry," he said. "I thought . . . that is, I didn't mean to hurt your feelings."

"Well, you did."

"But I didn't mean to—"

"I heard you the first time." Sandy sniffled. Her eyes were filling with tears.

"Please, don't cry." Gallagher put his hands on her shoulders, guided her into a seat. "Here, why don't you relax?" He looked imploringly over at Mike as she settled down. "C'mon, tell her I didn't want to insult anybody."

"I think she said she heard you tell her."

"But nobody warned me she was on your *team*."

"You didn't give us a chance," Mike said. "Sandy's been helping with our research, though it's probably beside the point."

Research? Sounded good, I thought. My boyfriend, sort of, was handling the situation with aplomb.

Not so Sandy. She just continued to get tearier. Call me a sucker, but I felt for her.

"Tommy swore he didn't love his wife and told me we were meant to be together," she said. "He bought me everything I wanted—"

Gallagher looked at her. "Everything?"

Sandy nodded. "And more."

Gallagher kept looking at her.

"Big spender, huh," he said.

"Like you wouldn't believe," Sandy said. "Then he cheated on me with someone else."

Gallagher scratched the back of his neck. "In other words," he said, "Thompson's a cheating cheater."

Sandy nodded, weeping. "What kind of man does that?"

"Don't think I'm being fresh, but having a dish like you, he'd have to be nuts to step out of line." Gallagher scratched his head. "Especially, you know, considering his other option . . ."

He seemed to ponder his own words a moment. And he wasn't alone. They'd made me ponder too. What did he mean by *other option*? Could it be he knew about Jessie? And why put her down? A lot of guys would've been glad to have an extramarital fling with her.

I exhaled. What in the world was wrong with me? Or had I *not* just gotten irked hearing Gallagher take an implied swipe at my friend's mistress appeal?

Meanwhile, Gallagher had finished ahead of me in the pondering race.

"You want a Kleenex?" he asked Sandy. "I'm sure I've got some around here."

She nodded again, her cheeks wet. "I'd appreciate it."

Gallagher stood up, walked across the room, and yanked a tissue from a box on the reception desk—and as he did, Sandy turned to give me a sly wink and a smile.

I looked at her in astonishment. That's S-U-C-K-E-R. In case anybody wants to spell it out.

"There you go," he said, handing the tissue to her. "Look, I know you don't want to hear this again, but I'm sorry I made you cry."

"That's okay, it isn't really you."

"It isn't?"

"No." Sandy sobbed. "You started it. But now I'm crying about something else."

"You are?"

She nodded. "I'm remembering Tommy's lies. And his threats."

Gallagher straightened.

"Wait a minute," he said. "He threatened you?"

"Not only me," Sandy said. "Also the woman he cheated on me with. The one from Pigeon Cove."

His eyebrows crunched together.

"Lina?" he said. "Gee, that's hard to believe."

I looked at Gallagher. So did Mike.

"By 'Lina,' " I said, "do you mean Lina Fipps?"

He stood there looking back at us,

"Lina Fipps was having an *affair* with Tommy Thompson?" Mike said.

Gallagher swallowed with a loud gulp, mortified. He clearly realized he'd slipped up big-time.

"I thought . . . that is . . . when Sandy here mentioned he had a girlfriend from the Cove . . ."

"I meant someone else!" she said in a choked voice. "I can't believe Tommy had *two* other girlfriends! From the same town!"

"Talk about spreading it around," Gallagher muttered under his breath.

Sandy inhaled, her chest heaving under the top of her dress till it looked ready to burst. Then she broke into fresh tears.

We were all quiet a few seconds, Mike and I looking thoughtful, Gallagher looking at Sandy as she bawled away.

"Want another tissue?" he asked her.

"No, thanks."

"You sure? I got plenty in the box—"

"I'm fine, really. I've been tossed aside before. My mother always said we're born with expiration dates."

"We?"

"Women," Sandy said.

"Oh." He made a sympathetic face. "You look plenty fresh to me, for what it's worth."

Sandy batted her teary lashes at him.

"Why," she said, "it's so sweet of you to say that."

I managed not to clutch my stomach.

Meanwhile, Gallagher predictably kept his attention on Sandy as her chest shook with sobs. And did a passable job of keeping his eyes in his sockets, I ought to add.

"Might be none of my business," he said. "But you mind my asking why Thompson made those threats to you?"

"He dumped me and I wanted an explanation," she said. "That's all the reason he needed."

"And the girlfriend? I mean the one you knew about. He have the *same* reason for doing it to her?"

Sandy opened her mouth to answer, but choked up before she could

"We have no idea," I said, jumping in. "But she's left town without a word, and we'd like to find her if we can."

Gallagher looked at me. "I thought you said you were writing a story on Getaway Groves. How you figure that's got anything to do with whatever went on between Thompson and the woman who took off?"

"Nobody said it does," Mike replied. "We just don't know that it doesn't."

Gallagher seemed confused.

"It's like working on a puzzle," I said. "Ever build a jigsaw?"

"No. Well, when I was a kid, I guess—"

"You'd start by sorting the pieces, remember? Put the edge pieces in one pile, and make another pile with pieces that had the same colors or markings on them, and then build a section at a time. Until the whole thing was finally assembled."

Gallagher stared at us for a long time, looking hesitant. It was as if he was having a debate with himself.

"What is it you want to know about Thompson?" he said.

"Anything you can tell us," Mike said.

"My name stays out of it?"

"If that's how it has to be."

Gallagher nodded.

"Tommy wrote out the checks," he said. "It's wild, when you think about it. Kyle asking him to open that escrow fund to keep the Getaway Groves cash away from Lina."

"And then Tommy having an affair with her," I said.

"A cheating cheater," Sandy said miserably. "When you know him the way I do, it isn't the least little *bit* wild."

I found myself feeling sorry for her as she honked into her tissue.

"What was it that halted construction?" Mike asked.

Gallagher shrugged.

"Thompson must've made his last payment right around the beginning of September," he said. "This was for work I'd already done. Then maybe a month, six weeks later, I go ahead and lay out fifty thou for building supplies."

"Your own money?"

"Yeah."

"That sounds like a lot."

"It is." Gallagher shrugged again. "I could've waited for the cash upfront, but never figured a hotshot like him would actually stiff me. Plus, I wanted to be sure the project kept rolling on schedule."

"Have you gotten reimbursed yet?"

Gallagher shook his head. "I must phone Thompson once a week," he said. "Sometimes he says he's busy and needs to call me back. Sometimes he ducks me and has the receptionist answer. Every so often he even promises the check. But it never comes. And when it doesn't, I get an excuse. There's a new one every time."

Mike considered that in silence. Something that might've been a bulldozer rumbled and clanked out in the equipment yard.

"Did Kyle and Drecksel know about all these delays?" he said after the racket died down a bit.

"Not at first," Gallagher said. "Even *I* didn't realize it. Thought it was the usual stall tactics. When you're running a business, people expect you to deliver on time. But try getting them to pay when they're supposed to. Sometimes they have cash flow problems. Or wait for a new fiscal quarter. Whatever. They'll hang you up for a hundred reasons. But the longer I waited on Thompson, the more I started to think what he was doing wasn't just par for the course. And I wanted to get compensated."

"Did you finally tell Kyle?"

"Yeah."

"When was this?"

Gallagher gazed at him for a long moment.

"About two weeks before he died," he said.

Whoa, I thought.

I didn't let my mouth drop open, and I didn't jump to conclusions. I was determined to show restraint. But I had to automatically ask myself if the timing was a coincidence.

"How did he react?" I said.

"The way you'd figure," Gallagher said. "Went to Tommy's office and asked him about it."

"And what was Thompson's explanation?" Mike asked.

"That Lina and her divorce lawyer got a judge to put a freeze on the escrow account. They were claiming it was really set up for Kyle to hide away cash he didn't want figured into a settlement."

Mike looked at him. "If I were Kyle, I'd have been mad as hell," he said. "Thompson's his personal accountant. How does he not pass that along?"

"Fipps wanted to know the same thing," he said. "Thompson told him he was sorry and was sure the freeze was temporary. Called it a bargaining chip. Said he didn't think it was important to bother Kyle with it."

"And Kyle believed him?"

"I don't know. I suppose he might've. He and Tommy went back a ways."

"How'd you feel about it?"

Gallagher shrugged.

"Didn't make a difference how I felt," he said. "Whatever the reason, I couldn't move ahead with the condos till I got my payment. Or enough of it to start covering some of my expenses."

A moment passed. I thought Gallagher had done an okay job of tiptoeing around Mike's question. Except for one thing. And I was just about to bring it up when Sandy beat me to the punch.

"I don't understand," she said. "Tommy's supposed to protect Kyle's money from Lina while he's fooling around with her?"

Gallagher gave her a look.

"You got to wonder about it, don't you?"

"More than wonder," Mike said. "It sounds like a blatant conflict of interest."

One that was bound to leave Kyle in a seriously compromised negotiating position, I thought. And then I decided to push ahead and ask Gallagher something else that had ticked my curiosity,

"How do you know Tommy and Lina were having an affair?"

Gallagher turned to me. I waited as the bulldozer, or whatever it was I'd heard in the yard, revved up again. This time it wasn't alone—there seemed to be a number of other tractors coming to life out back.

"This stays in this room," he said finally.

I nodded.

"I mean it." He let his eyes move to Sandy and Mike. "Stays right here between the four of us. Anybody ever asks me about it, I deny the whole thing, understood?"

It was their turn to nod.

Gallagher cleared his throat. "I was close with Lina before she met Tommy," he said. "Real close if you catch my meaning."

I looked at him, incredulous. "You and Lina *too*?"

Gallagher's shoulders slouched.

"We met last spring. I went to Kyle's house to pick up some blueprints, and he wasn't there. And we got to talking, and one thing led to another," he said. "I didn't plan it. It just sort of happened. But she and Kyle were already done anyway. They were both moving on. Looking for his and her replacements." He paused. "Lina had this cabin, used to belong to her parents. A little place we'd hook up every so often."

"And when did Tommy Thompson come into the picture?"

"Must've been right around last July. Kyle and Drecksel threw their launch party for the Groves. There was a groundbreaking ceremony over on the South End, and then drinks and food over at Kyle's. Thompson was there, and I noticed him and Lina kind of drifting away from everybody. Together, you know. But I didn't think much of it. Guess I should've seen what was happening when it was in front of me, but I didn't."

"Join the club," Sandy said.

Gallagher smiled wanly.

"Hand me a membership card. I'm in," he said. "Anyway, things cooled a little between me and Lina after the party. But I just figured, no biggie. They could heat up again just as fast. I knew she went to the cabin every weekend in the summer, so I decided to stop by. This was, like, August or so. And when I got there—" He broke off for a second, cleared his throat. "When I got there, who was snoozing in a hammock out front but Tommy Thompson? Wearing nothing besides a pair of shorts. *My* shorts, in fact. Even I'm smart enough to know he didn't tire himself out mowing her lawn."

I was thinking hammocks seemed to be a running theme when it came to major discoveries involving the Fippses. And wondering if this was the same hammock I'd found Kyle in. Somehow I knew I'd never view hammocks as the de rigueur summer item again.

Sandy rose from her chair and moved toward Gallagher.

"You poor man," Sandy said. "Just dredging up that awful memory . . . you need a hug."

I watched them from where I sat. Something told me

the little blip of heartache Gallagher had felt over Lina was about to pay off with the hug of a lifetime.

"Your cheating cheater cheated with *my* cheating cheater," Sandy said, spreading her arms wide.

"There's plenty of that to go around," he said.

And melted oh-so-willingly into her embrace.

Chapter 15

It was quarter to seven in the evening when I pulled my Caliber into the parking lot behind City Hall for my first night of office cleaning there.

I'd felt out of sorts since midafternoon, and suspected that was a residual effect of my visit to Gallagher Construction, which had started me wondering if everybody in the general Boston area was slinking around with everybody else's husband, wife, or girlfriend. Considering that Ed Gallagher's revelations came at a time when Mike seemed more concerned with Sandy Savoy's life than mine, they'd really put me on tilt and—

No, wait. Hold up.

That wasn't fair.

I wasn't fair, pinning everything on Mike. Or maybe anything on him. Not when I'd gotten all fluttery over Chief Alejandro Vega that night outside the police station. And not when my mind kept cutting back to how he'd looked at me as I'd driven off, or how hard it had been to tear my eyes away from his. I'd told myself over and over it was only in my imagination. But somehow I knew I was done with that.

I'd always been a one-man-for-me kind of person. In the seven years I was married, and during the entire two years Paul and I lived together before making ourselves official, I'd never been tempted to stray. But these days I didn't know how much exclusivity I wanted. Or expected. Or was prepared to offer Mike. Or anyone.

Tilted. At an unfamiliar angle. That was how I felt.

The whole tangle of secret affairs involving Sandy, Tommy Thompson, Lina Fipps, Ed Gallagher, and who *knew* how many more parties—it had stirred up thoughts and feelings I wasn't close to being ready to deal with.

Later was better. Later had to be better.

I hadn't wanted a committed relationship with Mike. But I hadn't thought about anyone else, or so I'd insisted to myself until something about the past few hours made me acknowledge I had. I suppose it was hearing about so many lies. The deceitfulness, the sneaking around—I could never handle it. I really couldn't. It was too complicated.

Still, my desires scared me more than a little. I knew I would have to be up-front if I acted on them. The alternative to honesty would be easier in the short run, which was what made it such a temptation. In the end, though, it was always cruel and unfair to everyone involved.

I would need to make my choices and decide what I was going to do, and I understood I couldn't put it off indefinitely. But I also understood that the time hadn't arrived yet. There was *later*. And right now, I was glad I could concentrate on my work.

The parking lot was deserted after business hours, and I had my pick of spots close to the building. I took one outside its service entrance, then cut the Caliber's motor and went around to the cargo hatch. It was very dark outside, the sky moonless and starless. Only a single helmeted old lamp pole stood to brighten the lot because of city ordinances that restricted how much lighting could be used—something to do with the glare it cast on nearby residences. This left me very grateful for the SUV's interior lights as I reached into it for a collapsible laundry cart I'd bought especially for my big new job.

After I'd unfolded the cart, I got my bag of tricks, Oreck vacuum, and dust mop out of the hatch and carefully put them into it. Then I wheeled the whole shebang toward the entrance, letting myself in with one of several keys I'd gotten from the custodian, a grizzled but friendly guy named Rick who'd been working at City

Hall since LBJ was president and had volunteered to give me a tour of its three floors the same day Tommy Thompson confirmed my hiring.

Rick had also kept his promise to leave a few lights on for me tonight. The ground-floor entry hall was at once spare and expansive, with a granite floor, seven-foot-tall windows, a directory, a couple of benches against the wall, and a huge public notice board announcing everything of community interest from the next bean supper to the latest neighborhood rezoning proposal.

I was facing the board as I stepped through the service entrance, a heavy, glass-paned oak door almost identical to the front door over to my right. Standing guard on one side of the main entrance was a six-foot-tall snowman figure with a top hat, coal eyes, a carrot nose, twig arms, and a plaid scarf around his neck. Directly over my head was a circular black iron chandelier entwined in dried vines—these sprayed a silver or pewter color and festooned with colorful baubles and gilded fruit and nuts. On my right, a wide, banistered staircase climbed to the upper stories, and a glance in that direction revealed a wood-carved French Victorian le Pere Noel, or Father Christmas, in a corner of the landing above me. Tall and thin, with a flowing beard, he carried a knobby, crooked walking stick and wore a long robe and peaked cowl the original color of the white pine from which he'd been crafted. Tyler Binkman, Pigeon Cove's most well-known carver, had made about a dozen quaint Old World Santas for the town, and my friend on the landing was one of three or four in City Hall.

Despite those holiday touches—or in a weird way, because of them—I found the atmosphere kind of spooky. I guessed part of it was the size of the place, coupled with its being empty instead of totally filled with people as it was during business hours. But the decorations unquestionably added to the feeling. Something about them didn't fit, not at night when the corridor was dim, and still, and silent. It was almost the opposite of cheerful, as if someone had gussied the place up for a party that had to be hastily called off, wasting all the elaborate preparations, and leaving my friends Frosty and Father Christmas to stand vigil over the evacuated corridors and offices.

The Haunted Christmas Cleaning Bash, I thought. *Another Sky Taylor and Her Bag of Tricks Chiller.*

Luckily, I couldn't dwell on that masochistic flight of fancy. I knew I had to get cracking, and I took a clipboard from my cleaning kit to read over the to-do list I'd jotted out.

Me being me, I'd made sure I was organized and would start with the basics I wanted to accomplish. Anything else I noticed along the way would be put on the list for my next scheduled night at City Hall. I had also set a time limit for each task to keep myself paced, a habit I'd carried over from my ad-writing days, when I was always squeezed by tight deadlines. Once I moved ahead with my plan, I would keep on moving ahead till I was finished.

That plan called for me to begin with the top floor and then gradually work my way back down.

I hauled my wagon upstairs, paused on the landing to catch my breath. Down the hall to my left were the conference rooms. On my right a doorless entry opened from the landing to the bell tower where Tommy Thompson would ring in the New Year—or more precisely to the spiral stairs leading up into the tower. Rick the maintenance guy had brought me inside during my guided tour, taking me all the way up to the bellringer's platform. It was pretty neat to stand there looking down at the historic buildings on Main Street . . . even dreamy, somehow. If only for a few moments, it had given me a sense of perspective and lightness and calm. I couldn't have explained why, not exactly, but there's no question it did. Up on that high, narrow perch, I'd been able to imagine what it was like to be a bird about to launch into the air.

I sighed. Right now, I could imagine cleaning well into the night unless I got busy. Turning into the hall, I pushed the cart toward the largest of the three conference rooms, a wide-open space with no rugs or extraneous furnishings—just a hardwood floor and a rectangular meeting table with about twenty chairs around it. There was an oblong bowl full of evergreen sprigs, red candles, and celosia blooms in the middle of the table, but that wasn't the room's main holiday attraction.

I could see another Father Christmas standing at the windows opposite the entrance. Wearing a fur-trimmed cap, an ankle-length coat, and carrying a polished staff rather than a gnarled walking stick, he was plumper than the first one—though still not quite jelly-bellied—and had a waggish amusement on his face that I couldn't help but associate with old-time Brit character actors.

Probably better company than his far too lean and serious Frankish alter ego downstairs, I thought.

"Oi oi, matey!" I said, and tipped him a wave.

He didn't respond, but I was sure he would have if he hadn't been made out of a tree. And he continued to look like a jolly good fellow.

Inside the conference room, I removed my cleaning kit from the cart, got a commercial garbage bag out of it, and clipped the bag to the cart. I wasn't expecting to find much trash, nor was there a whole lot in the wastepaper baskets, Pigeon Cove having cut a deal with a mill somewhere up in Maine that recycled its shredded paper into pulp.

That out of the way, I went into the hall, got a stepladder out of a utility closet Rick had showed me on his guided tour, and did my dusting. I took care of the moldings, windowsills, table, and chairs in order, and then climbed the ladder and did the corners of the ceiling. After that came the windows. And after that dust mopping and vacuuming the floor.

The other conference rooms were scaled-down versions of the main one and added a few more props to my haunted Christmas set. Room Two had a tall, narrow pine tree hung with assorted origami animals that a sign on the base said were donated by the Forestry Committee. In Room Three, the meeting table's centerpiece was a frosted vase of red flowers—anemones, roses, gerbera daisies, mini-carnations, and maybe a variety or two that I didn't recognize.

I did my thing in both rooms without any ghosts yelling "Boo!" while I was on the ladder, or worse, pinching me with pervo poltergeist fingers. That took about half an hour, putting me fifteen minutes ahead of schedule.

Being ahead of schedule was good. Very good, in fact. Especially when my imagination was getting the best of me, which tended to happen whenever it was most inconvenient and apt to make my hair stand on end.

Next stop, second floor, where the city council members had their offices.

I started with Tommy Thompson's, since it was the first off the stairway, promising myself I wouldn't poke around where I didn't belong. It was one thing to stick my nose in Thompson's affairs when I had my quasi-journalist's hat on. That I could easily quasi-rationalize. But when it came to cleaning there was nothing quasi about me. I was a cleaning professional. I had to abide by the rules of acceptable conduct for my line of work.

Although the reality was that nobody had ever written the book on it, let alone an actual rule. Or even a mono-syllabic word, come to think. Sure, it was understood that a place ought to be left tidier than it was when you got there. And, naturally, nothing you found in it except dirt and refuse ought to be missing after you left. But when did simple inquisitiveness cross the snooping threshold?

The question was a toughie, and I wasn't sure there was a clear-cut answer. My own policy was to avoid doing anything that bore even a semblance of snoopish conduct. Generally speaking. Like, say, when the potential snoopee was capable of firing you from a job you hoped would be your financial salvation.

And so I mentally compartmentalized. I forced myself to think of Thompson's office as being the same as anyone else's, and cleaned without any other agenda, and breezed my way along. I'd allotted twenty minutes to each office, but was done with his in ten. Somebody, maybe even Tommy, was keeping it spic-and-span. The trophies, picture frames, the braided antique rug under his humongous desk and chair . . . they were all spotless. So what if I suspected him of being a dirty thieving crook? His office was squeaky-clean.

I suppose a lot of people might have been glad for the chance to take a breather, but I felt almost remiss. There had to be something I'd overlooked. A fugitive dust ball, a gram of grime hidden somewhere out of sight.

You might say I obsess about this sort of thing. I'd argue that it becomes a challenge. A *tease*. Me against the unseen dirt. Hunter and quarry. Like the hounds in Thompson's hunting art, I wasn't going to be outfoxed.

This all goes to explain why I decided to move Tommy's chair back and gently run my Oreck over his rug . . . and how I stumbled on what was beneath it.

As I've said, it didn't look as if it needed so much as a touch-up. But nothing caused the fibers of a rug to deteriorate more than dust and dust mites that get in deep where you can't see them. And I knew the fibers of that particular rug were over two centuries old, making them naturally fragile and susceptible to decay. They deserved some special senior care, and that was what I'd purely, innocently, and unsnoopily started giving them when I pushed the vacuum under the kneehole of the desk—and then felt it hit an unexpected bump.

My forehead crinkled. It wasn't a big bump. But it wasn't a small one either. It had made an audible *clunk*, and jerked my arm a little when I struck it.

I thumbed off the Oreck and bent down for a peek. Something was definitely under the rug—the weave had bunched together where it stopped the vacuum's head. Luckily it hadn't caused a tear, but I figured it was just a matter of time before the fabric either snagged or had a hole worn through it from Thompson rolling his chair back and forth over the spot.

I put aside the vacuum and scootched under the desk on my hands and knees. I'd been asked not to move any of the building's furniture for insurance reasons—the

town government didn't want to be liable for my winding
up with a herniated disk. But I knew I wouldn't have to
do that, since the bulge was near the rug's outer edge.
I could easily raise a portion of the rug to get at whatever was causing it.

Which I did. And then saw what I saw. To my utter
surprise.

I'd uncovered some sort of concealed floor panel—a
six-inch-by-four-inch rectangle that had been cut right
out of the hardwood. There was an iron ring pull on top
that I could tell was meant to lie flat on its backplate
when the panel was set in place. But it had been accidentally left up, as it might be when somebody lifted the
panel. That explained what I'd bumped the vacuum
cleaner against.

I stared at it for a few seconds, remembering what I'd
told myself about sniffing around where I shouldn't. Not
that I'd done that on purpose. But it *was* done.

And what was done was done.

And now the itch to find out what was underneath
the panel was killing me.

Throes-of-a-dilemma time, I thought.

I squatted there under the desk, balancing my curiosity against my qualms about doing anything to invade
Tommy's privacy. I must have given it a full minute's
consideration. Okay, maybe thirty seconds—I wasn't carrying a stopwatch. But let's say I did experience some
real hesitation before I reached out to pull the ring, and
leave it at that.

The panel came up easily, revealing a metal door with
a keyhole in the middle. It reminded me of a postal box,
and clearly gave access to a locked compartment.

Crouched down over it, I suddenly felt a pang of conscience. Tommy Thompson held an important government position. He probably had important, well, stuff
related to his post that needed to be kept in a secure
place. So he had a floor safe in his office. Where was
the offense? And more significantly, where had I gotten
the nerve to uncover it? Yeah, sure, what was done was

done. That was some whiz-bang reasoning right there. But then, as usual, I'd gone one step further and done something else. And what was my excuse?

If it sounds like I'd about-faced, it's because I very definitely had. I was convinced I'd gone over the snooping threshold.

Way, way over.

But I could bawl myself out later, I thought. Right at that instant all I wanted was to get out of the office.

I put the wooden panel back where I'd found it, leaving the ring pull flat so it wouldn't harm the antique rug. Then I flipped the rug down over it, pushed Thompson's chair under the desk, and took my cart and rear end out into the hallway.

I cleaned the rest of the second floor, and then hustled downstairs to the first, where the town's administrative departments were located. Their doors all had glass panes at around eye level, and all the panes were decorated for the Twilight Zone Christmas party my imagination had concocted to make me wiggly. The pane looking into the county clerk's office had glitter snowflakes on it. The one on the door of the town treasurer's office had a red stocking full of Beanie Babies and satin bows hanging in front. The hall of records, a pair of silver bells fastened with sprigs of holly and red berries.

I stuck firmly to the plan of cleaning those offices. I was fast. I was thorough. I got them done, and I got out. And I did it without laying any more seeds of guilt and embarrassment for myself.

It was a little before ten when I left the building. Glad to be finished, I headed out the service door into the parking lot. It was snowing hard, and that surprised me. Three or four inches seemed to have fallen since I'd arrived at City Hall.

I didn't think I'd heard anything about another storm in the forecast. Or maybe I had, but wasn't paying attention. I'd been preoccupied with so many different things recently, I couldn't have sworn I'd even heard or watched a late weather forecast . . . not a smart way to go when you worked in the winter. Categorically dumb when you worked nights.

I paused on the stoop outside the entrance, blinking flakes off my eyelashes. Then I tucked my head down low, stepped into the parking lot, and pushed my cart toward the Caliber.

The wind was blowing through the lot in crosscurrents, scalloping the snow underfoot, whipping it around in agitated dervishes. Dark as the lot had been before, it was worse now. The lot's solitary streetlamp had become useless, and I was guessing snow had caked over its lens the way it might on the headlights of a car.

Reaching the Caliber, I unlocked and opened the hatch, happy once again to have whatever brightness the interior light could provide.

I'd begun unloading the cart when I noticed, or thought I noticed, a hint of movement over to my left. I barely caught it out the corner of my eye—it was just a rustle in the darkness and snow.

I was turning to check it out when . . .

I would tell you what happened next, but it's all a blur. What I *do* remember is that something hit me so hard it knocked me off my feet, practically dumping me under the SUV. I wasn't even sure where I got hit. Or what hit me. Just that I was up on my feet one second, and then the next was sprawling down there in the snow.

When I tried to stand, nothing was working. I couldn't get my bearings, and pain was radiating up from the vicinity of my leg to what seemed like everywhere else in my body. A wave of dizziness overtook me, and I was hot and cold at the same time.

I started to think about reaching for my cell phone and calling for help, but don't recall getting it out of my coat pocket.

Not before my awareness went as dim as the lights in the parking lot, and then dissolved to black.

Chapter 16

"Sky, you okay?"

I opened my eyes at the sound of the voice. Like the face above me in the darkness, it was drifting and fuzzy. But I knew right away they were connected to the same person and I mentally flashed on who I'd meant to call after—

After what? I couldn't remember. Or remember much. I'd left City Hall and headed for the Caliber. The rest was vague, though. It was snowing. At some point there'd been a sudden movement over to my side, and then the terrible pain in my leg. The next thing I'd known I'd been falling to the ground, groping for my cell. And then . . . nothing.

"Mike," I said, my vision still smudged. "Mike, what happened?"

"Whoa, I guess you ain't so okay," the voice said. "No way do I resemble Mike. And no, no way is he ever at the office this late."

I stayed motionless for a second, snowflakes coldly spotting my cheeks. The darkness didn't thin any. But the face looking down at me sharpened in my vision.

It definitely wasn't Mike's.

"*Bry?*" I said. My eyes had cleared enough to make out his cluster-piercings.

He nodded. "I figure the police should show any second. They told me an ambulance from Addison Gilbert might even beat 'em here."

"I don't need an ambulance," I said. "I want to get up."

Bryan looked at me.

"You seriously better stay right where you are," he said.

"It's *freezing* where I am," I said.

"That's 'cause you're lying out in the snow."

"I want to get up!" I said, and lifted my head. "You can either help me or—*ouch!*"

I squirmed. As far as exclamations went, "ouch" was subdued compared to how my leg had screamed out when I tried to move it.

"Dudette, jeez, I warned you . . ."

"I'm okay," I insisted. "C'mon. Give me a hand."

Bryan frowned with reluctance, but finally nodded. As he eased me to a sitting position, I felt something hard press against my back, glanced around, and realized it was my Caliber's rear bumper. It came to me that I'd been loading stuff into its hatch when I saw something move in the dark.

"Bry," I said, "how'd you know where I was?"

"You told me when you called," he said. "Don't you remember?"

I shook my head no, and almost *ouched* aloud again. It was throbbing like crazy and felt about the size of a beach ball. I guessed I'd conked it on my way to hitting the blacktop.

"I called you?" I asked

"Yeah. Well, sorta," Bryan said. "You dialed the main switchboard number and I heard it ring. And answered since nobody else was around."

All that was a blank.

"I must have thought I called Mike's office," I said.

"You must've," he said. "And that I was Mike."

I sat and looked at him. Sirens were warbling in the distance.

"What did I tell you?"

"Nothing, y'know, *juicy*. So you don't have to be embarrassed about being confused . . ."

"Bry, please. I'm really at a total loss. And I want to see if I can piece things together—"

"Got you. Sorry," Bryan said. "What you told me was

just that you were here and needed help. You were kind of mumbling, and then I lost you. I'm like, 'Sky, can you hear me now?' But you were gone. Which is why I busted it to get here." He cocked a thumb back over his shoulder at a beater Impala behind him. "I drove by the parking lot, saw you flat in the snow, and pulled into that spot. With it practically being a blizzard out, I would've missed you in the dark if your hatch wasn't open—that kept the suvvie's inside lights on."

I quietly let that sink in and then squeezed Bryan's wrist.

"Bry," I said, "thank you."

He made a shy face.

"Hey, it's no big deal—"

"Yes, it is," I said. "You're a good friend."

He smiled a little, and I managed to smile back. The sirens were getting closer.

"My leg hurts something awful," I said. It was pulsing against the denim of my jeans.

"Think it's broken?"

I decided to test it before I answered him, turning from side to side, and then bending it up at the knee before stretching it out in front of me again.

"No," I said. "I'm guessing it's bruised. Or maybe I just hope that's all it is. It felt like something hit me right under my knee."

Bryan knelt in front of me. The sirens had reached the street outside the lot, and I could see red lights strobing across his features.

"Ambulance is almost here," he said. "Or maybe it's the police. I called 'em the second I found you."

I nodded and moistened my lips with my tongue.

"You've got snow in your hair," he said. "Kind of looks like frosting on a cake."

"That must be why my head's so cold."

"You think?"

I nodded again, and Bryan reached out and gently brushed off the top of my head. A spill of talcy white powder dusted my shoulders.

Then I saw headlamps swing into the parking lot—or

more properly saw three sets of them, one behind the other. Light splashed the snow from the bars atop the vehicles' roofs, and their sirens were deafeningly shrill.

I glanced in their direction, shielding my eyes from the glare with my hand.

A patrol car led the way, followed hotly by the EMS wagon. A second cruiser brought up the rear.

They stopped nearby, their doors flying wide open. I saw Chief Vega get out of the lead car and make his way toward me ahead of his officers, the whole group of them carrying flashlights. Meanwhile, a pair of EMTs hurried around to the back of their wagon. I was pretty sure they were the same guys that had arrived when Carol and I discovered Kyle Fipps's body.

"Sky!" Vega knelt beside me. "What happened?"

That was, of course, the exact question I'd asked Bryan when I thought he was Mike.

I told Vega I didn't know, except for being fairly sure something had slammed my leg. In the ensuing fuss, I probably repeated that four or five times to him and the rest of the cops gathered around me.

I do admit to noticing that the chief's concern seemed more than strictly professional.

"You hanging in there all right?" he said.

"I'm fine." I watched the emergency techs come over with their gurney and motioned toward it with my chin. "I don't really think I'll need that thing—"

"We can't drive you to the hospital in our rig unless you're on it," said one of the EMTs. He was the guy who'd told me he was a paramedic at the Art Association. "It's the rule."

"Insurance reasons say you need to be horizontal," said his partner. "Besides, you might have some broken bones in that leg. Better you're stable and they don't slip out of place."

I looked at him.

"The leg doesn't feel that bad," I said. "I'm not even sure I need to go to the hospital."

"I'd suggest you do it anyway," Vega said. "There's no harm being on the safe side."

"If I were you, I'd take his advice and not refuse transport," said the first EMT. He looked at me. "Hey, don't I know you?"

"Sure, we know her," said the second medical tech before I could answer. "She's the one whose friend was singing lullabies to that likely DOA who turned out to be a definite DOA a week or two back."

I frowned.

"It was a wake-up ditty," I said. "We thought he was asleep."

"Well, there you go. I stand corrected," the tech said. He turned to Vega. "You don't mind, Chief, we need you to move out of the way so I can collapse the gurney and transfer the patient onto it."

My frown deepened. I didn't want to be transferred.

"I can get up on that thing," I said, and gave Vega a glance that was either pleading or insistent, I'm not about to tell. "I just need some help. Please."

Vega returned the look, holding it for a long moment. Then he slipped his hands under my arms.

"You have any problems, let me know, okay?"

I nodded, and he slowly assisted me to my feet.

"Sky," he said quietly as I leaned my weight against him. "Who do you think could have done this?"

"I don't know," I said.

"Nobody who might've had a reason?"

"I wish I could think of someone," I said. "But I really can't."

Vega stood in the snow and looked at me, holding me steadily under my arms as our gazes once again remained in lingering contact.

"Okay," he said. "We'll talk about it later. I'd just like you to get checked out by a doctor."

I nodded again, not moving or taking my eyes from his.

He was very warm, and his hands were very firm and strong.

I was suddenly short of breath. And I realized it wasn't because of any pain I was feeling, not right then, standing there against him in the snow.

"I need to call Chloe," I said. "And my mother . . . she's staying at the Fog Bell."

"Leave that to me," Vega said. "I'll handle everything."

"I feel so awful worrying them. Especially my mom . . . this is supposed to be her *vacation*."

"I promise to reassure them you're all right."

Vega's eyes still hadn't left mine. I didn't want them to. I wanted—

"We'd better get going," he said in a low voice.

"We'd better," I said.

I took a tentative step toward the gurney, and then another, leaning against him to shift some of my weight off my hurt leg.

"Patient's capable of self-locomotion," one of the EMTs said as I sat down.

"You want me to put that or 'ambulatory' in our report?" said the other.

"Stick to 'ambulatory'—it covers everything," said the first.

They nodded in mutual agreement, and the next thing I knew were wheeling me toward the back of the wagon.

I searched for Bryan as I was lifted inside and saw him standing off by himself, looking solitary and displaced behind the small group of town cops who'd responded to his call.

"Bry," I said in the loudest voice I could muster. "Hey, Bry!"

"Back here!" he shouted, waving his hand in the air.

I held up my own hand, waved back at him, and then was put aboard the wagon, one of the EMTs staying alongside me as its rear hatch slammed shut.

When we reached the hospital about fifteen minutes later, I was rolled into the emergency room, X-rayed, and then examined behind a curtain by a woman intern named Diaz. She was very nice. Of course, you need to bear in mind that Addison Gilbert was the same hospital where Dr. Darpan Maji, the county coroner, had examined the body of Kyle Fipps. The mere fact that I was getting looked over by Dr. Diaz instead of Maji might have influenced the positive impression I got of her, considering that he reserved his attention for sign-ins who happened to be deceased.

Happily I was alive and well. The X-ray images came out negative. Nothing was broken. I had a bone bruise in my leg, a nasty bump on my noggin, and some minor scrapes and scratches. Dr. Diaz gave me some Tylenol with codeine, scribbled out a one-time renewable prescription for a week's worth of the painkiller, and then told me to go home and get some sleep. The leg might swell overnight, she said. It was possible I'd have headaches for the next day or so. But she was confident I wouldn't be on one of Maji's slabs anytime soon—barring someone clobbering me on a more high-risk part of my body than my leg, she hastened to mention.

I was sitting on the cot in my gown, waiting for a nurse to bring my release form, when I heard laughter on the other side of the curtain.

Even if I hadn't recognized the laughs as coming from people I knew—that's right, people, as in there being more than a single laugher—I would have known they weren't of the jovial variety.

These were loud, high-strung, tension-releasing laughs.

Or to put it another way, Maha Deependra yogic laughs.

I could tell on impact with my eardrums that one of the cuckoo outbursts was coming from my mother.

The source of the other was a surprise . . . though maybe it shouldn't have been. Betty-Mom can be a dangerously subversive influence.

"Chloe? Mom?" I said. "That you?"

The curtain parted slightly as they swept through into my little examining area.

"You poor dear—this is horrifying!" Betty-Mom said, and gave me a big but delicate hug.

"Terrible," Chloe said, coming over next to kiss my cheek. "I don't understand why anybody would want to pipe you."

"How could anybody pipe *anybody*, Chloe?" Betty-Mom said. "It's sick and violent!"

The two of them stood on either side of me, looking across at each other.

"Hahaha ha-ha! Hahaha ha-ha! Hahaha ha-ha!" blurted Betty-Mom, sounding like Woody Woodpecker in those old Walter Lantz cartoons.

"Hoo-hoo, hoo-hoo, hoo-hoo, hoohoohoohoo!" Chloe let out. Her laugh was more Looney Tunes . . . kind of like Daffy Duck getting tickled.

Meanwhile, I was trying to figure out what they'd been talking about. And wondering when somebody on the hospital staff would arrive to throw them out of the ER.

"Pipe me? What do you mean, *pipe* me?"

"I mean pipe you the way that poor figure skater Nancy Kerrigan was piped," Chloe said, abruptly cutting short her laughter. "You remember—they told her whole story on Court TV. That other skater, Tonya Something-or-other, was competing with Nancy for a championship, and her boyfriend hired another man to hit her across the knee after a practice session."

"With a pipe," Betty-Mom expanded.

As if I hadn't already figured out that part.

I looked at them. "I still don't get it. How do you know all this?"

Betty-Mom sighed.

"Chief Vega told us it was a Gloucester fisherman," she said. "He was stopped for drunk driving by the same officers who came to help you at City Hall. After the ambulance drove off, I think they saw him weaving in the storm on Route 128. When they pulled him over, they saw a pipe sticking out from under his backseat, and got suspicious that he might have been the man who attacked you."

"From what we know, he confessed on the spot," Chloe said. "I'm told he felt very remorseful about it."

"So ashamed he was crying and begging for forgiveness," Betty-Mom said.

"A guilty conscience can be your worst jailer," Chloe said.

I ignored that obvious excerpt from her book of sentence sermons and sat there with an incredulous expression on my face.

"This is crazy!" I said. "Why would anyone single me out?"

"That's what the police wanted to know," Chloe said. "At first the man claimed he was so drunk he didn't know what he was doing. But they didn't believe him, and questioned him at the station. And I suppose he finally broke down and told them it was because of the Map Flap."

My eyebrows shot up higher.

"How's that have anything to do with *me*?"

Chloe looked at me.

"It seems to be a case of mistaken identity," she said. "I trust you're familiar with the term?"

I gave her an impatient glance. "Chloe, I may not be your match when it comes to knowing crime stories. But that isn't exactly some kind of obscure police lingo—"

"Don't get tense, it will make you feel worse," Chloe said. "What happened is the man says he ran into someone at a bar who was complaining about the tourist map situation, and that it made him angry."

"Alcohol can do that to people when they overdo things," Betty-Mom said. "This is why Lou and I always stuck to smoking grass in our day. With no more than a glass or two of mild sangria."

Chloe gave her a long look but didn't say anything. It made me remember why I'd spent my childhood in a state of perpetual embarrassment.

"I'm still not sure I'm following all this," I said, clearing my throat. "Are you saying the man thought I was involved in leaving Gloucester off the map?"

Chloe nodded. "He mistook you for one of the women on the Pigeon Cove brochure committee, and thought you were going home for the night."

Which would have made me scratch my head if the bump on it hadn't hurt so much. The Chamber of Commerce was a small building across town from City Hall. It seemed like a huge stretch to believe someone might get them mixed up. Stewed to the gills or not, a local guy would know the difference between the two. Especially a local guy who'd gotten riled enough about the map fiasco to run out in the middle of a snowstorm and whack someone in the leg over it. Or so it seemed to me.

"I don't know," I said. "This is too weird. I just have a feeling there's more to all of this than—"

"Hi, sorry to interrupt!" Dr. Diaz poked her head through the curtain, and then slid it open. "We almost have you ready to go."

I noticed she was carrying a pair of adjustable aluminum crutches—the sort that have padded cuffs that rest under the forearms.

"I don't think I need those things," I said. "I can walk all right on my own."

"I'm sure that's true," she said, sounding totally unconvinced. "But we can lend them to you free of charge as an outpatient service, and it isn't often you'll hear those words about anything having to do with health care." She smiled. "You might as well take advantage. With all the snow and ice outside, they might come in handy for the next few days . . . even if you only decide to use a single crutch."

I disliked the idea of using crutches. Or even *a* crutch. This is because I really disliked looking or feeling remotely helpless. I'd gotten used to taking care of myself. I'd had no choice in it after Paul died, but had been that way even before.

I didn't like it, but I accepted the crutches anyway, and listened to Dr. Diaz give me some tips for using them.

The rest was routine. Betty-Mom and I went to the checkout desk and took care of some paperwork. Meanwhile, Chloe got her Beetle from the visitors' lot and pulled it in front of the main entrance. When I left the hospital the snow was still walloping down, and I reluctantly decided to go with Dr. Diaz's single-crutch compromise walking toward the curb. We'd planned on stopping at City Hall so we could pick up my Caliber, but decided against it—the storm was too intense for us to make any stops.

It was a taxing, snailish drive to the Fog Bell. Snow had blanketed the road ahead of us, with thick puffs of it exploding against our windshield. When we finally crept up to the inn around midnight, Chloe offered to brew some tea, and a relieved-sounding Oscar even hollered from his studio that he'd join us in a minute.

I thanked them, but wanted to head straight upstairs. Although my leg was barking, I was anxious to turn on my computer, and almost unbelievably wasn't even thinking about being assaulted by a crazed, tourist map–obsessed fisherman armed with a pipe. The one and only thing on my mind was that I had an e-mail to write.

"Sky! I'm so glad you're home!"

This was from Sandy as I walked in my door. I'd halfway expected her to be out somewhere. Maybe dancing naked in the storm like a preternaturally well-endowed snow elf.

She hadn't gone out that night, though. Nor, for a change, was she walking around the place unclothed. Granted, her lacy white robe flowed delicately over a nightgown with a hundred-fathom curve for a bustline. But it was refreshing to see her more or less covered up.

"I heard what happened," she said. "Don't worry, I fed Skiball dinner and tucked her into her little kitty-crib. So just go ahead and and relax while I run a bath for you."

"A bath?" I said.

"With Moroccan rose otto," she said. "It's steam distilled."

"It is?" I said.

Sandy nodded.

"From petals harvested at dawn in the Valley of Roses," she said.

I stood in the entrance looking at her. *Shades of Betty-Mom*, I thought.

And then I found myself thinking something else as well. Since the afternoon I'd met Sandy at the *Anchor*, my default reaction to encountering her had been irritation of the extreme variety. Yet it was hard not to see her gesture as anything but very sweet . . . putting aside any consideration that being piped, clunked in the head, and sent to the emergency room might have temporarily disabled my instincts for self-preservation.

"The captured dawn light's good for you," she went on. "It helps with everything from muscle aches to sensuality—and you can take my word for it. Dancing around a pole every night means I've got to avoid one and nurture the other."

I looked at her. Sure, the part about the light sounded iffy at best. But I couldn't deny that the rest of what she'd told me had a weird ring of authority.

Still . . .

"Sandy," I said, "I really want to sit down at my computer—"

"Go ahead. It'll take me a little while to get things ready," she said, and then carefully relieved me of my crutches, helping me out of my coat before I could insist on doing it on my lonesome.

A minute later she swooshed off toward the bathroom, stopping briefly to hang the coat in the closet.

I went into my bedroom, took a peek inside Skiball's wicker carrying case and preferred sleeping quarters. Just as Sandy had said, she was curled up in back, sound asleep.

Sitting down in front of my computer, I turned it on, and waited as it booted up.

Before typing even a single word of my e-mail to Jessie Barton, I knew exactly what I was going to write.

Chapter 17

The snow stopped falling sometime near dawn. It left a ten-inch accumulation on the ground, with windblown drifts topping out almost as high as the enormous black-and-blue welt on my leg.

By eight o'clock that morning I'd tuned to WBZ-AM's traffic and weather reports, which said the Newburyport/Pigeon Cove rail line was expected to be entirely cleared of snow before midday . . . and that train service had already resumed with intermittent delays.

An hour earlier, at seven, right around when I'd gotten out of bed to check my e-mail for the first time, Mike had found out about the Mad Piper of Cape Ann from the police blotter, worriedly called to see how I was doing, and volunteered to drive my Caliber over from the City Hall parking lot after I'd reassured him I was okay.

He reached the inn at nine, after my fourth and final e-mail check, and joined Chloe, me, and—rarity of rarities—Oscar downstairs for coffee and muffins. Sandy and Betty-Mom had slept in, taking care of me the night before having apparently tuckered them out.

"I need to head over to the office and catch up on this and that," Mike said a half hour or so later. "But I don't have much to do there today, and can be back at noon to help you out with things."

I appreciated the offer. I also didn't want him returning.

"I'll be okay," I said. "I've got Chloe and Oscar if

I need anything. And Sandy, once she rises from her daytime slumber."

Mike had looked at me over his coffee.

"You sure?" he said.

"I'm covered, Mike," I said. "Those painkillers the doctor gave me will probably knock me right out."

I'd sounded very convincing. That was because I was telling the truth. The pills would have put me in a drowsy fog.

Except that I had no intention of taking them.

Mike headed off a little while afterward, phoning for a car service to bring him back to his place so he could drive his Mini Cooper over to work. By then Oscar had already lurched out of sight to start tooting his clarinet, and Chloe was on the phone to someone she'd enlisted in her annual Christmas toy and clothing drive.

After Mike left, I'd gone upstairs, done my usual tippie-toe past a dead-to-the-world Sandy, shared some quality playtime with Ski in my bedroom, and then searched online for the street directions I would need.

I had driven past the Back Bay Hilton in Boston a time or two, so I knew approximately where it was. But I didn't want to attempt driving a long distance that day, not with my bum right leg being stiff as a board. Having to step on the gas and brakes on the highway would be too uncomfortable, not to mention dangerous.

From the Internet trip map, it looked as if the safest and most convenient way to get to the hotel was to take the railroad to North Station and cab it from there.

I left the Fog Bell at eleven o'clock, drove to the nearby station, and waited in my Caliber with the heater blasting. At a quarter to twelve I got out and single-crutched it to the platform.

The southbound train arrived right on schedule at noon and had me at North Station a little over an hour later. Flagging down a taxi upstairs was no problem, and the ride to Belvedere Street added maybe another fifteen minutes to my trip.

I got out, negotiated a snowbank with the cabbie's assistance, and limped across the sidewalk to the Back Bay

Hilton. As I passed under the blue awning above the entrance, it struck me that the large, twentysomething-floor hotel was probably within a stone's throw of Sandy Savoy's condo tower. Considering who I'd come to meet at the Rendezvous Lounge and Café in its lobby, the irony couldn't have been any sharper.

Jessie Barton had beaten me to the punch and was already at a table having a coffee. She'd always been one for dramatic accents to her appearance, but looked more subdued than I'd gotten used to seeing her. The reddish highlights in her hair were toned down, her skirt suit was smart but conservative, and she'd stuck to the basics with her makeup. I thought she looked good, though. Insecure under all her feminine bravado, Jessie had always seemed unaware of how naturally pretty she was. I'd always felt her features would have been less contour perfect, but maybe more attractive, before her repeat visits to the cosmetic surgeon.

I watched her for a minute, then started over to the table. I was midway across the lobby when she saw me, our eyes making contact.

I smiled instantly. I couldn't help it. She looked nervous, and probably couldn't have helped that. When she saw my crutch, she started rising off her chair to give me a hand. But I waved her back into it.

I sat down opposite her, propping my crutch against an empty seat at our table.

"Sky, I feel so awful," she said.

"Thanks, Jess. I missed you too," I said.

She smiled wanly. "I meant about your leg. And you being assaulted. I could hardly believe my eyes when I read your e-mail."

I shrugged.

"It's just a bang," I said. "How's the coffee?"

"Okay, I guess. Nothing like Bill Drecksel's."

I knew there was no implied sarcasm in the remark. Jessie had always been the one person in town who actually enjoyed drinking Bill's tepid-dishwater brew.

I gave the menu a perfunctory glance and put it down. When the waitress came, I ordered a cup of the house blend and a chocolate chip cookie. I wasn't really hungry, but hot coffee was always a go with me.

We were quiet. Jessie still seemed uneasy.

"So," she said. "Here we are."

I nodded. "We are definitely here."

Jessie drank some coffee, lowered her cup, and sat staring into it for a bit

"I owe you an apology, Sky," she said then.

"You didn't do anything wrong."

"Or right." She shook her head. "We're friends. I should've let you know when I was planning to leave town."

"I won't argue it," I said. "Why didn't you?"

"I couldn't work up the nerve. I felt that you'd want to know my reasons. And that I'd either have to lie about them or come clean about certain things I wanted kept secret."

"Like your affair with Tommy Thompson."

Jessie looked at me.

"In the old days, I'd have insisted on some gossipy quid pro quo. I don't confirm or deny that bit of information until you say where you got it."

"It's a long story, Jess."

She gave me a small, wistful smile. "Isn't everything?"

She had me there.

We were silent as my order arrived. The cookie was big and the chocolate chips gooey. I took a bite, sipped my coffee. The flavors mixed tastily in my mouth.

"Did you know Tommy was having relationships with other women?" I asked.

"Not all along, if that's what you mean. But at the same time, it never would have shocked me. And even when I began to suspect it, I wasn't jealous. That came later."

"You fell in love with him?"

"No," Jessie said, and paused. "He was fun. He took me out to wonderful places, showed me a good time. And he was, you know, attentive. Physically. Does it sound terrible of me to say that's all I wanted from him?"

I looked at her.

"If you'd asked my opinion, I would have told you I was opposed to seeing a married man. As for the rest, Jess, you're a big girl. It's for you to decide what makes you happy. I'm just wondering when the jealousy became enough of an issue to drive you away from Pigeon Cove."

Jessie smiled humorlessly again.

"There'd been signs that he was involved with other women for a while. The mysterious calls on his cell phone that he wouldn't answer. The business trips, so to speak," she said. "He'd always told his wife our little three- and four-day vacations were business trips, and I wasn't so naive I didn't think I was getting fed the same crock. But I was staking no claims, Sky. And I have to be honest. It wasn't until I knew I was being edged to the sidelines that it bothered me."

"How'd you come to feel that way?"

"Edged out?"

I nodded

"A pair of gorgeous double-drop diamonds-in-platinum earrings showed me the light," Jessie said. "He actually left them in his coat pocket one night that he stayed over at my place. In their blue Tiffany's box, with a romantic little card written out to 'Sandy.' I'm not ashamed to admit I called the store and got a price quote. Care to guess at it?"

"Jewelry's never been especially my thing," I said. "If I had to take a stab, I'd say four, five thousand dollars."

Jessie was shaking her head.

"How about making it ten thousand," Jessie said. "And then some."

I blinked.

"Yeeow," I said.

"My thoughts exactly," Jessie said. "Tommy wasn't a cheapskate. But he'd never spent like that on me, either. And I resented . . . no . . . I *hated* knowing he would do it for someone else." She shrugged. "I suppose that puts me in the unflattering role of the woman scorned, Sky. It was that basic."

I broke a piece off my chocolate chip cookie, put it in my mouth, and thought for a while. Thinking's always best undertaken while one enjoys a mouthful of cookie. "Tommy's pretty well-heeled, but his pockets aren't bottomless. Didn't you wonder how he got the financial wherewithal for spreading the wealth?"

"Why would I need to wonder?" Jessie said. "I knew he'd been involved with Getaway Groves."

"From Bill Drecksel?"

"Yes, Bill told me Tommy set up the escrow account for its construction expenses. This was when the Fippses filed for divorce. Bill guessed Tommy helped Kyle shift some of his personal savings into the fund . . . and that he was juggling paperwork so Lina wouldn't find out how much was being stashed away."

"Sounds underhanded," I said. "Maybe borderline illegal, though it'd be complicated to prove if the accounting was done right."

"And that might have just been the tip of the iceberg. A little birdie told me Tommy accepted payoffs from Kyle in exchange for giving the rubber stamp to Getaway Groves building permits."

My eyes widened.

"Now we're crossing the border into no-doubter criminality," I said. "Care to say if your birdie bears any resemblance to Bill?"

Jessie paused, suddenly looking defensive.

"I won't go there with you, Sky. But I want to be clear that he wasn't part of it. If he conveniently looked away, it was because he was so eager to get the condos built. They're his dream."

I wasn't sure I was convinced of Bill's total obliviousness. You had to admire her loyalty to him, though.

"Jess," I said, "did you know construction on the Groves slowed to a halt before you left town?"

She looked at me. "You realize I know where you're heading with this, Sky."

I nodded. "Across the border into the deep, dark woods," I said.

Jessie was silent, staring down into her coffee cup

again. After a long moment, she brought her eyes up to mine.

"I know when things add up," she said. "Of course I was aware of the slowdown. Bill complained that the builders weren't getting paid, and said Kyle was furious, and intended to ask Tommy point-blank why the checks weren't cut. Not coincidentally, that's around the time I found a ten-thousand-dollar gift for a woman named Sandy in Tommy's pocket." She turned her cup between her fingertips. "What was I supposed to think except that he was siphoning money from the escrow fund?"

"Do you know if Kyle ever confronted him about it?" Jessie shook her head.

"No, I don't," she said, and then gave me a meaningful glance. "But it so happened that Tommy's pocket planner—he uses very stylish leather ones made in England—slipped out of his sport jacket one night when we were together. It also happened that I found it after he left, and accidentally opened it to a date when he was supposed to be going on one of his business jaunts. And I saw he'd marked out a weeklong cruise for two to St. Croix."

"A cruise that didn't include you," I said.

She nodded.

"I lost it, Sky. I really did. And then *I* confronted him," she said. "I wanted to do it to his face but couldn't make myself wait. So I called his cell and hit him with every dirty deed I knew about or suspected. The shady political favors, the embezzling, his cheating with other women . . . everything."

"And what did he say?"

"Not much at first. I could tell it was because he wasn't alone . . . you know how people's voices can sound different over the phone? I mean, when someone's around and they don't want to be overheard."

I nodded.

"Well, I was sure he was with his wonderful, costly Sandy," Jessie said. "That only made me spin further out of control. I told him I was thinking about going public, letting the press and the cops decide whether there was evidence to support my claims. And I must've pushed his buttons, because then it was *his* turn to lose it. Tommy threatened me, warned me to shut up or else. He said that if I opened my mouth something terrible would happen to me, and that he'd make sure nobody ever connected him to it."

"Was he specific about what he intended to do?"

"He didn't have to be. Tommy has a way about him sometimes. It's hard to explain. But I knew he was serious."

"And that was when you told him you had the key," I said.

Jessie and I held each other's looks.

"You've been talking to whoever was with Tommy when I called," she said.

"What happened to you not wanting an equal trade?"

"I want to know about *her*," she said, pulling rigidly erect in her chair. Her gaze had sharpened. "Why he chose her over me."

I was quiet. I'd eaten the last of my cookie and was wishing I had another chunk to break off. It would have given me something to do besides sit there looking back at her.

"I can't tell you," I said.

"Can't or won't?"

I shrugged but said nothing.

Jessie stared at me for another long moment, then produced a long sigh, her posture relaxing.

"When he threatened me, I told him about the key I'd 'found' tucked into a flap in his planner. It was an impulsive thing. I didn't know what it opened. But it was a Medeco key, the kind you can't copy without having an authorization card. And I had a hunch it was important."

"How'd Tommy react?"

"He was furious. But I think it was more because I'd had the audacity to take the key from his planner than out of concern that I might somehow use it against him. He had a duplicate. And I didn't know what it opened. And he knew it." Jessie shrugged. "He *still* knows it. I don't think he's ever been afraid of me or anything I might do to him."

I decided to back up for a second.

"Jess, tell me something," I said. "I still don't know where you were these last three or four months. All this time . . . sending me e-mails, and e-cards . . . have you been in the area?"

She shook her head.

"When I first left town, I went to stay in California . . . a tiny vacation bungalow in Venice that one of my ex-husbands' family members use as a time-share. I figured I'd lick my wounds, maybe come back to the Cove after a while. But though my feelings didn't hurt any less after a couple of months, I had to vacate it for another relative. So I came back to this area and rented a place outside the city."

"Why didn't you let any of us know? Me . . . Bill . . . *somebody*?"

Jessie hesitated, cleared her throat. "I felt too humiliated, Sky. And too scared of Tommy. That's the best explanation I can give you."

We sat for a while, an island of silence amid the bustle of the café and lobby. I wasn't sure how to react to what I'd heard. Yes, I was sympathetic to Jessie. But I was also angry with her for keeping Thompson's secrets. I didn't know how she could live with herself knowing he'd probably stolen a small fortune from Bill and likely ruined his dream of building Getaway Groves.

Then, for what must have been the hundredth time since I found it, I pictured the secret panel I'd stumbled upon in Thompson's office.

"Jessie," I said, "when I sent you my e-mail last night, I didn't know when you'd answer, or if or when you'd be able to meet—"

"Hearing about what happened to you, how could I not do it right away? Especially being this close, Sky. No matter what you might think of me, I'll always consider you my friend."

"It means a lot to hear it, Jess. We'll always *be* friends." I paused. "I'm glad to see you. And grateful you came. But I still need what I told you I needed in the e-mail. It can't wait."

Another silence. It lasted almost a full minute. I could see the conflicting emotions play across Jessie's face as she considered my words.

And then, finally, she reached into her purse, pulled out a key ring with a single key attached, and dropped it in my hand.

"Thank you, Jessie," I said, closing my fingers around it. "I think I understand what it took for you to do that."

She gave me a slow, slow nod.

"Go get him," she said.

Chapter 18

I was on the commuter train back to Pigeon Cove when I remembered to check my cell phone messages. I'd turned the ringer off during my rendezvous with Jessie at the Rendezvous, but had felt it vibrate on its belt clip several times while we were talking.

There were four voice mails. The first was from Betty-Mom—she and Chloe had read the note I'd left for them and wanted to be sure I didn't push too hard at the office. Mike called next to touch base.

The other two messages were from Chief Vega. The first was a considerate *hello, hope-you're-feeling-better.* The second caught me off guard.

Sky, please give me a buzz, the message said. *The man who attacked you has been talking. We should discuss it.*

The time stamp logged the message at three p.m. Less than an hour ago. I pressed the CALLBACK button, reminding myself to un-scrunch my forehead. Scrunching was a bad habit of mine. The harder I thought, the more my brow creased up. And all the thinking I'd done over the past week or so amounted to an open invitation for wrinkles.

Vega answered his phone.

"Hi, Chief," I said.

"Sky, I was just about to try you at the newspaper. I buzzed Chloe a little while ago and she said you were there."

Lucky I called first, I thought.

"Sorry I didn't get back to you sooner," I said. "I just listened to my VMs."

"No problem," Vega said. "But I need you to come down to the station as soon as possible. My message pretty much gave the reason."

"The guy you picked up last night . . . what's he said besides what he already told you?"

"That's just it." Vega paused. "This is more about what he *wants* to say. And not to the police."

I let that register a moment.

"He wants to talk to *me*?"

"Right," Vega said. "His name's Dave Gillis, incidentally. We checked him out and he's what he claims to be. A down-on-his-luck fisherman, wife and kids, rents an apartment in Gloucester. He's been in minor trouble for a few alcohol-related misdemeanors. Disorderly conduct, reckless driving, and so forth. But he's got no prior criminal record, no history of violence, nothing that would predispose him to physically go at a total stranger—"

"Chief Vega," I said, "I appreciate you telling me all this. But what words do I really need to hear from him that can't wait?"

"You don't owe him a second of your time, if that's your point. Bear with me on this, though," Vega said. "Gillis has been having pangs of regret since we picked him up. And now that he's sober, he seems completely distraught over what he did."

"Maybe he should've done me a favor and huddled with his conscience before doing it," I said. "Besides, he can be repentant in front of a judge if he wants."

"I won't argue with you there. The thing is, I have my doubts about parts of his story."

Do not pucker the brow, I admonished myself. "You mean his confusing City Hall with the Chamber?"

"And getting you mixed up with another woman," Vega said. "Seems you've been thinking along the same lines I have."

"Some," I said. "Believe it or not, my mind's been elsewhere today."

Vega kind of grunted, but didn't comment on that.

"Listen, Sky," he said after a second, "we'd have already brought Gillis to the county jail out in Middleton if not for last night's snowstorm. But it's taken the plows a while to clear all the local roads, and it seemed reasonable to keep him here in a holding cell an extra day. With him wanting to apologize to you directly now, I figured it's a perfect chance to see if he opens up about anything besides what he's admitted to."

"Wouldn't a lawyer advise him against it?"

"Against even talking to you at all, sure," Vega said. "But he's waived his right to legal counsel." He paused again. "I'd really like to use this opening to our advantage. And I thought you might feel the same."

I considered that for a few moments, examining exactly how I did feel. Then I made my decision.

"I've got some work that needs wrapping up," I said, and calculated roughly how long it would take me to reach the Cove. The train, I noted, had just chugged out of Salem, which wasn't quite halfway up the line. "Can you give me about an hour?"

"That sounds fine," Vega said. "Want me to send a patrol car over to the *Anchor*?"

Not unless you plan on it picking up somebody besides me, I thought.

"No, thanks. I can drive."

"I meant so a couple of my men could accompany you from your office. In case you need a hand with anything, or have trouble getting around."

"That's okay, really," I said. "My leg hasn't been a major problem."

"All right, then," Vega said. "See you in a while."

I got off the phone with him, then called Chloe to let her know I'd be stopping at the police station on my way home. "I'll tell Betty you'll be late," she said. "Did you accomplish very much today?"

"Not in the writing department," I said. "But I did get hold of the material I wanted."

Which wasn't a lie.

The train chugged into the Pigeon Cove station forty

minutes later. Maybe it was the deepening late-afternoon cold, but my leg was aching despite my assertions to the contrary, and I found myself grateful to have a crutch to lean on as I limped from the platform to the Caliber. Inside the SUV, I sat for a minute warming up and letting the pain subside . . . or maybe wishing it would. Then I drove on over to the station.

Vega met me at the front desk a minute or two after the dispatcher buzzed him to say I'd arrived.

"Sky, hello," he said. "You look a whole lot better than you did last night."

"Quit with the flattery," I said. "Didn't I already promise I'd cooperate?"

He seemed nonplussed. "No, I mean it. You do—"

I smiled to let him know I was joshing.

"I'd sincerely hope I look better," I said, trying not to let on that my leg wasn't feeling all that great. "When you saw me I was being hauled off to the emergency room in an ambulance."

Vega smiled too now.

"An EMS vehicle," he said. "Those guys who drove you off are touchy about being called ambulance drivers, remember?"

I thought back to the night of the Art Association party.

"Yeah," I said, "I do."

Vega looked at me. "Would you like something to drink? There's coffee, soda, water . . ."

"I'm fine, Chief," I said. "I'd just like to get this out of the way."

He nodded, motioned toward the entry through which he'd appeared. "Gillis is back in the interrogation room," he said. "We'll make this as brief as possible."

At a glance, the interrogation room, in true Pigeon Cove style, almost could have been a small conference room in an ordinary corporate setting. Spare but clean and well lit by overhead fluorescents, it had a tan wooden table with some chairs around it, a couple of poinsettias atop a file cabinet, and a watercooler in the corner. Of course, the pistol-toting officer who stood outside in the corridor, giving Vega a nod as we passed him, wouldn't have been the norm in corporate America. And on closer look, I couldn't help noticing the video camera mounted above the door and the metal grate over the windows.

Inside, Dave Gillis sat with his back to the door, his hands linked together and resting on the table. A big, rangy guy of about thirty, he wore jeans and a flannel shirt and had long brown hair pulled into a ponytail that fell straight below his shoulder blades. Though he'd barely moved his head when we came in, I felt him watching my progress as Vega showed me around to a chair opposite him. Then, as I sat, and the chief took my crutch and leaned it against the wall, I thought I saw his eyes snap over to it for a split second before they quickly returned to looking at me . . . and then just as quickly dropped down to study his hands again

"All right, Dave," Vega said. "You wanted to apologize—here's your chance."

The room was quiet. Gillis examined his knitted fingers. I could see the muscles of his jaw bunching together.

"Dave," Vega said, "we aren't going to wait all nigh—"

"I didn't know you were so small," Gillis said. It seemed an effort as he brought his eyes up from his hands to my face. "I couldn't see too good in the dark."

I found myself staring angrily at him.

"You saw well enough to come at me," I said. "You didn't have any trouble connecting that pipe with my leg."

"I was all boozed up," Gillis said. "I—I guess I got you confused with somebody else . . ."

"Who? A *different* woman who's half your size?"

Gillis opened his mouth, closed it. Then he shook his head.

"I'm sorry about what I done," he said. "Damned sorry. It was that map thing. Gloucester bein' left off it, y'know. My wife's a maid at one'a the motels, makes her livin' on tips from summer people. And me and some of the guys . . . well, we had some drinks, and got to talking about how it was gonna hit our families in the pocket come summertime—"

"No," I said. "Stop."

Gillis looked at me.

"How long have you lived in this area?" I said.

"What do you mean?"

"It's a simple question," I said. "How long have you lived here on Cape Ann?"

Gillis kept looking at me.

"I'm gonna be thirty-three come March," he said. "My father and grandfather was born Gloucestermen, and so am I."

"And you want me to believe you couldn't tell the difference between the Pigeon Cove City Hall and the Chamber of Commerce? A three-story granite building versus a little saltbox on the Wing?"

Silence. Chief Vega stood nearby with his hands in his trouser pockets, his gaze fixed on the plants atop the file cabinets. Willis's jaw muscles worked some more.

"I wish I could take back what I done," he said. "It makes me feel low as a bug, and I'll take what's coming to me for it. But I don't know what else I can tell you."

"How about the truth?" I said, looking him straight in the eye. "You say you're sorry, and maybe I even sort of believe it, but that isn't enough. Because there's more to this than you're admitting. I want to know why you really attacked me."

Gillis swallowed.

"I made a mistake," he said hoarsely. "A damn mistake. Can't we leave it at that?"

"Not if you were put up to it," I said. "If that's how it is, something else is bound to happen to me. But I guess you couldn't care less."

I turned in my chair and struggled to my feet, wondering where all that had come from. Or maybe not so much wondering where as how it had suddenly pulled together for me. Because I knew it had been swirling around in the back of my mind for a while—maybe even since the night before, in the hospital.

I hadn't figured it all out, not yet, but I was thinking Tommy Thompson had to be involved.

"Sky, hang on." Vega reached for my crutch and started handing it to me. "Let me help you with this—"

"No, don't leave," Gillis said. "Please. Sit down . . . I mean the two 'a you. 'Cause this might take me a bit to put in words."

I stood with my hands braced on the table, looking from Vega to Gillis.

"Please," Gillis said. "Please stay."

I took a deep breath, nodded, and sat. Then Vega lowered himself into a chair beside me and we waited.

"I just wanted a little Christmas money," Gillis said after a minute. "Got it from somebody who had plenty."

"Give us a name," Vega said. It was the first thing he'd said to Gillis since we'd come into the room.

Gillis looked at him but said nothing.

"It's no good otherwise, Gillis," Vega insisted. "We need you to name him."

Gillis inhaled, exhaled. His hands were clenched so tightly in front of him that their knuckles had turned chalk white.

"Not him," he said at last. "Her."

I blinked with open surprise.

"Her?" I said.

Gillis nodded.

"Lina Fipps," he said.

Chapter 19

"It wasn't easy getting hold of these documents," Mike said, tapping the crammed manila file folder on his desk. "Everybody at the city clerk's office is in preholiday mode. They're trying to clear away the work in front of them, not dig around for something new to gum up their works."

"You mean they weren't ecstatic to see a reporter from the local weekly?" I said.

Mike smiled. "Let's just say nobody was offering me any eggnog."

Sandy Savoy make-believe shivered in her chair.

"Brrrrr," she said. "Michael, hon, I don't even want to imagine what they might have stirred into your glass if they had."

Sandy's remark made me wonder if customers at Silk N' Lace and the Sugar Shack were treated to a complimentary laxative cocktail when they got out of line.

I smiled and reached for my coffee. It was something like my tenth booster cup that day, which was noteworthy because I'd gone to bed early the night before. Between my trip to meet Jessie Barton and finding out about Lina, I'd been exhausted.

I hadn't slept a wink, though. Same reasons as above—they had not only made me tired but kicked my thoughts into hyperdrive. The upshot was that I spent most of the night wishing I'd get drowsy and hugging Skiball, who left Sandy's bedside to pay me an obligatory cat call.

Morning hadn't come too soon. I don't know about you, but nothing drives me crazier than a losing battle with insomnia. In my opinion it's better to get stuff done.

After breakfast, Chloe hustled off to run some errands and I wound up pitching in on the housework with Sandy and Betty-Mom, doing whatever light stuff my bum leg allowed. That helped take my mind off things, and made me so tuckered that I finally was able to nap for a couple of hours. Then, waking up to a late-afternoon phone call from Mike, I decided to do what I'd lied about having done the day before, which was head over to the *Anchor* and put in a few hours' work on my column.

It wasn't my only reason for going in. Not nearly. Just as it wasn't Sandy's reason for tagging along with me. Or maybe I should say giving me a lift, since we'd taken her Audi over from the inn. Her Royal Shapeliness, Queen of the Amazon, having deigned never to let a lowly Dodge serve as her palanquin.

Anyway, I'd told Mike on the phone that I had gotten in touch with Jessie, leaving out the fact that we actually met up in person . . . and that she'd given me a key that I had a strong hunch would fit the lock of a certain hidden floor panel in Tommy Thompson's office. I wasn't sure why I'd kept that a secret, and hadn't felt like examining my motives too closely. All I knew was that my tongue had stuck to the roof of my mouth right when I'd been about to divulge the information and I'd decided to hold it back from him.

I had, however, shared everything I'd been told about Tommy carte-blanching the construction of Getaway Groves. And that had prompted Mike to make a trip to City Hall, and led him to convene our little summit at the newspaper.

Now he flipped open the folder as I sat there and stretched my leg, wanting to prevent it from stiffening up on me.

"These permit applications originally passed through the Codes office before being filed by the clerk," he said.

"That was another thing I had to be careful about. I didn't want to push too hard and make anyone too curious about why I wanted the papers. It could be a problem if anyone in Codes finds out about my interest in them."

"And gives Thompson a heads-up that you asked for copies," I said.

Mike nodded.

"We don't know who might be in cahoots with him," he said. "Tell you the truth, the way scuttlebutt bounces around bureaucratic departments, I'm not sure it was even possible to avoid tripping alarms. Tommy's a popular guy, despite what the three of us think of him. And, who knows, it might turn out he hasn't done anything to violate the law or his oath of office."

"What about basic ethics? From what you told me, it looks like he rushed to approve every single permit request attached to the Groves project."

Mike gave me a shrug. "The documents I got from the clerk make it pretty apparent to me he wasn't a neutral examiner. If a zoning or environmental issue created a hitch in issuing an approval, the city council would put the problem to rest with a legislative act. In every instance, Thompson was its principal backer . . . he'd draft a new ordinance, push it through the voting process, then tag the ap for quick review by Codes. But fast-tracking an application doesn't automatically equal dishonesty or a conflict of interest. You can argue it's suspicious, sure. But it's hard to prove cronyism in a small town where everybody knows everybody else from the time they're schoolkids."

"And seems to be sleeping with everyone else's wife or husband," I said.

"No surprise to me there, Sky," Sandy said. "If you want to see daddy grow hair when the missus isn't around, come see what goes on once he walks into the VIP lounge at my club."

I looked at her.

"Grow hair?"

"Like that guy in those old movies who'd turn into the Wolfman when the full moon got in his face. You know . . . *aah-whoooo!*"

I was quiet for a second. Hey, nobody'd forced me to ask.

"So what's your next step?" I said, turning to Mike.

He spread his hands.

"More of the same," he said. "I'll need to review these papers again, see if anything jumps out that either proves Tommy's abused his authority or might lead to conclusive evidence. I also want to get hold of other related documents, since this is just a sampling of what was available. But it's going to take a while . . . Another visit to the clerk's office is out till after the first of the year. And I'll want to step lightly so there's at least a chance Tommy doesn't catch on."

I patted my leg. The spot where I'd been hit was swollen and tender under my jeans—stretching it only helped so much.

"Can't blame you, given what that fisherman did to me," I said. "Or maybe I should say what he claims Lina Fipps paid him to do."

Mike swiveled his chair around so he was directly facing me.

"I called Vega about that this morning," he said. "He was pretty open with his information."

"Did the police question Lina yet?"

"She's driving up from the Big Apple," Mike said. "In the company of a high-priced defense attorney."

I nodded. When Vega had gone to talk with Lina at her home the night before, her live-in housekeeper told him she'd left for New York to spend the holidays with her brother, Renault, the master choreographer.

"It gives me the willies," I said. "He assaulted me for, what, a couple of hundred dollars?"

"And might've crippled you if he'd been sober enough to land a clean blow . . . or drunk enough to slip up and hit you in the knee," Mike said. "From what Vega told me, Gillis's story that he did some handyman work for Lina last summer checks out. With the fishing industry being in bad shape, he's been picking up extra cash taking odd jobs around the Cove and hired on to weatherproof her deck or whatnot. I think it's plausible she'd turn to a hard-luck guy like him to do her dirty work . . . if he's telling the truth about the rest."

"You mean that she found out I was prying in her business, and wanted to scare me off her trail."

Mike nodded.

"I'm wondering what could push her to such lengths," he said. "She'd have to be a borderline mental case to have hired Gillis just because of your run-in at Grace Blossom's."

I shrugged. "You'd figure it would take more than that, but who knows?"

"Do you think someone ratted you out?" Sandy said.

"It's occurred to me," I said. "Again, though, I can't figure out who it would be. Not Finch Fontaine . . . she's anything but friendly with Lina."

"How about Gallagher?" Mike said. "He seems a possibility."

Sandy was shaking her head.

"You're wrong," she said. "Not Edward."

We both looked at her. *Edward?*

"You sound very certain," Mike said.

"I am," she said.

"Any reason in particular?" I said.

Sandy shrugged. "Why would he do it? He has nothing to gain."

"Maybe not," Mike said. "But he did tell us he had a thing going with Lina."

"Once upon a time," Sandy said. "But he's over her now."

We both looked at her again.

"Is there something here you want to share with us?" Mike said.

"Only that you shouldn't be suspicious of Eddie because Lina's his old flame," Sandy said. "He wouldn't blab. All he wants is to get Getaway Groves back under construction."

Mike didn't say anything. Neither did I. But I'd been

unable to fend off a sudden image of her comforting Gallagher against her pillowy bosom the other day.

I sighed, glancing at my wristwatch. It was three o'clock, getting kind of late. I could ponder that another time.

"I need to sit down at the computer and do some work," I said. "My column has to be filed by the end of the day tomorrow."

Mike grunted. "You might as well go ahead—it seems to me we've covered everything for now anyway," he said. "What're you writing about this week, incidentally?"

I shrugged.

"Trust, loyalty, and the holiday spirit. With some cleaning tips thrown in."

"Nothing too broad, huh?"

I smiled and slowly rose to my feet.

"Do you want me to hang around a while?" Sandy said. "We can go back to the Fog Bell together."

I shook my head. "Appreciate it," I said. "But you should go on ahead. I'm hitching a ride with someone else."

Mike stood too now, helping me steady my crutch under my arm.

"I'll walk you to your office," he said, and gave me a confidential glance. "I want to let you know about that dinner date with your mom."

I regarded him a second, nodded. Then we stepped out into the hall

"So," I said as we neared my door. "You want to tell me something?"

Mike stopped, looked around as if making sure nobody was in earshot.

"Yeah," he said finally. "But it isn't about a dinner date."

"I kind of figured, since we don't have one. With or without my mother."

Mike was quiet another moment.

"Vega wasn't the only investigator I talked to today,"

he said in a low voice. "About an hour ago, I heard
from someone at the coroner's office."

"Dr. Maji?"

"I have my contacts," Mike said. "It's probably best
just to leave it at that."

I looked at him. "And did whatever this contact told
you have anything to do with Kyle Fipps?"

Mike nodded.

"Fipps's autopsy results are about to be released," he
said. "The conclusion's going to be that his death was
the result of homicide. All the indications are that Kyle
was poisoned."

I let that sink in and released a sigh.

"That's terrible," I said. "I won't say it comes as a
total shocker, though."

Mike gave me a nod, hesitated. "Look, I'm not sure
what it'll mean for you. Or whether there's any connection to what we've been looking into."

"But you think it's possible."

Mike shrugged.

"I'm not prepared to offer a guess right now," he said,
his voice dropping another notch. "It won't help to start
piling suspicion on top of suspicion until we learn more
about Thompson's dealings. But after this whole business with Lina . . . I felt you should know what's happening. And try to be a little extra careful until we sort
things out."

I nodded.

"I will," I said, and squeezed Mike's arm. "If kissing
and groping weren't inappropriate in the workplace, I'd
thank you properly right now."

Mike smiled. "I'll be here at least another couple of
hours," he said quietly. "I don't know who's giving you
a lift home, but was thinking tonight *could* be the night
I meet your mother."

"Actually, it can't," I said. "I'm cleaning at City
Hall later."

Mike seemed surprised. "Shouldn't you put that off
till your leg feels better?"

"I'll manage," I said. "It's a new job and I won't skip out on it my second time around. Besides, I'm hoping to break in a new assistant."

He looked at me.

"Who's that?"

"Can't tell you," I said. "I promised it'd stay under wraps."

"Oh." Mike paused. "Is this is the same person who's giving you a lift?"

I put my finger to my lips.

"You're not the only one who's obliged to stay hush-hush about certain things," I said. "A promise isn't worth making unless it's keepable."

"Keepable?"

"I think that's a word," I said, and grinned. "Talk to you later. My computer beckons."

I turned into my office. Aside from my cleaning tips, the writing was a struggle. Trust and loyalty. I'd been thinking a lot about those qualities, and how important it was to hang on to them when it seemed people everywhere around us gained satisfaction through cheating and deceit. It had seemed an easy choice to weave those into some kind of holiday theme, but I didn't quite know how to pull them together. I was trying, but it wasn't working, I couldn't get to the nub of whatever it was I wanted to say. Maybe I was dodging something—the franker I was with myself, the more honestly and directly I felt I could communicate with my readers. When I got stuck, it usually meant I was trying to avoid dealing with an issue.

I guessed that could have been it. Or maybe it was that I'd just seen *too much* cheating and deceit lately. Though it might have been something as simple as my leg bothering me after I'd sat at my cramped little desk for a while. I didn't know. And I didn't have all night to figure it out.

At a quarter past five, I knocked off for the evening, put on my coat, grabbed my steadfast and stalwart crutch, and went down the hall to poke my head into the webmaster's office. Nobody was there, so I headed upstairs.

As I approached the employee lounge, I caught a whiff of something and paused a moment, wanting to get the proud smile out of my system. Then I went inside.

I found Bryan in the kitchen wiping down a countertop. He stood with his back to the entry, a cleaning cloth in one hand, my bottle of reused vinegar in the other.

"Hi, Bry," I said, knocking on the wall behind him.

He whipped his head around, startled by the sound.

"Sky, hi!" he said.

I leaned slightly into the kitchen. "We'd better quit with the rhyming before it gets idiotic."

Bryan gave a nod to show he'd caught my meaning.

"Wouldn't want to have Dr. Seuss flashbacks," he said.

"Nope," I said. "Bad enough we had to endure the deluded teachers who thought we actually *liked* those books."

"Hey, what do you think got me started on body piercing?"

We stood there swapping grins.

"This place looks spotless," I said.

"You mean it?"

"I wouldn't kid you."

"I used your stinky vinegar," Bryan said. "Did the coffeemaker, then the counters."

"I can see that."

"Smell it too, I bet."

I nodded.

"So," I said, "you still helping me out tonight?"

"Gonna try my best to make it," Bryan said. "I need to do some last-minute site maintenance, but figure I can drive you home first, come back here, take care of business, then meet you at City Hall."

"You don't have to knock yourself out," I said. "If I can bug you for that ride home, we'll start your formal clean-freak apprenticeship another time."

Bryan made a face.

"The ride's no bother, Sky. Like I said, I *want* to be there. Give me five minutes to finish up and we'll head out to my car."

I looked at him. He was definitely becoming my studded, tattooed prince.

It was six o'clock when he dropped me off at the Fog Bell and then went chuffing away in a cloud of exhaust smoke. I bumped upstairs to my apartment using my crutch, changed my clothes, and kissed Skiball repeatedly on the nose and forehead while she feigned annoyance with a range of very vocal squeaks and mewling noises. Next I clunked downstairs for a quick lasagna dinner with Chloe, Betty-Mom, and Sandy . . . Oscar being inconspicuously absent because of a rehearsal for his woodwind trio's Christmas concert.

"Are you sure you don't want me to tag along?" Sandy said as I inhaled some pasta from my plate. "I'm ready for action anytime."

I politely declined, trying not to think double entendre.

"I'm already expecting an assist from someone," I said. "Appreciate it, though."

And then I snatched up my coat and bump-clunk-shambled out to my Caliber. I wasn't going to let on, but my leg seemed to hurt the most late in the day, and it was really smarting now that evening had come.

I was driving along Main Street toward City Hall, when I noticed the goings-on at the police station. Its lighted entrance was just ahead to my right, and a pair of officers stood waiting there on the pavement by a black Lincoln Navigator. The Nav's front doors were open, and I could see a person climbing out each side. Coming around from behind its wheel on the street side was a big, thickset man in a dark overcoat and muffler with a bulldog face and a full woolly head of silver hair.

Meanwhile, Lina Fipps was stepping out onto the sidewalk opposite him in the same eye-searingly bright red coat she'd worn the other day at the plant shop.

As she emerged, I saw her make an angry face at the

officers, heard her raise her voice at them through my
windows, and slowed for a closer look. Curious about
what she was shouting, I reflexively pushed the window
control near my elbow to lower it about a third of the way.

"—tell you this is disgraceful!" Lina hollered. "How
dare you people insult me like this! Make me come back
up from New York for nothing!"

I lagged past the station, astounded by the scene. Lina
carried on some more as the woolly-haired man, who
was holding a briefcase, tried to steer her around the
cops toward the station entrance. I assumed he was the
defense lawyer Mike had mentioned.

And then she caught sight of me and stopped dead
on the sidewalk. Since there weren't any other cars on
the road at that moment, I guessed my headlights might
have been what drew her attention. Or maybe she noticed me by pure chance.

Unless of course she simply possessed a malevolent
sixth sense that was tuned to my personal frequency.

Whatever made it happen, all I knew for sure was that
Lina turned to look at me just as I came rubbernecking
past the station, her eyes spearing mine through the Caliber's partially open window.

An instant later they opened so wide I could clearly
make out their whites against the darkness of the street.

No exaggeration.

"You again!" she shrieked. And I do mean *shrieked*.
"You! Again! Scrubwoman! Why don't you mind your
own business?"

Seemingly on its own, my finger jabbed the control
button to bring up my window. At the same time Lina's
attorney hurried her along toward the police station with
renewed purpose, his arm a thick bar across her back
and shoulders.

And then I snapped my head around toward the windshield and became rigid in my seat. I knew it was partly
the unexpected eye contact with Lina that tensed me up.
But some of it was the sheer, unmitigated enmity I'd
seen in her contorted features and heard in her shrill,
hysterical voice.

And, I mean, *scrubwoman*?

Looking straight ahead, I left the police station behind and headed farther down Main Street to the town center and City Hall.

If only I could have left my anxiety behind too.

I wasn't thrilled pulling into the darkness of the parking lot, and liked the prospect of walking through it even less, though my anxiety wasn't exactly sudden. I'd been feeling trepidation whenever I thought about my first time coming back at night. The hardest thing for me psychologically was just leaving the protection of the SUV—I needed several deep breaths, and a brief inner pep talk, before I could muster up the gumption. After that, it was all about forward motion, and concentrating on what I had to do.

And so I dropped my crutch into the wagonload of cleaning supplies, leaned on the wagon's handle to take some weight off my leg, and then hustled toward the building, trying not to let my imagination run wild as I put one foot ahead of the other.

I was proud of myself. I only almost jumped out of my goosebumpy skin once, right as I got halfway across the lot. And I had an excuse, since that was when a strong gust of wind sent a discarded fast-food container skittering out of the shadows in my direction.

Fortunately it wasn't a very big meal container. If it had been inclined to attack, I would've been able to fend it off with my crutch before it made its move.

Rick the maintenance man had been his conscientious self and left some lights on . . . the same number of lights he'd made sure were on last time, though somehow the hallway didn't seem nearly bright enough to suit me tonight. Then again, I supposed I wouldn't have minded if every single bulb in the building had been left to shine.

Under the metal chandelier, I waved hello to Frosty, who continued to stand watch beside the main entrance. It didn't offend me a bit that he didn't reciprocate. I preferred that he stayed on the attentive lookout for trespassers.

After a moment's pause, I wheeled the cleaning cart toward the stairs.

"Bonsoir," I said as I reached the oddly stern French Santa on the second-floor landing.

Like his colleague the snowman, he didn't answer.

"Hey, that's okay. I wouldn't want to distract you guys," I said. "It's always best sticking to your routines when you're on the job."

I thought that was decent advice. If I had intended to take it myself, which probably would have been the smart and unhypocritical thing to do, I would've gone straight up to the third floor to work my way down.

But I didn't go up to the third floor. I'd already decided to make a stop on the second.

I turned past Le Pere Noel, rattled my cart down the hallway to Tommy Thompson's office, and then paused again outside it. My heart thumping in my chest, I reached into my jeans pocket and slipped out the key I'd gotten from Jessie Barton.

I stood there with my fingers clenched around it.

"Don't," part of me whispered.

"Who're you kidding, *let's go!*" said another part of me.

Lately, I'd been hearing a lot out of Voice Number Two.

A whole lot.

Before Voice Number One could say, "You've lost your puny little mind," I went into the office and headed straight over to Tommy's desk with my flashlight in hand. Going around the desk, I pulled out his chair, crouched, and then crawled into the kneehole, folding back the rug to reveal Tommy's hidden floor panel.

Holding my breath, I pulled open the panel and slipped the key into the lock to the compartment beneath it.

It fit perfectly. And turned smoothly with a soft little click.

And then I had the compartment door open.

I thumbed on the flash and aimed its beam into the

compartment. Inside were several stacks of banded bills and maybe four or five large, bulging brown envelopes. I could see that the bills were of the hundred-dollar variety. The envelopes had words written on their faces in heavy marker pen. One said RECORDS. Another said, DEEDS. I saw more writing on a third envelope but couldn't quite make it out, and angled the head of the flashlight for a better look.

"I told you not to move the furniture, Sky. Insurance reasons, remember?"

No, that wasn't what it said on the other envelope. It was a voice from behind me—one that I recognized instantly.

I jolted in shock, the top of my head banging against the bottom of the desk so hard I saw stars. Shifting dizzily around in the cramped kneehole, I got my first look at the person who'd come up behind me—and then all at once noticed some sort of object in his hand.

"What's that?" I said from under the desk. "What have you got in your hand?"

I'd asked the question out of panic and hadn't expected an answer. But I got one anyway . . . got my answer even as the stars dispersed from my vision, enabling me to see exactly what Tommy Thompson was holding out in front of him.

He grinned now and came toward me with the long-needled syringe.

"Insurance," he said.

Chapter 20

"You've done all the cleaning you're ever going to do, Sky," Tommy said. "Come out of there."

Yeah, right. Somehow that didn't seem like a good idea.

Keeping my eyes on him—and on the needle in his hand—I edged backward into the open space under the desk. The reception room was about fifteen feet behind me across the office. And beyond that, the outer hall. But even without my bum leg slowing me down, it would have been almost impossible to wriggle out from under the desk before Tommy moved around it and blocked my way to the door. The injury just made things worse.

I wouldn't be able to escape, at least not like that. The fifteen feet to the reception room might as well have been fifty.

I felt a fresh surge of panic inside me but squashed it down. Somehow, I needed to keep my head together.

"Get up," Tommy said. And came closer to the desk. "You're putting off the inevitable."

I forced my voice to work.

"What do you want from me?" I said. "What's in that needle?"

Tommy moved forward again. I could smell his expensive cologne now. Another step or two and the tips of his riding boots would be poking under the desk.

"What do you *suppose* is in the needle?" he said. "Take a guess."

I didn't answer.

And then Tommy suddenly bent forward, his free hand reaching out under the desk. I automatically drew away, but couldn't move far enough back before he grabbed my wrist.

"Let's have that guess," he said. "You and your friends seem to like figuring things out . . . and let's neither of us pretend we don't know who those friends are."

I tried to pull free of Tommy's grasp and couldn't. He just tightened his grip around me, pressing his fingers into my arm.

"Your relationship with Ennis is hardly a secret," he said. "Did you think I wouldn't be aware of it? That I wouldn't find out he's been sniffing around Codes, or check his records applications to see which ones he copied?" Tommy grinned. "I know your cleaning schedule, Sky. After learning about Ennis's visit, I decided to stay after hours tonight. Call it a logical precaution."

Tommy's smile broadened as his fingers dug in deeper.

"Yeeeouch!" I said, flinching.

Tommy stared under the desk. "My strength shouldn't come as a revelation, Sky. Surely you don't see a weakling when you look at me, do you?"

I didn't answer. I was too terrified, and figured the question was rhetorical . . . though maybe it wasn't. If anybody on earth seemed vain enough to fish for compliments under the circumstances, it was Tommy Thompson.

"Talk to me, Sky," he said. "*Communicate.* If you'd rather not discuss Ennis, we can exchange personal Sandy Savoy stories. I have plenty to share."

Tommy looked at me and chuckled. I figured right off that he'd registered my surprise at his mention of Sandy.

"Yes, I know my old flame is in the Cove," he said. "I told you I wanted to discuss your *friends*, plural, didn't I? A woman like Sandy can't come and go around town—stay at the homey Fog Bell Inn—without being noticed. She's an outstanding piece of eye candy . . . even on the rare occasions when she keeps her clothes on."

I didn't say anything. Tommy twisted my wrist hard enough to make me wince again.

"You're not very chatty tonight, are you?" he said. "Well, maybe we should have stuck with our original topic of discussion. At least that seemed to pique your interest."

I stayed quiet, saw him raise his syringe.

"Tell me what you think is in the hypo," he said with a smirk that even the Marquis de Sade might've labeled as unpleasant. "A narcotic overdose that will gently put you to sleep forever? A slow, agonizing toxin? Guess, Sky. *Guess*. Do it or I'll break your wrist."

Tommy wasn't making an empty threat. To prove it, he gave my hand another sharp, painful wrench.

I looked up at him through the tears that had sprung into my eyes.

"No," I said. "I won't play along."

"Then I'll drag you out here and finish this," Tommy said. "And don't worry—I'll make sure your body rests where it won't be disturbed. Unlike Kyle's."

Tommy yanked at my arm and I went sprawling. Then he pulled again, using too much force for me to resist. Wrenched partway from under the desk, I felt a stinging rug burn on my belly as the bottom of my sweater rode up over the waist of my jeans.

I looked up into Tommy's face. It still wore that cruel, smirking expression. The repulsive creep was enjoying himself. Having a grand old time.

That got me steamed. I mean, really, really furious.

"Jerk!" I hollered, slamming my flashlight down on the back of his hand. "Let me go, you stupid lummox!"

Stupid lummox?

Tommy cried out, and not because I'd called him names. He kept holding on to me, but his fingers had loosened their grip. I had given him a solid whack, and could hear my poor, trusty flash's shattered guts rattling around as I raised it for a follow-up.

The second time I hit him, it was smack across the knuckles.

That did the trick. As he staggered back on his heels, Tommy's fingers reflexively unclenched from around my wrist. He was shaking his hand in pain and howling at the top of his lungs.

I wasn't about to stay there on the floor waiting for him to recover.

I gulped some air and jumped to my feet. It was the extent of my immediate plan, and I stood there deciding what to do next. Broadly speaking, I wanted to stay alive. Putting some distance between me and Tommy and his syringe seemed a good start toward that objective.

I took a quick step past him, wanting to bolt around the desk for the door. Unfortunately that single step was all I managed to take before my bum leg grabbed between the ankle and knee.

"Yeeee-oooouch!" I screamed. Sure it was repetitious, but that was low among my concerns. I had to say see-you-later to Tommy. Had to run. And it wasn't much help having my calf muscle cramp up, probably from kneeling under the desk for so long. The pain was excruciating. Worse yet, the leg wouldn't bend. It felt stiff as wood.

I tottered in front of the desk a moment, keeping my weight on the leg, right back to not knowing what to do. Then I saw Tommy coming from over to one side, and realized that knowing wasn't all it was cracked up to be. I had to get away from him. Limping, bunny-hopping, it didn't matter how.

I glanced hurriedly around for my crutch, didn't see it at first, then remembered it was in the cleaning cart and almost went to get it out. But with Tommy on the move again there wasn't time. If I stopped to reach inside the cart, he'd be on top of me.

I needed to find something else. But *what*?

It came to me in a bolt. The solution was there before my eyes. Right where I'd left it.

"I'll get you!" Tommy was hollering as he lunged at me with his needle. "Get you!"

I ignored the clutching pain in my leg and threw myself at my cleaning cart, seizing the handle with both hands, leaning my weight against it just as I'd done out in the parking lot.

Well, okay, not *just* as I'd done. In the parking lot, I hadn't had a diving start.

It made a difference.

As I grabbed the handle, my momentum pushed the entire cart forward, and then the next thing I knew it was rolling across the room, gathering its *own* speed while I clung to it for dear life, carried along for the ride.

"Ooooweeee!" I shouted. In dire and terrible moments, there was comfort in reverting to an old incoherent standby.

Tommy was right behind me, so close I could hear the soles of his boots slapping the floor, hear his panting breath, even hear his teeth clicking angrily together. Somehow I managed to wrestle control of the wagon before it completely hauled me off my feet. Then I spun it around the desk and half rolled, half rode it through the door, across the reception room, and over to *its* open door, gaining a few steps on Tommy in the process.

I'd no sooner jockeyed the cart into the hall than someone appeared in front of me, right outside the office door. I gripped the handle as I suddenly recognized who it was, swinging the cart sideways to avoid a head-on collision . . . and even so almost crashed into her full tilt, rocking her on her heels.

"Sorry, Grace, I—"

The rest of the sentence froze on my tongue as I tried to slow my whirling thoughts and make sense of things. What in heaven was Grace Blossom doing out here in the hall?

"Grace?" I said, gaping at her in shock. "What's going on?"

"Sky," she said, "I'm sorry. But I told you, I won't let anyone take what's mine."

"Grace, stop her!" Tommy hollered behind me. "Stop that scrubwoman now!"

Scrubwoman? Twice in a single night? At least now I knew what Tommy and Lina said about me behind closed doors.

But my immediate concern was Grace. Her eyes locked on mine, she stood motionless as I heard Tommy come plunging through the reception area.

Then it hit me. *Tommy and Lina. Lina and Grace. Tommy and—*.

"Omigod," I blurted. "You too!"

Grace reached both hands out, grabbed the sleeve of my sweater.

"Hurry, baby!" she said. "I've got her!"

Actually, that wasn't true. All she had was my sleeve, and maybe some of my arm. Leaving the rest of me free to move.

I think I might have screamed again as I swung the cart around hard, swung it toward Grace this time, side-swiping her with all my strength. She staggered away from me, the breath kind of woofing from her mouth, her fingers letting go of my sweater to clutch her stomach. Before she could regain her balance, I bashed her with another swing of the cart that sent her flying backward through the corridor and against the wall to my right, her head striking it with an audible *clonk*.

As she sagged to the floor, I whipped the cart to my left, determined to reach the stairs at the end of the hall. There was no time to let up—a glance over my shoulder had revealed Tommy emerging from his office about two or three feet behind me. His face a knot of anger, his hair flying in every direction, jabbing the air with his syringe, he looked like he'd escaped from an asylum.

"I won't let anyone ruin me!" he hollered. The words echoed flatly in the hall. *"Not Kyle! Not Jessie! And certainly not some scrubwoman!"*

Call me nonconfrontational, but sick and tired as I was of being insulted, I wasn't about to stick around and argue. Shoving the cart forward, I pushed off my good leg to boost it toward the stairway, then let it do the rest and whoosh me along down the hall.

I reached the landing in what felt like a heartbeat and

tilted the wagon up onto its rear wheels to brake it. From his customary spot in the corner, the gnarled old French Santa came across as especially grim—and I thought I knew why. With my body shaking all over, I looked downstairs, then back around toward Tommy, and at last disconsolately settled my eyes on the wagon.

That was when I realized I'd started crying.

The wagon had gotten me as far as the landing, but lugging it downstairs would only be a hindrance. The best I could do was get my crutch out of it, hang on to the banister for support, and try to reach the ground floor ahead of Tommy—and *then* somehow beat him out of the main entrance.

I wasn't optimistic about my prospects. I'd be too slow limping along without my trusty set of wheels. But I couldn't take it with me.

From here on in I was on my own.

I tucked the crutch under my arm, gripped the handrail, and started downstairs, aware that Tommy's footsteps were quickly coming closer.

I went down one step, two, three, telling myself not to look back. There was no sense in it, my leg had completely locked up, and looking would only slow me even more. I told myself not to look back, to keep looking ahead, whatever happened.

Then I heard him. He'd reached the second-floor landing and then started down after me, his footsteps banging loudly on the stairs.

"Scrubwoman!" he shouted. "Where do you think you're running?"

Keep moving. Don't look back. Don't—

Tommy grabbed my shoulder, jerking me off balance. It wasn't like when Grace had gotten hold of me. He was much, much stronger, and it hurt the way it had when he'd grabbed my wrist. I didn't know if I could get away from him.

He was down on the step above me now, pulling me back against his chest.

"No!" I screamed. "Let me go, you sicko. Let go!"

Tommy pulled me farther back. I kept fighting him,

but it wasn't doing any good. His fingers wouldn't un-lock.

Then I felt him shifting around above me, and knew without looking that he was preparing to jab me with his needle.

"Relax," he said. "Make it easy on yourself. The less you fight, the quicker it will be."

He gave me another backward wrench. Out the corner of my eye, I saw him raising the syringe in his hand— and that was when I heard more footsteps.

Only now they were coming from below.

"Sky, dudette, what's wrong? Where are you?"

I recognized the voice and felt my heart leap in my chest. "Bry! Bry! Help! I'm up here!"

Bryan Dermond appeared from the ground-floor hall-way, paused to look up for the briefest instant, and then was charging upstairs.

"Hey, yo!" he shouted, pointing at Tommy as he bounded up the steps two at a time. *"Hands off her!"*

Tommy became motionless. I mean, stopped moving altogether. I felt his entire body tense and I strained to break away from him again. And then my arm came free of his hand.

I would never know if he let go of me at that moment, if I took advantage of his surprise and pulled myself from his grip before he could recover, or if it was some combination of both. Either way, I managed to get loose, stumbling down a couple of steps with a force that threatened to propel me headlong to the bottom of the staircase, and would have if I hadn't thankfully managed to grab hold of the rail.

The next thing I knew I heard Tommy beating it up-stairs. I had time enough to turn my head and see him spring onto the third-floor landing before Bryan scram-bled past me in close pursuit.

"Bry, watch out for his needle!" I yelled after him.

"I'm on you like Krazy Glue, you freaked-out doper freak!" Bryan shouted to Tommy's back.

Which made me terribly afraid that he hadn't quite gotten my meaning.

I watched Tommy cut through the entry to the bell tower with Bry on his heels, then turned and began following them as fast as I could, hopping-skipping back up the steps pretty much on my one cooperative leg.

It was right as I stopped to catch my breath on the landing that I noticed an old-fashioned red fire alarm box on the wall above it. The glass pane that once covered the T-handle was gone, probably had been for decades. *Good*, I thought. I'd never seen the sense in making people stop to break that glass in an emergency.

I reached for the handle, pulled it down hard, and heard the fire alarm begin to jangle earsplittingly throughout the building as I plunged through the tower entrance.

Then I was at the bottom of a short spiral staircase. I could see its risers winding up along the tower's curved fieldstone wall under some dim lights—fixtures that must have been wired into the same circuit as those Rick had turned on for me in the corridor.

I gripped the steel handrail, swung onto the stairs. My heart was pounding. I'd glimpsed thrashing, flailing shadows on the walls, heard scuffling sounds on the bell-ringer's platform up above. And then Tommy: "I won't be ruined! Not by a bum like you!"

"Bry!" I shouted. "Hang on, I'm coming!"

There was a scream from the platform.

A shrill, frightened, awful scream, followed by a thud, and then a clang that echoed stridently inside the tower and made the fire alarm seem muted by comparison.

"Oh no!" I screamed. *"Bry!"*

Dragging my bum leg along, cursing it for having slowed me down, I rushed up the few remaining stairs to the platform,

"Bry, what's happening?" I was shouting. *"Bry—"*

A hand steadied me as I reached the top.

"Relax, dudette. Things're cool."

I stood on the platform, Bryan tightly holding my arm. Right in front of us, several feet below the platform, the Paul Revere bell hung suspended between a pair of large parallel girders, tolling away as the clapper repeatedly struck its sides.

Tommy Thompson was on top of the pealing bell, his arms and legs wrapped around it, straddling it for dear life as it swung back and forth underneath him. I stared at the unbelievable sight for a moment, then looked through the tower window opposite the platform and saw the flashing red lights of fire trucks and police cars arriving down on Main Street. Their sirens dopplered up and up through the cold night air to join the dissonant chorus of the Revere bell and the fire alarm.

Then Bryan said something from beside me, but I couldn't hear a word above the deafening racket around us.

"What was that?" I said, pointing to my ear.

He leaned closer and nodded toward Tommy.

"He called me a bum before he fell," he repeated with a frown.

I looked at Bryan, smiled, and kissed him on the cheek.

"Never mind his dirty mouth," I said. "I thought it before, and I'll tell you right now, Bry—you're my studded prince."

Chapter 21

"It's going to be very odd tonight," Chloe said.

"Having someone other than Tommy Thompson ring in the New Year?" I said.

Chloe nodded, walking to my right on Main Street while Betty-Mom strolled along on my opposite side.

"He's been ringing the bell for twenty years as council president," she said. "But I suppose that tradition's come to an end."

I gave her a little shrug and strolled along toward City Hall, the wintry air nipping at my cheeks. Actually, Tommy had rung the bell, just a few days early, and in a different manner than anyone might have anticipated. But I didn't mention that.

"He might've gone a long way toward preserving that tradition if he hadn't been a crook," I said. "Instead he decided to rip off the government left and right."

"The government and your friend Bill Drecksel," Betty-Mom said.

"And let's not forget Kyle Fipps," I said. "That's what really pushed him over the edge—Kyle threatening to audit his books. If Tommy hadn't gone overboard helping himself to the money in the Getaway Groves escrow account, he'd still be presiding over tonight's ceremony instead of Chief Vega."

Chloe nodded again.

"Greed loses what it has gained," she said.

I looked over at her.

"That actually makes sense to me," I said.

She looked surprised. "Why shouldn't it, dear?"

"Maybe because *nothing* from your sentence sermon book makes sense."

Chloe waved a gloved hand.

"It isn't from that book," she said. "The silly thing was much too confusing—I returned it to the swap shop after Christmas."

I bit my tongue and walked on in thoughtful silence. *Greed loses what it has gained.*

That had been true enough for Tommy, Grace Blossom, and to a lesser extent Lina Fipps.

It was all still pretty incredible to me. While Thompson was telling Lina he loved her—and secretly advising her how to get her hands on the condo money he was holding in escrow for her husband—he'd been having an affair with Grace, her best, oldest, and maybe *only* friend in town. At the same time, he was dipping into the money to lavish it on Grace, Sandy Savoy, and heaven knew how many other women. Kyle and Bill's grumbling about the missed payments to the construction company had started things coming to a head, but according to Chief Vega, Kyle's insistence on digging into Tommy's books was what really raised Tommy's anger and paranoia to critical mass . . . and made him convince Grace to order the pong pong tree whose seeds he used to murder Kyle.

The pong pong, and the castor bean plant that had produced the ricin poison he'd meant to inject me with.

Both were legal plants that Grace had easily gotten hold of for her shop. Between her and Tommy, they'd cultivated quite a deadly garden.

I shivered. Even now, after everything that had happened, I found it difficult to understand what Tommy had expected when he'd stuck his hand into Kyle and Bill's fund. How could he think they wouldn't see what he was doing with their money?

Of course, it was tough to know exactly what *anyone* involved in the messy, complicated business had been thinking.

Lina, for example. A shrewd, devious, mistrustful

woman. Yet, she had confided in Grace about her affair with Tommy, and told her in supposed confidence that the two of them were scheming to get hold of the escrow fund as part of her divorce settlement. At the same time, she had remained clueless about Grace also carrying on with Thompson . . . *and* been manipulated into having me attacked, something she blabbed about after Vega let her know Grace and Tommy had been an item. As Vega understood it, Lina grew concerned about me poking around in her business the day I ran into her at the flower shop. She'd told Grace as much afterward, and that had made Grace *and* Tommy wonder about me too—especially since Grace was well aware I'd been friends with Jessie Barton, and that I was dating Mike Ennis, the crime reporter at the *Anchor*. The last straw for Tommy, I supposed, was his getting wind that Sandy Savoy was staying with me.

Finally, when Grace suggested that Lina do something to scare me off, Lina came up with the piping idea. And when somebody in the city clerk's office tipped Tommy off about Mike's visit there, he'd decided to stick around City Hall later that night to keep a guarded eye on things . . . and had convinced Grace to come along with him as a lookout.

The irony was that he had known nothing at all about my meeting with Jessie. Or my having the key to his lockbox. Not till he'd found me crawling around under his desk.

Tommy, Lina, Grace . . . between all of them they'd had so much, until their greed had taken everything from them.

Now I walked between Chloe and Betty-Mom. All around us Pigeon Covers were out on the sidewalk, nearly everyone headed in the same direction. At City Hall, the Paul Revere bell would soon be tolling the promise of a New Year.

"This is magical, Sky," Betty-Mom said as we reached the building to stand among the thickening crowd. She looked up at the tower. "Really magical."

"Glad you stuck around town an extra few days?" I said.

She smiled. "This is such a special occasion for you," she said. "How could I possibly miss it?"

I looked at her, smiling too. Then I glanced around the milling courtyard. At its far end, Sandy Savoy and Ed Gallagher stood necking like a couple of teenagers on hormonal overdrive, their arms wrapped around each other. Both wore glittery New Year's Eve hats. I wouldn't have thought Sandy would notice me, but as my eyes fell on her, she looked up and gave me a high, enthusiastic wave hello.

I grinned, waved back. Then I felt Betty-Mom squeeze my arm.

"There's your significant other, right where he said he'd meet you," she said, motioning toward the wide granite entrance stairs. "You'd better go see him . . . the countdown's going to start before you know it."

I nodded, knowing I had to hurry.

Mike kissed me as I came up to him, his hands on my waist.

"Big night," he said.

"Yeah."

"Festive."

"Sure is."

"And loaded with star power."

I swatted his shoulder. "Okay, enough. Cut it out."

"We finally getting together with your mom after the ceremony?"

"She wouldn't have it any other way."

"And how about after?"

"Your place," I said.

Mike pulled me closer to him.

"Don't forget that black silk thingie," he said.

I smiled, my lips brushing against his. "It's already in my overnight bag," I said. "Doesn't take up much space."

We stood there quietly for a few minutes. Then, still holding me close, Mike glanced at his wristwatch.

"It's a quarter of twelve," he said.

I nodded.

"You have to go," he said.

I nodded again.

"Break a leg, Sky," Mike said.

I chuckled. "Just when I can finally get around without a crutch?"

It wasn't often that Mike looked embarrassed. But he did then, and I thought it was sort of cute. I kissed him lightly again, pulled away.

"Later," I said, and turned toward the stairs.

The bell tower didn't have much standing room for visitors. Its narrow platform only had space for the bellringer—usually the city council president—and the police chief.

Tonight, it was just me and Vega, who was fiddling with the rope on the platform.

"Sky," he said as I neared the top of the spiral stairs. "There you are!"

I looked at him.

"Am I late?" I said.

Vega shook his head.

"No, no," he said. "Guess I've just been anxious for our honorary town ringer to arrive."

I smiled, stepping onto the platform beside him.

"You didn't have to do this, Chief," I said.

"It's Alex," he said. "And I wanted to do it. It's no fun being up here by myself."

I looked at him, nodded.

"Alex," I said. "Thank you."

He handed me the end of the rope, and we stood looking out the tower window at the busy street below.

A few minutes later, one of the senior city councilmen poked his head through the tower door and announced that he was about to head out to start the countdown. We had our own set of loudspeakers in the tower to let us monitor it as it blared from the PA system set up near the main entrance.

"Ten, nine, eight, seven, six, five, four, three, two—"

At midnight on the dot, I pulled on the rope to ring the bell. Then, still holding the rope, I looked over at Veg—ah, Alex.

And saw him looking back at me.

I couldn't hear what he said right then, not with the crowd cheering merrily on the street, and the bell ding-donging like crazy in my ears. But there weren't too many words to it, and it didn't take all that much effort to read his lips.

"Happy New Year," he said. "I'm crazy about you, Sky."

I stared into his emerald eyes a whole lot longer than I should have.

"Uh-oh," I said at last.

And let me tell you, I meant uh-oh *big time*.

Sky Taylor's Cleaning First-Aid Kit (for Home and Office)

Here's a kit that should handle most cleaning emergencies.

We'll start with something to hold your cleaning items. As I mention in chapter 5, I use a spacious old metal Red Cross first-aid kit that I bought for under a dollar at the thrift shop. But they're not always easy to find, and those plastic modern first-aid kits that look like flattened lunch boxes work almost as well—you can find them in the pharmaceutical or camping departments of most general merchandise stores and supercenters. *Make sure to prominently mark the word "Cleaning" on the outside.* The provisions that come with the kit won't be wasted—just put them in your medicine cabinet or existing medical first-aid kit.

Once your cleaning first-aid kit's mounted on the wall, you'll be ready to stock it. Here are ten essential items you should include:

1. A handheld whisk broom. Trim the bristles down about one and a half inches so it fits into the kit. The shorter bristles give you a nice, solid, compact sweep and will break less easily than long ones. Also, the longer the bristles, the more likely it is that dust and dirt will slip through them. As an alternate to a whisk, you can use a stiff three-inch-wide paintbrush.

2. One or two leaf-notebook-type cardboards will make handy nonskid dustpans. Keep a roll of duct tape in the kit—you can tape the edge of the card-

board to the floor for an easy and thorough sweep. The duct tape is also handy for lifting pet hair, lint, and the last little bits of your sweep-ups.

3. Getting back to brushes for a second—I always keep an assortment of smaller ones in the kit. These work well when you're removing spots, or doing corners, computer keyboards, and other hard-to-reach areas. Don't spend money on new brushes—instead use your worn-out toothbrushes, basting brushes, one-inch paintbrushes, and so on.

4. Fels Naptha laundry soap. This is a staple of my fully stocked bag of tricks, but I also suggest storing half a bar—or a mostly used one—in your first-aid kit. With the Fels Naptha, you're covered in the event of any spills, stains, and quick-fix laundering emergencies.

5. Travel-size screw-top toiletry bottles filled with your choice of window or all-purpose cleaners, wood soap, ammonia, and vinegar.

6. Non-soaped steel wool for ground-in whatevers.

7. A dozen folded heavy-duty paper towels. Fasten them together with a paper clip and they won't fly around when you open your kit!

8. A cloth rag, rolled up tightly to take up minimal space. Use it for wipe-ups, dusting, dabbing, and buffing.

9. Five or six Ziploc storage bags. They're neat and convenient trash bags for swept-up dirt and your used paper towels. Once they're sealed there's no chance of odors from spills or cleaning products . . . and you can go to a nearby sink or cooler and fill them with water!

10. Assorted large and small safety pins. For unexpected rips and splits, not to mention holding curtains back.

An added suggestion: When stocking your cleaning first-aid kit, don't remove the alcohol, antiseptic wipes, and adhesive bandages that come with most store-bought medical kits. You'll be glad you kept them if you cut or scrape yourself while cleaning!

Read on for a sneak peek at
the next Grime Solvers mystery
from Suzanne Price

NOTORIOUSLY NEAT

Available April 2009 wherever books are
sold or at penguin.com

Spring had arrived in the town of Pigeon Cove. Well, spring with an asterisk. The snow was gone, the grass was green, and tulips lined our garden paths like cups of brightly colored paint.

It was cold, though. Not just sort of. It was c-c-*cold*. The coldest spring Covers could remember.

That's why the shivery asterisk, if you're wondering. Since moving to New England, I'd found out that the cold could stick around until the Fourth of July or so.

Still, I was primed for the new season. This was partly because I was also good to go for my first official date with the dashing police chief, Alejandro Vega—or Al, as he kept asking me to call him—with not a thought in my mind about Mike Ennis.

Okay. Let's add another of those pesky, clingy little asterisks to the word "not."

But I'll get to Mike in a while.

Mike wasn't now.

Now, with hesitant spring and tentative romance in the seasonably wishful air, I, Sky Taylor, was pretty darned ready to focus on dinner with Chief—um, Al.

Happily, I'd found my sexy but too-light-for-the-weather clothes the slightest bit loose as I'd put together my outfit. Thanks to hours of murdering myself at the Get Thinner Gym, I was at my all-time slimmest after a winter of noshing on hearty stews, creamy chowders, and sugary cakes and muffins—making me feel downright

glamorous in a pair of skinny black pants and my mother's latest fashion concept, the so-called kite tunic.

If you haven't caught on to Betty's new chicy-chic,
retro, hippie-dippy designer clothes online marketing
Web site, I should explain that her tunic—item number
five on her e-catalog's "Asian Vibrations" page—was actually a tapered tuxedo shirt dyed pink and then hand
painted with dozens of pastel origami-type cranes flying
through the air. And while I'm explaining things, I might
as well mention that there was a special reason for my
Japanese-inspired style that evening. This being that Al
and I were having dinner at a Japanese restaurant.

It wasn't just your average old sushi bar.

An old waterfront manor renovated in the style of a
traditional Japanese shoko's minka, it was the most popular new eatery on the North Coast. Though the food
was scrumptious, its atmosphere was responsible for a
lot of the hoo-hah about it, and a big reason there were
no open reservations till Saint Swithin's Day . . . unless
you happened to be the police chief or some other
local VIP.

Of course, going out for Japanese is never just about
the food. Or shouldn't be. It's about an aesthetic, too—
doing more with less to maintain the balance of nature's
beauty. At Shoko's, with its spacious interior and mix of
low traditional tables and American-style teakwood
table and chair sets, diffuse lighting through rice paper
shoji doors blurred the lines between the dining room
and the landscaped garden outside.

The chief—that's to say, Al—had arranged to have
one of the traditional tables set aside for us, thinking we
should have the total experience. But when our lavish,
delicacy-filled bento boxes arrived, he seemed mildly
worried about his choice.

"You're sure you think it's comfortable on this mat,"
he said, patting the tatami underneath him. "If you'd
rather have a chair, I'll ask for a regular table—"

"This is wonderful. I wouldn't want us to be anywhere
else," I said, which was absolutely true. In fact, I'd never

known there'd be a hibachi built right into the table to keep us toasty warm even with the patio door open.

I popped a seaweed-wrapped *onigiri* into my mouth and devoured it.

Chief Al, meanwhile, looked as if I'd just partially eased his concern.

"How about your leg?" he said. "It's okay now? I mean, okay enough for us to sit on the floor like this?"

"Been fine for ages." I resisted the urge to do a demonstrative knee flex and show I was fully rehabbed after the Christmas whacking I'd gotten from a drunken fisherman. "As far as that goes, Bry deserves serious credit."

"The kid who used to do Web stuff for the newspaper?"

"Bryan Dermond, right."

"He's gone full-time with you?"

"A couple months back," I said. "His assistance with some of my tougher cleaning contracts gave me a chance to take it a little easier."

That was also the unadulterated truth. My sweet but frightfully pierced and studded assistant had turned out to be a *huge* help, proving to be as creative as he was reliable, especially when it came to using fewer chemical cleaning products in our effort to go green . . . something that he'd likewise convinced me to do.

Chief Al picked up a shrimp with his chopsticks. My own chopsticks swooped at the *negimaki*, a grilled beef and scallion roll I'd been eyeing since the waitress brought our meal.

It was well on its way into my mouth when I heard a loud commotion from over by the patio, across the dining floor to my right and—

Wait. Whoa. Strike that.

"Commotion" is a way too general term here, as well as an understatement verging on the ridiculous.

"Commotion" doesn't come close to describing the shrill screams of confused, horrified diners and servers, the loud crash of chairs and dinnerware, or the simultaneous and totally freak-out worthy chorus of barks, grunts, neighs, and squawks that accompanied the rest of that bestial cacophony.

I'll mention the hoofbeats later. This is mainly because my brain was on a ten second time delay as far as realizing that was what they were. But it's is also because I should probably talk about the monkey first.

The monkey was what jolted me out of my utter shock and disbelief as it snatched the *negimaki* from my chopsticks with a furry—and almost human—paw and then eagerly popped it into his rubbery, smacking lips.

Now, I will gamely admit he was a cute monkey. A very, very cute monkey, in fact. Not that I've ever been aware of *un*cute ones. This particular primate, however, was only a foot or so tall and had big twinkling brown eyes that said he probably liked sharing a good laugh every once in a while. Later I would learn he was a trained capuchin named Mickey who knew how to make popcorn, operate a DVD player, and really preferred peanut butter sandwiches to stolen rice balls.

But later's for later. Since I already have to explain all about Mike and me, we'll add Mickey to the list. The two have names that are alphabetically proximate anyway.

Right then and there at Shoko's Madhouse, I only wanted to pull myself together and figure out what in the world was going on as the creature gulped down my bento box offering, grunted contentedly, and then sprang from the table to my lap with a kind of soft, fur-butted thud before wrapping his scrawny monkey arms tightly around my neck.

"Chief Vega!" I hollered, unable to even blame myself for reverting to his title under the circumstances. "It's a monkey! We've got a monkey at our tab—"

Then I cut myself off. Not because I was dumb enough to think the chief wouldn't have noticed the thing giving me a hug. But because I'd suddenly realized Vega had leaped up to his feet from the tatami and was staring gape-eyed at the very large and diverse menagerie of critters charging in our direction—and every other direction, racing around the room in a chaotic frenzy.

As I also got to my feet, my shrieking, grinning, food-grabbing simian pal still wrapped affectionately around me, a greyhound came springing through the patio door behind a pony or miniature horse—not being Jack Hanna or Doctor Doolittle, I didn't know which it was. But its hooves were clopping and clomping pretty loudly as the dog ran into a tiny kimono-clad waitress, knocking her to the floor, saki glass–laden tray and all.

Sprawled on her back among the spilled drinks, she shouted something that sounded like *"Hidee-na!"*

I didn't know what that meant. But it sounded panicked. Justifiably.

This is what I remember of the next minute or two's confusion:

The horsey/poney thing galloping past the waitress and knocking over a cabinet full of china. A llama—that's right—a *llama* spitting in the teacups of mortified customers I recognized as Rena and Ritchie Freund, the saltwater taffy makers. Dishes crashing to the floor as maybe a dozen cats pounced and skidded across tabletops. Chairs toppling over as a honking white goose harassed Henry Stootz, the hairdresser. And then Gazi del Turko's poor little girls Evie and Persha squealing with delight—yes, right, delight, they're *kids*—as a peacock strolled into the place behind the rest of the zoo crew, regally unfanning a large plume of iridescent blue tail feathers.

When the police came dashing into the restaurant behind the zoo crew, it was oddly anticlimactic. Well, I shouldn't speak for everybody. Although the waitress with the saki tray had collected herself, a cashier with a phone in her hand was still screaming her lungs out in Japanese.

For the record, the word she was hollering was *"Omawani!"*

Which, I learned later but will tell you right this very instant, means, "Cops!" I don't want to make you wait for everything.

And then one of the officers—it was my old square-jawed friend Conners—pulled to a halt in front of us.

"Chief Vega," he began breathlessly, pausing an incredulous beat to notice the huggy monkey in my arms. "Chief . . . it's the veterinarian across the road. Someone's murdered her."

I squeezed Mickey, who I did not yet know was named Mickey, tightly in my arms.

"Dr. Pilsner?" I said with horror. "*Gail* Pilsner?

He looked at me. I looked at him. And then we both just looked at each other with understanding as something downy quacked between my ankles.

The point was that Gail Pilsner wasn't just my cat Skiball's vet, she was practically every pet owner in town's favorite animal doc . . . besides being the only one to actually specialize in and board exotic pets like llamas.

I had obviously known Gail's office was across the road. I had also just seen a pack of escaped animals invade the restaurant, and heard a very distressed uniformed officer say the word murder in connection to the reason for their escape.

Who *else* would it have been but Dr. Pilsner?

I felt my spine stiffen, squeezed my monkey pal more tightly against my chest for comfort, and listened to Conners continue to fill in Chief Vega.

". . . think we have a suspect," he was saying. "Caught him red-handed, sir. He's talking a mile a minute in Spanish and we need you to translate."

A second passed. Somewhere in the restaurant I heard a terrific bang, followed by an exclamation that I would phonetically approximate as, "*Gua-ooo-laaah!*" I think it was bestial in origin, but it might have been a person who was really upset.

Then Chief Vega said, "I don't speak Spanish."

Conners looked at him, mystified.

"But I thought—"

"My ancestors were from Mexico," Vega said. "That doesn't mean I speak Spanish."

Conners reddened, embarrassed.

"Oh," he said.

"Right," Vega said.

"But we need somebody who—"

"I speak it," I said, freeing a hand from the monkey's embrace to raise it.

They both turned to me and I smiled kind of timidly.

"You do?" Chief Vega said.

I nodded.

"College minor. I lived in New York," I said.

Vega grabbed my elbow and started toward the patio door.

"We'd better hurry up," he said.

I hurried up.

Its cheek pressing against mine, my monkey pal hung on for the ride.

About the Author

Suzanne Price is the pseudonym for a nationally best-selling author. While Suzanne has never solved a murder, she's as quick with cleaning hints as her heroine is.

A PEACH OF
A MURDER

A Fresh Baked Mystery

Livia J. Washburn

*Fresh out of the oven: the first in a new series
of baking mysteries. Includes recipes!*

All year round, retired schoolteacher Phyllis Newsom is
as sweet as peach pie—except during the Peach
Festival, whose blue ribbon has slipped through
Phyllis's fingers more than once...

Everyone's a little shaken up when the corpse of a
no-good local turns up underneath a car in a garage in
town. But even as Phyllis engages in some amateur
sleuthing, she won't let it distract her from out-baking
her rivals and winning the upcoming
Peach Festival contest.

With her unusual Spicy Peach Cobbler, Phyllis hopes to
knock 'em dead. But that's just an expression—never in
her wildest dreams did she think her cobbler would
actually kill a judge. Now, she's suspected of murder—
and she's got to bake this case wide open.

**Available wherever books are sold or
at penguin.com**

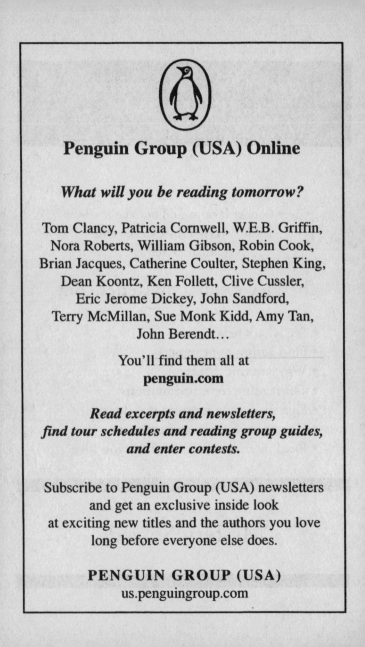